Luscious Craving

A CANDACE STEELE
VAMPIRE KILLER NOVEL

CAMERON DEAN

BALLANTINE BOOKS · NEW YORK

Luscious Craving is a work of fiction. Names, characters, places, and incidents are the products of the author's imagination or are used fictitiously. Any resemblance to actual events, locales, or persons, living or dead, is entirely coincidental.

A Ballantine Books Mass Market Original

Copyright © 2006 by Parachute Publishing, LLC.
Excerpt from *Eternal Hunger* by Cameron Dean copyright © 2006 by Parachute Publishing, LLC.

Published in the United States by Ballantine Books, an imprint of The Random House Publishing Group, a division of Random House, Inc., New York.

BALLANTINE and colophon are registered trademarks of Random House, Inc.

This book contains an excerpt from the forthcoming book *Eternal Hunger* by Cameron Dean. This excerpt has been set for this edition only and may not reflect the final content of the forthcoming edition.

ISBN-10: 0-345-49254-4
ISBN-13: 978-0-345-49254-8

Cover illustration and design by Tony Greco

Printed in the United States of America

www.ballantinebooks.com

OPM   9   8   7   6   5   4   3   2   1

"*D*ammit, Candace," Ash said, taking a step closer. "I want you. And all you do is fight me."

Out in the desert, beneath the light of the stars, I took a step closer.

"And if I stopped fighting?" I asked, my voice low and husky. "Not forever. Just for tonight. What would you give me if I stopped fighting you, Ash?"

He bent his head, then put his mouth to mine, and the world exploded in a shower of sparks. Ash's hands were on my breasts, trailing fire in their wake. There was no patience in his touch. Other nights were for explorations, for going slow. Not this one. On this night Ash and I desired one and the same thing: to take what we wanted.

Also by Cameron Dean

PASSIONATE THIRST

For JoAnn,
with many thanks

One

It gets cold in Las Vegas at night, especially if you are alone.

But after working all night in a casino designed to resemble a hyped-up *Tales from the 1001 Arabian Nights*, called the Scheherazade, shlepping drinks in instruments of torture masquerading as high-heeled shoes, fending off ass-pinchers, watching newlyweds lose their nest egg on a single roll of the dice, sometimes, the cold, thick darkness is exactly what I crave.

Tonight was one of those nights.

Besides, I'm used to being alone.

"G'night, Candace," the night doorman said as I left the Sher through the employee exit that leads to the parking garage.

I got into my car and drove home slowly through the neon-lit streets. This is the hour when the night is at its coldest, at its darkest—the hour just before dawn. The time that normal, everyday people dread, when their eyes suddenly fly open in the darkness and it occurs to them to wonder if this will be the day when the sun declines to rise.

I never worry about this myself. When you've seen the things that I have, you know the truth: Truly major shit doesn't give a damn about the time of day, and it sure as hell doesn't go by anyone's alarm clock. If it's coming at you, all you can do is duck. Or run. And even then, chances are more than a little good it's going to get you anyhow.

I pulled the car into my driveway, then, draping a long woolen coat over my shoulders, I started walking. My feet made absolutely no sound on the sidewalk.

Down my street, past another, and suddenly, it's there before you: the Mojave Desert, nestling at the feet of the Spring Mountains. You can smell the desert long before you get there, just the faintest tang of sage on the air. It can find you when you least expect it, even on the Strip. Las Vegas is pure boomtown, spreading into the desert in a constant invasion that lasts for miles. But the desert is a worthy adversary. It does not give up. Between the condos and the malls and the brand-new developments that seem to sprout up overnight, the Mojave is always there.

It was exactly what I needed tonight.

I chose my favorite spot—a small hollow in

what, later in the day, would be the shade of a boulder—and sat down, letting the coat fall back behind me. I pulled my knees up to my chest, wrapped my arms around them, and gazed upward. You have to know how to look to see the Vegas stars at night. But I was good at it. I ought to be. I did it often enough. A bittersweet pleasure, a test I insisted upon giving myself. I closed my eyes, then opened them again. The stars were still there, and so was my reaction to them.

Where are you tonight, Ash? I thought.

Ashford Donahue III, the man I loved. The vampire I hated. Just my luck that he was both. The first time I met him, I could have sworn the stars were in his eyes. The last time I saw him, he was walking out. He had sworn not to come back. If I wanted him, it was my move. And I hadn't made it. Not in six long months. On nights like this, I wondered why. Nights like this made me want to forget the pain, the past, the blood. On nights like this, I still wanted Ash. The taste of his skin. The feel of his mouth.

"You shouldn't be out here alone." A voice in the darkness made me jump up; instinctively, I pulled out one of the sharp silver wands I wear in my hair. But I wasn't frightened. What I felt, and tried hard to conceal, was a completely different emotion: joy.

Joy. Because Ash was here, with me in the darkness of the desert night. . . .

"Ash! What the hell are you doing here?" I demanded, trying to conceal the powerful feelings Ash provokes in me. Feelings I am not particularly proud of, by the way. I have fought against them over and over, long and hard. I've lost every single time.

"Do you have to ask?" he said, stepping out from around the boulder. "You're starting to develop patterns, Candace. That can be dangerous, you know."

I slid the silver wand back into my hair. There was no sense calling attention to it. I don't think Ash knows what I do in my spare time. I hunt down vampires and kill them. Not just any vampires. The ones like Ash, who, by virtue of their high rank in the vampire hierarchy, feed on live human blood. He was the one who inspired this particular hobby, in fact. He once tried to drink mine. The truth is, I'm lucky to be alive.

"Do you watch me, Ash?" I asked now. "Is that what you're saying? If I want you, I have to come to you, but in the meantime you like to watch?"

"No, Candace. That's not what I like," he said as he took a step closer. He was standing beside me now. In the predawn darkness, his eyes seemed to kindle with their own light.

"You want me to say it? All right: I want you.

That's why I watch you. That's why I'm here. I'm willing to admit my need. I always have been. All you do is fight me."

I felt a strange madness seize me then. Out in the desert, beneath the light of the stars. I took a step closer.

"And if I stopped fighting?" I asked, my voice low and husky. "Not forever. Just for tonight. What would you give me if I stopped fighting you, Ash?"

Almost before I finished speaking, he gave his answer. I think we both knew what it was going to be.

"Whatever you want."

I took a second step, and then a third, our bodies now touching. "You," I said. "I just want you. You're all I've ever wanted."

He bent his head, then put his mouth to mine, and the world exploded in a shower of sparks. Ash's hands were on my breasts, trailing fire in their wake. There was no patience in his touch. Other nights were for explorations, for going slow. Not this one. On this night Ash and I desired one and the same thing: to take what we wanted.

He brought his hands together at the front of my T-shirt, fisted them, then tore the shirt apart. I wasn't wearing a bra. Ash growled, low in his throat, filling his hands with my breasts like a greedy child. Pushing them together, then up toward his mouth.

The action pulled me to my tiptoes. Another moment and I would lose my balance.

"Hold on to me, Candace," I heard him gasp as the movement of his tongue shot fire straight down to my legs. "Hold on."

I put my hands on his shoulders, and felt the world fall away as Ash lifted me, to lie me down. His hands were a blur of motion against the fastenings of my jeans, and then I felt the cool desert air on my legs as he drew the jeans down and off. The silk panties I wore went right along with them. I felt the rough texture of the wool coat against my skin. I lay back, gazing up at him. I was completely naked; Ash, completely clothed.

He leaned over me, bringing my lips to his for a lingering kiss, then stroking a hand straight down the center of my body. I watched it, a cool, pale white against my tanned skin, both saw and felt the way my body tightened at his touch. His fingers reached the triangle of curls between my legs, and he stopped, his eyes on mine. In them, a question. Slowly, my eyes never leaving his, I slid my legs apart, then bent my knees, tilting my pelvis up. Offering myself, opening myself to this lover as I did for no one else.

"What do you want, Ash?" I asked.

"You."

"Then take what you want."

He leaned down, pulled my knees onto his shoulders, and kissed me, openmouthed. Tongue thrusting deep inside me, then sliding out to slick across my clit, fingers tightly gripping my butt. I writhed against him, all but helpless in my need.

"Ash," I gasped out. "Ash, I want . . ."

I heard him laugh then. "I know what you want, my love. I always know what you want. The only problem is, you can't always have it."

He put his lips against my clit, then vibrated them wildly, even as his fingers slid inside me. In and out. In and out. Faster. Deeper. Harder and harder. Until I heard myself give a hoarse cry of pure pleasure. Felt my body arch up, pull taut. And then I was coming, the world shattering around me; the sky above, a sea of shooting stars.

I sat straight up in bed, my bedroom echoing with my own cries of passion. The sheets were a tangled mass at the end of the bed, my legs spread open, wide.

God, I thought. *Oh, sweet, merciful Jesus.*

I sat up, pulled my knees to my chest, hugged them tightly, and told myself I would not cry. *A dream. It was only a dream,* I chanted, over and over. So vivid, even in my own bedroom I believed it was real, a literal slice of my own life. The passion so potent, I had actually climaxed. But it was only a dream, a dream I had summoned up myself.

Of passion fulfilled, and unfilled. Desire sated but never satisfied. After six long months of silence, six months of relative peace, I had awakened from a dream of Ash where all it had taken was just one look for me to throw myself back into his arms.

"I know what you want. The trouble is, you can't always have it."

As if I didn't know. As if he hadn't taught me that, himself.

Damn, damn, damn, I thought. *You are not going to do this, Candace. Do you hear me? You are going to put a stop to this, right here. Right now!*

I had wasted enough of my life agonizing over things I couldn't have. It wasn't a long list, but Ash was sure as hell at the very top. Well, I was finished with that bullshit behavior. Done. No more. I released my knees, swung my legs over the side of the bed, and stomped to my window and threw the curtains open. Bright morning sunlight streamed into the room, making my eyes water. I stayed at the window, gazing out upon the bright, clear winter day, until my eyes were dry as bone.

Only then did I turn away and set off down the hall. *I'll run a shower,* I thought. As hot as I could stand. I would wash the dream of Ash from my body even if I had to scald it off. Then, like a phoenix rising from the ashes, I would begin again.

Build anew, again. Never mind that I had made myself such promises before. This time I would make them stick. I would make new choices, stick to my guns.

But even as I gave the hot-water faucet a vicious twist, I wondered: How could I build anew when my foundation was the same thing it had always been: a broken heart?

Two

Hours later, in the cool of a new Vegas night, I drove back to the Sher. I had spent the day doing simple, everyday things. Running errands. Watering the garden. Washing clothes. As a result, I was feeling calmer, less raw.

The Sher is one of those casinos whose looks definitely improve at night. The exteriors of some casinos are brightly painted, so they glitter in the Vegas sun. The Sher is desert brown during daylight hours. It's at night that it truly comes alive, a tribute to the restorative powers of neon. A brightly lit sultan's palace filled with incredible riches, all just waiting for one of the thousands who come to Vegas each year, hoping to strike it rich. *Open sesame,* it seems to say. *Come on in and be the next Ali Baba.*

But it's different in the back where the employees come to work. If the tourists can't see it, why waste money? Simple parking garage, a few offices, and everyday streetlights. I parked the car, then made my way toward one of the plain doors set in what could have been mistaken for the rear of a Home Depot.

"I must be getting old," James mourned as he saw me approach. "Seems I just said good night to you a couple hours ago."

"What can I tell you?" I asked. Though it was true I was a little early. "Time flies when you're having fun." I held up the security badge hanging from my jacket's zipper.

"Don't give me any lip, now, young lady. The boss wants everything perfect for that big tournament. I get sloppy, my ass gets canned." He sent a leer in my general direction. "Yours, too, even if it is nicer than mine."

I gave an eye roll, the expected response. Though I had to admit, James had a point on both counts. The Boss, Randolph Glass, was a stickler for high standards. Fail to pass muster, and you're looking for a new job. My own was reasonably secure, but then I do have a somewhat unusual skill-set. One of which not even Randolph is aware: I can sense vampires.

A useful skill to have in Vegas, as it turns out. The undead like to party as much as anyone else. In particular they like the casinos, where they can use their heightened abilities to try and change the odds through a technique vamps call "establishing rapport." Not surprisingly, this does not go over very big with management. The one thing Vegas casinos do not ever want to do is lose money.

I don't know how my direct boss, the Sher's head of security, Al Manelli, knows about the existence of vampires. Our relationship is strictly military on this point: Don't ask; don't tell. Rousting a vamp while on cocktail-waitress duty is how I first caught Al's eye. I've been a member of his security team ever since, a thing my fellow Sher employees know full well. What only Al, my best friend Bibi Schwartz, and I know is the full extent of my duties: to help keep the Sher as vampire-free a zone as humanly possible.

Challenging enough under the best of circumstances. But, as James had just reminded me, even the best of circumstances were about to go hog wild. For the next several days, as the holiday season counted down to New Year's Eve, the Scheherazade would play host to the No-Limits Foundation Charity Poker Tournament, one of the biggest benefit tournaments around. With the proceeds going to benefit severely ill and disabled children, the Texas hold 'em round-robin would kick off tonight, then run nonstop till midnight, New Year's Eve, with elimination games running around the clock. The tournament would be broadcast on cable, drawing both pros and amateurs from all across the country. Even a politician was going to be involved. Senator Cabot Hamlyn, considered by many to be the front-runner for the Democratic presidential nomination, had signed up to play.

The No-Limits event was the reason I had come in early. The usual casino setup had been changed slightly to accommodate all the new action. I wanted to check things out. If there's one thing I've learned in the last year and a half, it's to do my best to avoid surprises. With a final nod to James, I passed through the Sher's employee door.

The locker room was empty. It wasn't regular shift change time. Though I've never had it officially confirmed, I've always suspected that somebody's Uncle Vinny got the Sher a deal on paint, and the employee locker room is where it got used up. The walls are painted an institutional green; the lockers a blue so bright it hurts your eyes.

With quick, practiced movements, I got out of my streets and changed into my cocktail-waitress costume. *I Dream of Jeannie* gone extremely naughty, an absurd concoction of bright pink velvet and chiffon that covers what needs to be covered and not much else. I swept up my hair, pinning it in place with my silver chopsticks.

Not chopsticks, really. Stakes. Silver stakes. Silver is a purifier. When it comes to causing a vampire pain, silver is second to none. And it's a whole lot more subtle than lugging a bunch of wooden stakes around.

I took a last glance at myself in the mirror, then headed out onto the main floor of the casino. No matter how ritzy the hotel or exotic its theme, all of the Vegas casinos are the same in their heart of hearts. Slot machines ring the exterior, with the table games—craps, blackjack, roulette—farther in. There's always a section set off just for high rollers.

I stopped for a quick check of the poker area. For the Texas hold 'em tournament, the poker tables had been divided from the rest of the casino by a half wall of columns. The players were already in their chairs, eyeing each other as they waited for the first elimination round to begin. There were at least three dozen tables set up, along with the TV cameras that would document every minute of play straight through the final game. Only six players would qualify for that New Year's Eve game, and I couldn't begin to guess who would make it that far. When I was certain there were no vampires at any of the poker tables, I moved on.

I was halfway across the casino when I felt it: a sudden shot of cold. This was the feeling I hadn't gotten at any of the poker tables, the one that tells me there's a vampire around. My ability to sense vampires is a strange side benefit of the night in San

Francisco when Ash decided to give a whole new meaning to the promise "I'll make you mine." A promise he had attempted to make good on by draining me of blood in the elevator of my apartment building. I'm still not precisely certain why he didn't finish the job. I had managed to pull free and stagger out into the hall. And that's where I would have bled to death if not for the quick actions of my friend Bibi, who found me there. As I recovered, I found that the little love bite Ash had given me had left something special behind.

When a vampire is near I get cold all over. Most of the time it's just a mild chill. But if the vamp is truly powerful, the cold seeps into my skin and gnaws at my insides. The vamp I was sensing now was midlevel. Not a human bloodsucker, but still scum. I let my eyes sweep the casino as my legs carried me in the direction of the cold. A fine-boned, black-haired man was standing at one end of a craps table. Chances were good I would never have noticed him at all if he hadn't set off my vampire radar. He was dressed like a typical tourist in jeans and a polo shirt.

Tourist my ass, I thought. For all his careful camouflage, he wasn't behaving like one. Tourists shooting craps always do the same thing: They watch the dice roll along the felt. This guy was focused on the boxman, Larry, who announces who gets paid off and how much. *Rapport in action,* I thought. This was my vamp, and he was trying to improve his odds. I sauntered a little closer, trying to figure out my next move. The table was crowded, so I would have to be reasonably subtle.

You're a cocktail waitress, Candace. Act like one, I thought. Quickly, I snagged a forgotten drink, set it on my tray, then sidled closer to the vampire.

"Excuse me, sir," I said brightly.

Not very original, but it did the trick, broke the vamp's concentration. I saw Larry shake his head and blink, hard.

"Hey, I'm playin' here," the vampire said, his eyes still on the boxman. Clearly, this guy had seen *Midnight Cowboy* one too many times.

"I'm terribly sorry to disturb you, sir," I apologized at once. "But if I might speak with you for just a moment?"

He turned to snarl, then paused as he got a good look at my harem-girl outfit. I saw his gaze slip down my front to settle on my cleavage. *Two can play at the distraction game, pal,* I thought.

"Do we get to talk in private?"

Slimy creep, I thought. I let myself flush. "I—" I began, then stuttered forward, as if I had been hit in the back. The drink flew off my tray and down his front. Perfectly good bourbon, sacrificed for a good cause.

"What the hell?" Furious, he dabbed at his shirt with a drenched handkerchief. "Watch what you're doing, can't you?"

"Omigod. I'm so, so sorry," I said at once. I yanked a napkin from the tray and began to help him wipe. "Of course, the casino will arrange for your clothes to be replaced. If you'll give me your name and tell me where you're staying, I would be happy to arrange that for you."

The vampire hesitated, his expression considering. He wasn't about to give me the address of where he nested during daylight hours. "I just got here," he said finally. "I haven't checked in yet."

"Then let me take you to speak to my manager. He'll authorize the chit for the costs to launder or replace your shirt." I gave him my brightest smile, leaned a little closer. "Nobody's going to care if you're really a local. Let me do this, and you can use the chit to gamble instead, if you want."

Larry leaned over when the guy hesitated. "Go ahead," he said. "I'll save your place."

The vampire grinned. "All right."

"This way, sir," I said, motioning toward the nearest exit sign. It led to a staircase that didn't get used all that often, and then mostly by employees. The official procedure I had established with Al called for me to usher any bloodsucker out of the casino by the closest exit possible, preferably quietly. And that's what I intended to do.

I led the way down the stairs, listening to his footsteps and gauging my chill level to determine how close the vamp was. He was one riser above me. In a more public exit, I would have asked him to go first. But I could hardly do that when I was the only one who knew where we were going. That's when he did it: He reached out and touched my ass. Sliding his hand between the layers of chiffon that danced down my legs to get to as much bare skin as possible.

The truth is not pretty, but it is the truth.

I lost it. All my hatred, my disgust for vampires, my self-disgust for loving one, came to a head in one brilliant, crystalline moment.

With a shout, I pivoted on one heel, drove the tray I was still carrying straight into his stomach. The vampire doubled over in pain, and I brought my knee up beneath his chin, knocking him over. He fell backward, spread-eagled on his back. Before he could so much as get an elbow beneath him to lever himself up, I was kneeling down beside him. One hand grasping his shiny, dark hair.

"What the fuck?"

"Watch your language. There's a lady present," I snapped. He bucked, but I held him down. With my free hand, I slowly slid one of the silver stakes from my hair. The vampire went still at once. I pointed the sharp end toward his face, brought it down, stopping less than a quarter inch from his right eye.

"You know what this is?" I asked. "You know what it can do to you? I want to hear you say it."

"Yes!" he said, his voice high and tight with panic. "I know. I know."

"Give me one good reason why I shouldn't use it, you bloodsucking ass-pincher."

"Wait a minute. Wait a minute," he squawked. "I know something."

I smiled. "So do I," I said. "I know lots of things. What can you possibly know that would induce me to spare your miserable existence?"

"There's a con set to go down," he was babbling like an infant now. "A big one. It's going to ruin your tournament and the casino. I can tell you all about it. You have to let me go."

I changed the angle of the spike, brought it down to nick his cheek. He gave a hiss of pain as the skin where the silver had touched turned dead white and began to flake off.

"Tell me now."

"Okay, okay!" he choked out. "It's high-tech, real cutting-edge stuff."

I gave a snort. "That much, even I know. Everything around here is high-tech. That's how casinos run. There isn't an inch of the casino floor that's not under observation from every angle you can imagine."

As a matter of fact, somebody somewhere is probably catching me on tape right now. I was going to have to speak to Al about that. I brought the spike closer, an eighth of an inch from the vamp's eye this time.

"That's not enough, and we both know it. Give me more."

"New Year's Eve. It's set to go down on New Year's Eve, the final game of the poker tournament. That's all I know. I swear to God."

I stared down at him for a moment, battling my own desire to stake the sonofabitch and be done with it. But I had the feeling he was telling the truth. And if I took this vamp out, I would be breaking my own vow. High-level vamps, human bloodsuckers only. Anything else was just too risky. I had been incredibly stupid to let my temper get the best of me in the first place, as a matter of fact. I had tipped my hand to the fact that I could tell a human from a vampire. I could only hope he was so terrorized that revealing the secret would never be in his best interests.

I pulled the stake away, stood up, stepped back, and motioned for the vampire to follow suit. He did so slowly, as if expecting me to pounce, to change my mind.

"This meeting never happened. Have you got that straight?" I asked. "We both walk away, forget all about it. But you come into my casino again, my memory will make a miraculous recovery. Are we all clear about what will happen then?"

He nodded.

"Good," I said. "Now get out."

I pointed down the stairs. The vampire hesitated for about two seconds, then took off like a shot. I waited until I heard the door yank open, then slam behind him before I tucked the stake back into my hair and picked up my tray.

I had to get to Al Manelli's office.

The security office is on public display, not far from hotel registration and the main entrance, there to show guests that nothing is going to happen to them, or their winnings, while they're at the casino.

I knocked and Al opened the door slightly, then wider.

"I've been wondering when you would show up."

"I hope you snagged that tape," I said.

He nodded as he closed the door behind me. "Already on it. So, Nerves," he said, as I plopped down into his one and only guest chair. "Care to tell me what the hell is going on?"

Nerves is Al's nickname for me. Short for Nerves of Steele. Al Manelli looks exactly like his name suggests: short and powerful as a fireplug. The truth is, he looks just like a mob enforcer. The rest of the truth is that he's got a big soft marshmallow for a heart. He's a great guy, and an even better boss.

"I'm sorry about what just happened, Al," I said. "I'm really sorry. But I did learn something you might want to know."

Quickly, I explained my interview with the vampire. I kept to the facts, not discussing my own lapse in judgment and poise.

"You don't look too surprised," I said when I had finished.

Al gave a sour laugh. "That's because I'm not. There've been rumors about a con at the tournament from the very beginning. Randolph and I have done our best to keep them quiet. They're probably rumors, nothing more."

"But you don't know that for sure," I prompted.

"No. No, I don't. You know, sometimes I wish Clooney and company had gotten caught robbing the Bellagio and been slapped in jail at the end of *Ocean's Eleven*. Maybe that would keep all these idiots from trying to knock over casinos."

"You're taking this threat seriously," I said. "Why?"

"Well, I pretty much have to, don't I?" Al replied. "Big celebrity tournament, broadcast all over the country. Something goes south anytime during it, and the Sher would never recover. Particularly not if it happens on New Year's Eve."

"So what are you doing about it?"

"Increased security presence on the casino floor," Al said at once. "But I must admit, what you've just told me does add a new wrinkle. One I can't say I like very much."

"That would make two of us," I replied. "But it's not very likely vampires would be directly involved in the con itself, Al. It's just not their usual style. Way too high visibility."

"Under normal circumstances, I agree," Al responded. "But I don't think I can afford to leave any stone unturned here, Candace. Maybe we should follow up on the fact that this vamp knew something.

"Scout around a little," Al suggested. "See if you can find out if the bloodsuckers really are involved. And you might check in with Chet McGuire in IT. He'll be able to fill you in on the tech end of things, the security system in particular."

"Chet McGuire. Information technology," I said. "Got it. Meantime, I'm off the floor?"

"After tonight, yes," Al nodded. "For tonight, I want you to stay in the casino, see if anything else shakes out. After that, try whatever other sources you have to. The No-Limits tournament is a very big deal, Candace. Absolutely nothing can go wrong."

"Where have I heard that before?" I murmured, as I got to my feet. "I'll do my best, Al."

"I know you will," Al Manelli said. "That's why I watch your back. But you need to watch yourself. I saw you in that stairwell, Candace. You looked pretty damn close to losing control."

"It won't happen again, Al," I said. "Believe me when I say that's the last thing I want."

"I do," Al Manelli said. "Now get out there and find out what we need to know."

I returned to the floor, feeling shaken by what I wasn't willing to admit to Al. I had done more than come close in that stairwell. For a few desperate seconds, I *had* been out of control. Furious with every single vampire in the world. Furious with myself. And all because a dream had shown me a truth I didn't want to face.

I could hate every single vampire on the planet, and it wouldn't do me a damn bit of good. Not as long as I was still in love with one.

Three

Vampires and a con at the Sher. Now there was a combination made in Hell. Also one that didn't make a whole lot of sense. As I had said to Al, it was just too high profile. Not only that, vampires aren't really into high-tech toys. They much prefer their own mind games to any electronically induced ones. Best-case scenario therefore: My instincts were right. Al's were wrong. And I would essentially end up with the week between Christmas and New Year's off.

Meantime, my shift was finally over. A recharge of the mind/body batteries was definitely in order. I needed caffeine and food, in that order. That meant Ma's Original Diner. Neither Ma nor the diner are, in fact, original. But by Vegas standards, where things are built, torn down, only to be rebuilt and torn down half a dozen times more, the place practically qualified as a historic landmark.

"Morning, Candace!" Ma called from behind the red-speckled laminate counter as I came in the door.

She could have been forty or sixty. Her face was un-lined, her hair a dull gray. "Coffee?"

I nodded but didn't smile as I glanced along the narrow counter. *Well, shit,* I thought. It appeared that I was going to have a Goldilocks moment. Somebody was sitting in *my* chair. Or on my stool, to be precise.

A tourist, no less. Now, instead of my favorite spot, I was going to have to settle for the one next to it, the one with silver duct tape all over the top.

I stomped past the tourist, glaring behind his back as I went. Ma gave me a commiserating shrug. I plopped down onto the stool from Hell, glanced at the guy's plate. It looked pretty good. So did he.

"I'll have what he's having," I told Ma.

The tourist who'd stolen my chair had a tight, wiry build that seemed to radiate energy. His face was narrow, but he had wide, whiskey-colored eyes. His chin carried just the hint of a shadow, as if he, too, had been up all night. Right in the center was a cleft. I'm a total sucker for those. I kept my eyes on his as I watched him assess me. *Now here was a guy on the make,* I thought. Usually, guys like this totally turn me off. This morning was a different story. Maybe it was all the adrenaline run-ning in my system, a combination of my dream of Ash and the encounter with the vampire. Or maybe it was those whiskey-and-soda eyes. Either way, I could already feel my body pitching its case to my head.

Give yourself a holiday, Candace. Go with the flow.

"We could share," the guy finally said, and I found that I liked his voice. Deep and ever so slightly rough-edged. It suited the rest of him just fine. "There's enough to go around."

I let my tongue flick out to touch my lower lip, as if fantasizing about what the food would taste like, watched his eyes widen, and felt a little tingle of anticipation skitter along my spine. All of a sudden, I wasn't pissed off anymore. Instead, I was having fun.

"I don't know," I said. "I usually have a pretty big appetite. Besides, I don't even know you."

"I can fix that," he said at once. He offered a hand, and I placed mine into it. His grip was firm, his hand and fingers ever so slightly calloused. "Michael Pressman," he said. "Call me Mike and suffer the unfortunate consequences."

"I'll remember that," I said with a smile. "I'm Candace Steele. You even think about calling me Candy and same goes."

"There, you see?" Michael said. "Now we're old pals."

Ma set a steaming cup of coffee down in front of me and I retrieved my hand.

"Thanks, Ma."

"Don't mention it," she said. "Consider it bottomless, and it's on the house. Least I can do under the circumstances." Ma gave a snort and bustled off.

"What circumstances?" Michael asked, as soon as Ma was out of earshot.

I took a sip of coffee, even though I knew it would be too hot. "You're in my usual spot."

Michael's face went completely blank. "I'm sorry," he said. "I didn't know."

"No way you could," I replied. I took another sip of coffee. "But you do now."

Michael stood up at once. "I'll trade you," he said.

I let my eyes travel over his faded jeans, decided they could take the duct tape. "You're on."

I stood, then took a side step toward my regular stool. Michael stayed right where he was. He put a hand on my arm, as if to steady me. My body brushed against his, and, for one split second, my ass was snug up against his crotch. His other hand dropped to my hip, as if to hold me in place, and I felt a swift, hot stab of desire spear forward from where our bodies touched until it reached my groin.

I eased down onto my regular stool. Michael's hands stayed on me all the way, as if he were afraid, without him, I might fall down. Then he took the place that I had vacated and reached to slide his plate toward him. His forearm brushed against my breasts. I knew we both saw the way my nipples hardened. He speared a bite of omelet, held it out toward me.

"So, Candace," he said. "You want to share, or not?"

I took the fork into my mouth, then let Michael slowly slide it back out. I chewed, swallowed, then accepted a second bite. He turned his body all the way toward mine, his long legs on either side of my stool so that I was between them. I leaned forward, pressing my arms against the outside of my breasts so that they pushed toward him.

"That's good, thanks," I said. I took another sip of coffee. "What brings you to town?"

"I'm playing in the No-Limits tournament," Michael said simply. Then he made a face. "I guess you could say I have a sort of type-A personality. I got tired of running marathons, thought I'd try my hand at tournament poker."

"You must be pretty good," I observed. Not to mention loaded. The buy-in to the tournament was hardly chicken feed.

"I'm not bad," he answered with a shrug. "One of my friends just sold his software company. He's bankrolling me."

"That's a damned good friend," I remarked.

Michael laughed. "Tell me about it. But as I helped contribute to Josh's millions, I guess he's willing to share. I'm also his stockbroker." He took a bite of omelet, himself. "So, you're a local?"

"Actually," I said, "I'm a cocktail waitress at the Scheherazade."

"No kidding?" Michael said, his expression intrigued. "That's quite a coincidence."

"Isn't it, though."

He toyed with the food on his plate, his eyes on his fork. "Mind if I ask you something?"

"As long as it doesn't have anything to do with the casino," I said.

He shook his head at once. "Nothing like that," he said. "No. The thing is. I'm just sort of wondering . . ." He lifted his eyes to mine and I felt a punch of heat right through the gut. "How hungry you really are."

"That's kind of hard to say," I said. "But I'm pretty sure what I'm hungry for isn't on the menu at Ma's."

"We don't have to stay," he said.

"That's right. We don't."

"Half a second," Michael said. "Just let me settle up."

He pulled his check from beneath his plate, moved to the cash register at the far end of the counter. I stood, surprised to feel my head felt just a little light. *Anticipation,* I thought. The truth was, I liked the way my body felt, right at that moment. Cool skin, blood running hot. I joined Michael, and together we walked out into the parking lot. He headed straight for the stretch limo.

"You have got to be joking," I said.

He grinned. "Nope. You can blame it all on Josh." He rapped on the driver's window, and at once the tinted glass rolled down.

"Oh, hey, Mr. Pressman," a youthful voice said.

"Hey, Andy," Michael replied. "I'd like it if you'd just drive around the city for a while. Wherever you like."

"Sure thing. I can do that," the driver said. If he was surprised that his fare was no longer alone, he didn't show it. He made a move as if to get out and open the passenger door.

"No, no," Michael said. "Don't get out." He moved to the back of the limo, opened the door himself. I slid in onto the smooth white leather seat. The divider between the driver and the back was all the way up. Not only that, there were curtains pulled in front of it. Michael slid in beside me, shut the door with a sharp *slap*. I felt the car quiver, heard the door locks *snick* into place as Andy brought the engine to life. In front of the banquette seat stretched an ocean of plush, sky-blue carpet. I could have sworn the back of the limo had the same square footage as my office.

"So, what do you think?" Michael asked.

"Nice," I said. "Very nice."

He reached out, fisted one hand in the long-sleeved T-shirt I wore, and pulled me toward him. Leaning back against the locked door so that I sprawled across his chest.

"I was really, really hoping you would say that," he said. And put his mouth on mine.

Michael's mouth was firm and demanding. He nipped his teeth along my lips in quick bites that stopped just short of pain, while his hands slid down my body to cup my ass, kneading, stroking. I bit back, parting my lips, and at once he swept his tongue inside. I pulled it deep inside my mouth to suck, and heard him make a satisfied sound.

His hands moved up to tug the T-shirt from the slacks I wore. And then his hands were underneath the shirt and on my skin. The car took a corner. Gasping, I tilted to one side, then slid off onto my stomach on the plush carpet of the floor. Michael followed with a quick laugh. He knelt above me, arms and legs bracketing my body, hands already reaching for my breasts as he pressed his erection against my rump. I threw back my head. He bent his head and caught my earlobe between his teeth, biting down, hard. One hand still beneath my shirt, he reached with the other to push it forward, pull it off. He released the clasp of my bra and my breasts swung free. He put his mouth on my bare back. Fingers digging into my hips now, he ran his tongue along the length of my spine.

"I want to fuck you, Candace," he said, his voice husky. "Deep and hard. I want to hear you scream when you come."

"You're the one who's going to scream," I said, and heard him laugh, low in his throat.

He reached for the fastening on my pants then, undoing the button, eased the zipper down. Repositioning me so that my upper body rested on the leather seat, he drew the slacks, and the brief scrap of silk I wore beneath, down my legs and off. Then, quick as lightning, he rolled over onto his back, sliding beneath me as he spread my legs once more. He ran his hands up the backs of them, then slid around to the front. My breath began to come in hard, quick gasps. He pressed his mouth to my clit, slicked his tongue across it once, twice, three times, then pulled it into his mouth to suck.

I threw back my head once more, pressing my breasts against the soft, smooth leather, warming it even as my skin warmed. With one hand, Michael stroked along my ass. The other followed suit, then moved forward, his fingers sliding inside. I gave a guttural cry as I pressed against them, driving them deeper. My whole body was on fire now. His fingers inside me, their rhythm fast, then faster. I felt him take my clit between his teeth, and gently bite down. I did scream, then, as pleasure pure and hot as lightning shot straight through me.

"No," I gasped out. "Not yet. No. It's not enough."

I heard him laugh. Felt the vibration of it deep in my own body. He released me, his fingers leaving my body on one long, slow glide. His mouth left my clit to travel up across my belly. I put my palms on the edge of the seat, pushed myself back, and felt him leverage himself into a sitting position beneath me to take one breast into his mouth. I was writhing against him, desperate to feel his skin on mine. I leaned back, my bare crotch resting squarely on his still-denim-clad one.

My eyes on his, I undid the buttons of his shirt. Slowly. One by one, while a humming silence filled the car. With one hand, he continued to tease one of my nipples, plucking until it stiffened and ached. I pushed the fabric of his shirt away, bent my head, ran my teeth along his nipples. I felt his hand tighten on my breast, heard him make a strangled sound. And then my hands were undoing the fastening of his jeans. Shifting my own body away, I pulled them down and off. Beneath them, he wore a pair of fine silk boxers. I ran my hands up across the front, where his cock pushed forward, then slipped them inside the waistband and drew the boxers off.

And then he was reaching for me, pulling me up his body, positioning me above him. Bowing my body back, pushing my hands up to brace against the roof of the car, he pulled one breast deep into his mouth even as he gripped my hips, then urged me down. I rocked my body back and forth, taking him deep, then deeper still. He gave a groan. Slowly, as if measuring every inch of him, I began to move my hips, up and down. Michael's fingers dug into my hips.

"More," he choked out. "Faster. Harder, Candace. More."

I let myself go then, tumbling forward over him, hips pistoning up and down as he thrust to meet me, stroke for stroke. His hands raced up my back, then moved to find my breasts, capturing my nipples between his fingers, squeezing hard. My breath clogged in my throat.

"Do it," I heard him say. "Do it, Candace. Come."

On a great, hot surge of pleasure, I felt my body release, felt Michael thrust up, then go still even as

I clenched around him, his cock stone-hard. And then he was moving again, moving wildly, body bucking up into mine as he came in his own turn, hands gripping my ass as he drove us both on. I lay sprawled across him, my breath coming in ragged gasps.

"You didn't scream," I said, when I could manage to speak.

He gave a spurt of laughter I felt all the way to my core. He brushed the hair back from my face and gave me a long, slow kiss, then let those whiskey-colored eyes smile into mine.

"I didn't, did I?" he said. "Oh, well. There's always next time."

The Strip was pretty quiet as I drove toward the turn that would take me to my house. Images of Michael and our ride through Vegas played in my mind, arousing me all over again. I forced myself to push them away. *You have a job to do, remember?* I said out loud as I headed for home. I idled at a stoplight, sliding my cell from my bag and hooking the earpiece into my ear. Then I punched in Blanchard Gray's number. Blanchard works at the medical examiner's office. We pretty much keep the same hours. For me, it was so I could keep the Sher free of vampires. For Blanchard, the situation is a little more basic.

Blanchard Gray *is* a vampire.

I guess you might even say he's *my* vampire. If not for me, Blanchard wouldn't exist at all. I had come upon him literally being sucked dry in an alley not long after I moved to Vegas. By the time I had offed his attacker, Blanchard himself was too far gone. I hadn't been able to save his life, but I did manage to keep him from dying the horrible death of someone teetering between the living and the undead. In return, Blanchard helps me when he can, serving as my eyes and ears in the vampire underground.

If anyone would know whether or not a vamp con was going down, it would be Blanchard. Now all I had to do was convince him to tell.

"Blanchard, it's Candace. We need to meet," I said, when his voice mail picked up. "Unless I hear back otherwise, I'll expect you at Cisco's at seven tonight. You don't show, I'm coming looking for you."

That ought to do it, I thought, as I severed the connection. It was in Blanchard's best interests to keep a low profile when it came to our relationship.

I turned down my own block. Now that the business end of things was out of the way, at least for the time being, I could go home and catch a little shut-eye. With any luck, I would dream of Michael this time.

Four

It was a chilly night. The fog rolling in from the bay was as dense and dank as wet cotton, wrapping the city in a desperate woman's embrace, a mistress who knows that, even as he takes his pleasure deep inside her body, her lover has already forgotten her. The kind of night most humans prefer to spend indoors, preferably not alone. Light and sound, color and warmth, breath and touch—these are the ways to beat back this sort of night. Those who venture out do so from necessity, not choice.

Except for those like me.

I am a vampire.

A vampire in trouble, I thought, somewhat wryly, torn between elation and annoyance. A vampire who had just done the very last thing that he expected: lost his heart. To a human woman.

I turned a corner, heading toward the waterfront. The fog was even thicker here, rolling along the sidewalk as if it had a specific destination in mind.

It shouldn't have happened. It's as simple as that. And I wasn't so certain I wanted it to, if the truth were told. I may lie to others when it suits me, but I make it a point never to lie to myself. Self-delusion is a luxury I choose not to afford. Dalliances with women are one thing. Swift, urgent encounters. Enticing seductions. I have feasted on many women, in more ways than I can count. But love, even the possibility of it, never entered the picture.

Not once. Not until tonight.

I quickened my pace, impatient with myself now. I had held a woman I desired in my arms, and I had let her go. Because at the moment I gave myself the pleasure I had delayed all evening, drawing out the suspense, increasing the anticipation for us both, I had discovered that what I was experiencing wasn't what I had anticipated after all.

I wanted her. That much was clear. But as I had held her close, teasing her lips with mine until her eyes drifted closed, I discovered a need I had not known I was capable of feeling. Not to dominate, or to control or devour in great greedy bites, but to be gentle and to cherish. To protect at all costs. And so I stepped away, disappearing into the night as unexpectedly as I had stepped out of it, and left her standing, eyes closed, bemused with passion, in the middle of the sidewalk.

No doubt she was pissed as hell.

Better that way, I told myself. Better for us both. The woman was clever and funny and sweet. The kind a man made promises to—promises he actually intended to keep. The kind of woman a man looked forward to coming home to at night. The fact that, at the very first glimpse of her—dark curly hair in seemingly permanent disarray and laughing, chocolate eyes—I had felt something hot and sharp and utterly unexpected pierce my heart and then stick fast like a barb. It shouldn't have mattered. I had tasted her lips, satisfied my own curiosity, and that should have been the end of it. I had no need for a now and forever sort of love. I had no need for love at all.

I reached the waterfront and let my steps slow to a stop, leaning on impulse against one of the tourist pay-to-view telescopes. I pressed my eye to the eyepiece, as if trying to catch a glimpse of the view. *Go home, Ash,* I thought. Even considering the possibility I might find happiness with a human woman, find happiness at all, was like gazing into this telescope. There was nothing to see. There was nothing there at all. My best, my only, course of action was to go back to the existence I had constructed with such deliberation. The world that, until tonight, had provided everything I wanted. Stop dreaming of six impossible things before breakfast. Stop dreaming, period.

Satisfied with my conclusions, I lifted my head and felt a sudden pain greater than any I had ever known shoot through my body. A million tiny daggers, dancing along the nerves of my frame, rattling my very bones. I could feel my body spasm, was utterly powerless to stop it. My vision hazed red, went stark white, then black. And then I remembered nothing more.

When I knew myself again I was in a small room, the light so bright it hurt my eyes. I was wearing my own garments, lying on my side. Every single muscle in my body ached. I lay still for a moment, sensing the condition of my own body. My head throbbed viciously, as if whatever had attacked me had driven an ice pick through the base of my neck, then twisted it straight up into my skull. My mouth tasted vile. But I could tell I had no major injuries. Slowly, careful not to jar my head, I put my hands flat beneath me and levered myself to a sitting position. I stayed that way for a while. Then, as soon as the room stopped spinning, I got to my feet.

Big improvement, I thought. The room didn't spin this time.

As if my ability to rise to my feet had been some

kind of signal, the door to the room opened and two men entered. The first was clearly a vampire. His eyes flicked over me, quickly, assessing my condition. I felt the faint touch of rapport. It isn't just humans who can be affected, manipulated by this skill. It works between vampires as well. I let it wash over me without consciously attempting to deflect it away. *Rapport works two ways,* I thought. The fact that this vampire had used it at all told me that he was not quite certain of me. Not quite certain of his own strength now that I was aware of him.

I am stronger than you are, I thought. A strength I would hold in reserve, for now. The thought that I had let myself get caught unawares by someone weaker than I burned like a cinder in my gut.

So much for the power of love.

The vampire snapped his fingers and the second figure stepped farther into the room. At the sight of it, the burning in my stomach got much worse, for an entirely different reason this time. The newcomer was a human man, his skin a pasty gray, his eyes flat and dull. Except for a loincloth, his body was completely bare, and riddled with bite marks, some of them fresh.

Drone, I thought. Of the most disgusting, pitiable kind. This human had been kept alive for just one purpose: to be a food source. Vampires feed on humans in many different ways, all of them with unpleasant results if you are alive. But this was the worst sort of existence imaginable. To be slowly drained, until your body was rendered incapable of rejuvenating itself. Then, most likely, this man would be torn to pieces, literally devoured.

"I am Simmons," the vampire said. He gave a second snap of his fingers and the drone stopped.

"I would say that I'm pleased to make your acquaintance," I said. "But there wouldn't be much point. We both know it would be a lie."

An expression I couldn't quite read came over Simmons's face. *He wants me to goad him,* I suddenly realized. Why? So he had an excuse to dole out punishment? And, in that moment, I realized what his expression held. Envy and fear in almost equal measure. The fear I understood. Comprehending the envy would take more time. He gave the drone a shove, and the man staggered forward, dropped to his knees at my feet. I saw his throat move as he swallowed, vainly trying to prepare himself for what he knew must come. *He is almost spent,* I thought.

"You will feed on this drone before we proceed," Simmons said, in a tight voice. "The effects of the means we used to bring you here can cause some regrettable weakness. The Chairman wants you strong."

The Chairman! I thought. With those two words, Simmons had told me what I needed to know. I wondered if he realized it. *Watch your step, Donahue,* I thought.

"Please thank the Chairman for his kind offer," I said. "Sadly, I think I must decline."

Simmons moved then, darting forward like a snake to strike, his act so sudden it caught even me by surprise. With a swift, brutal motion, he brought his arm up, clubbed me to my knees. The drone and I were now on equal ground.

"I don't give a damn what you *think*," Simmons said, his tone shrill. "What you *think* is not important. What is important is that the Chairman gets what he wants. *You will feed on the drone.* You will obey this order or suffer the consequences."

I rolled my tongue around the inside of my mouth, then spat the blood that had pooled there at Simmons's feet.

"Very well."

With a sound that might have been a snicker, Simmons stepped back. *He likes to watch,* I thought. A vampire voyeur. Just what the world needs.

I stared at the drone, silently willing the man to lift his eyes to mine. He did so at once. In them, I saw a desperate plea, a desperate hope.

"Please come closer," I said softly. Again, I saw

that flicker of surprise. No doubt because I had asked, not simply taken. The drone dropped to all fours, crawled closer, then straightened up once more. Crawling was the only thing that he was capable of. I reached out and took the drone's head gently between my hands, looking fully into his eyes.

"You know what is about to happen?" I asked. "Let me hear your voice."

"I know," the drone replied, his voice no more than a single thread of sound.

"What is your name?" I asked. "Are you still man enough to recall your name?"

Simmons made a restive movement, quickly stilled as the drone spoke.

"Carlyle," he said, his voice moving slowly over the syllables, as if afraid they might get away if he spoke too quickly. "My name is John Carlyle."

"Very good. That's very good," I said. "You know what it means, don't you, John? It means that when you die, you will die as a man."

I broke his neck then, one quick, hard twist. He fell forward, into my arms. Then Simmons was there, screaming in fury, the veins standing out in his throat. I caught a quick glimpse of the weapon that had been my initial undoing, a taser, before the world once more exploded in a series of bright, painful shards, then went pitch dark.

*   *   *

When I came to myself again I was seated in a chair, dressed in a robe of simple linen, its only decoration a pin depicting a red equilateral triangle. Before me was a table made of lustrous ebony, also triangle-shaped, in a room completely unadorned. I was seated along the triangle's bottom. To my left sat three men. Two to my right, with an empty chair between them. But all my attention was immediately drawn to the man I faced, seated directly across from me, at the triangle's apex. Not that he was a true man, of course.

We were vampires, all of us. Powerful ones.

All vampires are predators. Sensing one another, the depth and extent of our own powers, is part of how we survive. And so I knew at once that I was in the presence of power so immense and ancient my mind could hardly comprehend it.

"I'm afraid I really must apologize for Simmons," the man across from me said. *This was the Chairman,* I thought. It could be no one else. "A useful enough servant, but overzealous in his duties sometimes. The matter is being looked into. It may even be that you will be able to render us some assistance before it is done."

He shifted his head then, cocking it the way a bird does when it considers the best way to remove a worm from the ground. He raised one hand, a gesture that encompassed the other vampires at the table.

"Do you know who we are?"

His voice was like nothing I had ever heard before. It seemed to me that it reverberated through the room, inside my head. A single voice, but so much more. He had the most extraordinary face I had ever seen. I have never used this word to describe a man, but he was beautiful. His features were high and finely etched, but he had a full and sensuous mouth. And his eyes seemed to hold every secret in the world. Changeable as the sea, fathomless as the deepest well. Ancient and filled with inexorable purpose. His hair was long, falling to his shoulders in golden waves.

Fallen angel, I thought. For surely Lucifer had been beautiful as well. Beauty and evil so bound up together no power in Heaven or on earth could have pulled them apart. Only one thing marred his features. Below his right eye was a mark, like a single teardrop of blood. I knew what it was, what it had to be: It was the Mark of Thoth.

I have seen many things in my long existence. Fury, delight, agony, passion—I have seen them all. I believe there are only two things I have not seen with my own eyes: joy so great that not even the fear of its loss can cause it to dim, and evil incarnate. The second was before me now.

"I am waiting for an answer," the Chairman said, and I discovered that I still possessed a voice.

"I do not *know*," I said, careful to stress the final word. I saw the flicker of what might have been a smile.

"But if you had to hazard a guess," he said.

"If I had to hazard a guess, I would say that you are the Board."

A ripple passed through the room then, a soft sibilance that might have been a sigh.

"And what is the Board, can you tell me that?"

"No," I answered honestly. "Not entirely."

"Then say what you do know."

I could feel the excitement, the tension rise within me. Never had I been so close to such unmitigated, ancient power.

"The Board is an ancient organization," I said. *And you were their leader, even then,* I thought. *That is why you bear the Mark upon your face. You were branded by the god Thoth himself.*

"Originally, they were priests—followers of the Egyptian god Thoth. Second in power only to the great god Ra. Thoth, giver of speech and weigher of dead souls. Thoth of strong magic, even the power to become immortal. He wrote this and many other spells in the Book of Thoth."

"How poetic," the Chairman murmured. "Go on."

"The god's followers desired immortality, so they performed the ritual that would complete the spell. But Thoth was aware of them. He cursed their tongues. Instead of becoming immortal, they became unclean, undead. Drinkers of living blood. And so the first vampires were born."

The Chairman smiled. "Well done. You know the basic history. What don't you know?"

I made a split-second decision. If the Board had wanted to put an end to me, they would have done so before now. There was no sense in lying. The Chairman would see right through that. I could feel his power, *their* power, beating at the edges of my mind.

"I do not know why I have been brought here," I answered honestly. "I do not know what you want."

"And yet you do not ask," the Chairman said.

"Because I assume that you act with purpose. That I will be informed."

Again, a sigh seemed to pass through the vampires assembled in the room. The question was, was my response right or wrong?

"The questions you do not ask are about to be answered," the Chairman said. "You will rise."

I did so.

The Chairman raised his voice ever so slightly, as if speaking to unseen servants. "Bring in Sloane."

A door to my right opened, and a second vampire was brought in. He bowed deeply before the Chairman, then moved to stand at my side. Sloane was dark-haired, slightly shorter than I am, with a tight, muscular build. *Mean in close quarters,* I thought. And that's precisely where we would end up, sooner or later. I know an adversary when I see one.

"Parker Sloane, Ashford Donahue, you two have been summoned before the Board for the same purpose, the same cause. To be tested, that we may know your strength, determine which of you is most fit to join us, to become part of the great quest to restore our true power and be granted immortality."

The empty chair, I thought. There should be seven Board members, not six. Seven—ancient number of power. There was a vacancy on the Board.

"What sort of tests?" Sloane asked.

"Patience," the Chairman counseled. "All in good time."

I felt a surge of satisfaction, swiftly controlled. I had been right about Sloane. He would fight like a junkyard dog when cornered. But he was impatient. Impatience makes one do stupid things.

The Chairman tilted his head once more, and the Mark of Thoth caught the light. Head of an ibis, a bird with a beak great and curving as a scimitar. Body of a man. On his head, a full moon rising from a crescent. In one hand, Thoth holds a papyrus, to remind mortal men of the gift of speech that he bestows. In the other, a set of scales to weigh the hearts of dead humans.

There would be another such tattoo on his body, I thought. Directly in the center of his chest, where he had once possessed a beating heart. All those who became true followers of the Board, vampire or human, are so marked. But only the Board's original members would have born the god's mark directly on their faces. Once, there would have been seven. Now, there was only one. *The others had been used up in the long centuries of their existence,* I thought, as the Chairman drew on their powers to help him continue his own existence, continue the great quest of the Board.

I had been collecting information on the Board for many years, drawn by the tales of unimaginable power matched with almost unimaginable frustration. According to the texts that I had read, after Thoth had shattered their ritual, he had shattered his own power, as well—taken the Book of Thoth out of the world, then split his power into three parts called the Emblems of Thoth: the Heart, the Body, and the Tongue of Thoth. Only by reuniting them could the Board complete its ancient ritual and obtain the immortality they had desired for so long.

"How do you know the tests haven't started already?" the Chairman asked now. "There are many ways of judging worthiness, some of them quite subtle."

Once again he raised his voice. "Simmons!" he snapped.

The door through which Sloane had entered opened. Simmons, the vampire who had captured me, staggered in. His shirt was in tatters, his pants ripped and bloody.

"Approach," the Chairman commanded. "Stand between the supplicants."

Simmons obeyed at once. I watched the way his eyes flickered over Sloane. He didn't look at me at all. And in that moment, I understood. He had been punished because of the way he treated me. I was the cause of his humiliation.

"Between you stands a problem, gentlemen," the Chairman said, his voice melodic and low. "A problem one of you will now solve. Simmons is a tool who is no longer of any use. His judgment has become flawed."

A fine trembling seized Simmons's limbs. He seemed powerless to stop it.

"What would you do with such a tool?" the Chairman asked. "How should it be . . . disposed of?"

"End him, Chairman," Sloane spoke at once. As if pulled by a string, Simmons's head jerked toward him. *He had hoped for some redemption there,* I thought. The Chairman was right. Simmons's judgment was flawed. Sloane would redeem no one but himself.

"What cannot be relied upon cannot be used," Sloane went on. "He should be destroyed."

The Chairman's ancient, unreadable eyes rested on Sloane, then turned to me. "Would this be your solution also?"

"No," I said. "It would not. He may still be useful, Chairman."

"How?" Sloane broke in, his tone derisive. "You heard the Chairman. The tool is flawed."

"But not broken," I said at once. "This man seeks to please you above all else, Chairman. You and only you. He has forgotten that even you serve a greater cause. That is his lapse in judgment, his flaw. Instead of destroying him, withdraw your favor. Send him away. Cast him out. If you destroy him, he will be forgotten. But if he survives, he will be an example to all."

"No!" Simmons pleaded. "Do not listen, Chairman. Don't send me away."

The Chairman raised a hand and Simmons's voice choked off.

"I don't remember giving you permission to speak."

Tears began to track slowly down Simmons's cheeks, but he did not make another sound.

"An elegant and painful solution," the Chairman remarked. "I admit you interest me, Donahue. You show compassion for a human drone but none for your own kind."

"That one is not my kind, Chairman," I replied. "He is more drone than the human was. He has given up his will. That is an act I will never perform."

"Then you will lose," Sloane said at once. "For that is precisely what the Board requires."

I turned my head to look at him. "You think so?"

"Enough," the Chairman said. "Your solution is accepted, Ashford Donahue." As one, the members of the Board rose, as if the Chairman's words had been some sort of signal. "Show me the mark of your allegiance," the Chairman commanded Simmons.

The vampire's face had gone a sickly yellow. With trembling fingers, he drew away the remains of his tattered shirt to reveal the tattoo in the center of his chest.

The Chairman lifted his hands in a simple gesture, palms up. The other Board members mirrored it, their palms facing down. I felt a sudden current lance through the room, potent as an electrical charge. The hairs on the back of my neck lifted, the way they do when prey knows the predator is watching. Then the other Board members clasped their hands together, the sound echoing throughout the chamber. The Chairman held his, palms facing out, straight out before him.

"What was bestowed, I now take away."

Simmons's eyes went wide. His body twitched. He gave a great shuddering gasp. And then he simply began to scream as the power the Chairman directed at him stripped away the Mark of Thoth. The skin on his chest blackened, then peeled back, and still the power flowed. My hair was wild about my head now, the light from the power emanating from the Chairman's hands all but blinding.

Then the Chairman brought his hands together with a *clap* and the room went absolutely still.

"Take him away. It is done."

Still screaming, Simmons was led from the room. For many moments, no one spoke.

"You have both begun well," the Chairman said at last. "I have learned much tonight. You will go now, and at the next full moon, you will be sent for. Then you will face the first true trial. The Nigredo, the test of the dark. Until then, prepare yourselves as best you can. I suggest you use your time well."

"And when one of us fails?" Sloane suddenly asked. "What happens then?"

"Oh, but surely you know the answer to that already," the Chairman replied. "That, too, is a problem that must be solved, and it is your solution that will apply.

"The one who triumphs will join us. The one who fails will be destroyed."

Triumph or be destroyed. Not a hard choice to make. I didn't ask to be a member of the Board, but from that moment on, I made my decision. I would not let the Board beat me. I would win. I would be a member of the Board.

Five

I was the first one to arrive at Cisco's Bar & Grill that evening. Not a surprise. Blanchard is almost always late for our meetings.

I slid into a booth, one that would let me see both the door and the restaurant, then sat back and scanned the room. The walls were covered with replicas of old signs and toys that should have been thrown out decades ago. Not really Blanchard's style, or my own. But the advantage of Cisco's is that it's a fringe place, a place where both humans and vampires go. Sort of a demilitarized zone. Blanchard calls meeting in places like this protective camouflage, and I have to admit he's got a point. Since our old meeting place, Ed's Diner, had been bulldozed to make room for a new hotel, we had sort of been bouncing around. Cisco's was the current meet location of choice.

The bar was busy and loud. A sudden burst of sound drew my attention to three young men at a table near the kitchen door. Slicked-back hair. Narrow ties. Tailored suits that hadn't been stylish since the early 1960s. A tall, skinny guy with dark wavy hair was toying with a drink and laughing drunkenly. Vegas is full of Elvis impersonators. This guy looked more like Dean Martin. Beside him sat a short, dark-skinned guy who looked as if he weighed less than I did. *And that one's Sammy Davis Jr.,* I thought, as the coin dropped suddenly. Plainly, these guys were working on a theme. Sammy glanced toward me, and I looked away, suddenly realizing the truth.

They were vampires.

"So sorry I'm late," I heard Blanchard's voice murmur. Lifting off a black fedora that would have looked perfect on Annie Hall, he slid onto the seat across from me, then grimaced in distaste. "Don't these people know plastic is hell on fine leather? Don't *you* know?" He shot an accusing frown at the waiter who had materialized beside us. "Shame on you."

The waiter flushed. Blanchard can sometimes come on a little strong. Usually, it's because he wants attention or because he's attracted to someone.

"Two Cokes," I said. The waiter gave a nod and moved off. Blanchard shot me a look of reproach.

Blanchard Gray has the best sense of style of anyone I know. Female or male, straight or gay. He prefers dark colors, a contrast to his pale skin and bleached-blond locks. But a simple black leather coat wasn't enough. Tonight he had accented it with a cashmere scarf that must have cost him a week's wages. Deprived of our waiter, he winked at the next one to pass our booth.

"Blanchard," I said, my voice long suffering. "Flirt on your own time. We need to talk."

He shrugged off his coat and loosened the gray cashmere scarf. "Don't you know that boys just want to have fun?"

"That's what I want to talk to you about." It didn't take me long to tell him about the vampire at the Sher and the rumor about the con at the tournament. I kept my voice low, aware that just about anyone in this place might be listening. In general, vampires have excellent hearing. "Have you heard about any schemes aimed at the Sher?"

"Why on earth would my people be interested in something like that?" Blanchard asked in a tone that suggested he found even having to answer the question tiresome.

"My question exactly. I couldn't come up with anything that makes sense. Can you?"

He flung his hands into the air, and our waiter backpedaled, spilling Coke on his tray. His eyes on Blanchard's every move, he set the glasses in front of us along with some straws, then rushed away at approximately the speed of sound.

"Candace," Blanchard said in a tone of exaggerated patience, as if he were speaking to a child. "I can't believe you called a meet over this. You know my people wouldn't get anything worthwhile out of such a con. And face it, even though some bored vampire might get off on making the casino look stupid, we don't go for the big public spectacle."

Exactly what I've been telling myself, I thought. The trouble was, I was pretty damned certain the vamp I had threatened was telling the truth, and I just couldn't make the two facts line up.

"You know us," Blanchard went on. "We prefer to operate in the shadows. The bright spotlight's not a vampire's cup of tea. Not any of the ones I know, anyhow."

"What about *those* guys?" I asked suddenly, motioning toward the group at the back of the restaurant.

Blanchard half-turned in the seat to check out the Rat Pack posers in their early-sixties finery. He turned back with a roll of his eyes.

"Oh, them. Total low-level losers. Can you believe that they actually call themselves the *Bat* Pack?"

I laughed in spite of myself. "Not too subtle, are they?"

Blanchard shrugged while he downed a sip of Coke. "What can I tell you? The truth is, they're new to the realm of the undead. So they're totally into the power trip some new vampires get off on—until they figure out that even our world has its hierarchy."

My cell vibrated against my hip. I pulled it out, glanced at the screen, and couldn't help smiling. M PRESSMAN, the readout said.

"Someone special?" Blanchard asked at once.

"Maybe."

"Who?"

"None of your business," I replied. "But I'm going to take this. Sit tight a minute." Sliding out of the booth, I pushed the *talk* button.

"Hey, Candace," Michael's voice sounded through the phone. "I hope I haven't caught you at a bad time."

I looked at Blanchard, who was eyeing the waiter again, and the Rat—no, make that *Bat* Pack, who were eyeing the whole room. "Absolutely not," I replied.

"Excellent," Michael replied. "So, listen, I made

it through two more rounds. I feel like celebrating. Any chance you'd like to help? I'm at the Scheherazade, in the Desert Tower."

Only the swankiest wing in the whole hotel.

Okay, you can make this work, Candace, I thought. Getting involved with guests wasn't exactly against the law, but it was seriously frowned upon. Al wasn't going to be happy if he found me hanging out with a player from Randolph's precious tournament. Visiting Michael at the Sher was going to be . . . challenging.

Which also meant it could be fun.

"What's the room number?"

"Eleven hundred."

"Nice."

Michael laughed, the sound pleased and warm. I remembered what it had felt like to have his hands on my body, to feel his skin slide across mine. And knew, in that moment, I was going to take the challenge.

"About twenty minutes okay?" I asked. "I'm across town, and I need to finish up some . . ." I glanced at Blanchard. "Errands."

"Twenty minutes is fine. It'll give me time to figure out how to work the damned stereo so I can have some mood music on when you arrive."

"Try the *on* button," I said.

Michael was laughing as he rang off. I flipped my cell shut and considered my options. I could walk boldly into the Sher and cross the casino to get to the Desert Tower, an act that would mean I would be visible on dozens of security cameras, breaking the unwritten rule. Or I could slip in wearing a disguise.

"Blanchard," I said. "Any chance you'd let me borrow your hat and scarf?"

"Are you going to get blood on them?" he asked at once. Before I could answer, his eyes went wide. "Omigod. You're going undercover. Please tell me it's for a good cause."

"Actually, it is," I said, deciding an appeal to Blanchard's sense of the dramatic might be in order. "A romantic assignation. In forbidden territory."

"Love it, absolutely love it!" Blanchard declared. "Dare I hope forbidden fruit will also be involved?"

I bit down on my tongue to keep from laughing. Blanchard and I sounded like old gal pals.

"Only if I can get there in the first place," I said. "So, whattaya say?"

Blanchard held the scarf and hat out across the table. "They're yours. But I warn you, get anything on them and I'm sending you the dry-cleaning bill."

"Deal," I replied. I put them on.

"For crying out loud, Candace, not like that," Blanchard exclaimed. "I swear to God, you have the fashion sense of a fruit fly."

He stood, made a few quick adjustments, then stepped back to admire his handiwork. "Okay, *now*."

"Thanks, Blanchard. I really mean that," I said.

"Don't do anything I wouldn't do," he said with a smile.

I gave him one back. "That's for me to know, and you to never find out."

It was hard not to chuckle as I strolled through the casino. Not one of my coworkers so much as gave me the eye. Blanchard would not have approved, but I had added my long wool coat to the hat and scarf to cover up as much of my body as possible. As I walked toward the Desert Tower, the shops edging the promenade changed from gift shops with rude T-shirts and antacids to high-end designers. Fendi. Versace. Hermès. Dior.

I stepped into the elevator, hit the button for the eleventh floor. Several moments later, I stepped back out again, onto dark green carpet thick enough to swallow my feet up to the ankles. Room 1100 was at the far end of the hall to the left. Along the way, I admired the wallpaper with its arabesque style, the graceful tables of wrought iron and glass, topped by glorious flower arrangements. I rang the bell beside double doors with brass numbers set into what looked like a genie's lamp. This was still Vegas, and the casino was called the Scheherazade, after all.

Michael opened the door about three seconds after I rang. When he got a load of my attire, his handsome face split from side to side in a smile.

"That's quite a getup," he remarked. "Very . . ."

"Mata Hari?"

"I was going to say Boris, of Boris and Natasha, though the coat should really be a trench coat. You need the belt and lapels. Because then I'd look really smooth when I did something like this."

He grasped the front of my coat, tugged me inside, then closed the door behind me.

"Hi," he said.

"Hi, yourself." I took a look at him. A good, long look. "Speaking of getups." He was wearing one of the hotel's thick, plush guest robes.

"I just got out of the shower," he explained, raking his fingers through his damp hair and leaving it spiked. He took my hand, drew me into the dimly lit foyer. "Why don't you take the tour while I put something else on?"

"Don't change on my account."

He went still for a moment, his eyes lighting up as they took in what I was wearing once more.

"Please tell me you're naked under that coat."

"No," I admitted with a laugh. "But really good thought." I tilted my head, looked up into those whiskey-brown eyes. "Does this mean I don't get the grand tour after all?"

"Of course not."

Fingers linked, we went into the suite's main room. It was magnificent, with high ceilings and thick oriental rugs covering travertine floors. Beyond the low, sleek sofa, sliding glass doors led to a private balcony. There was a full kitchen with green granite counters and cherry cabinets. A dining room with a long, mahogany dining table beneath a crystal chandelier. Soft music played through speakers hidden somewhere in the walls.

I cocked my head. "You managed to figure out the stereo."

"I called in expert help. Even though you're not naked, I'd really like it if you'd take off that coat."

"I think I might manage that," I said with a smile.

I pulled off the fedora, tugged the scarf from around my neck, shrugged out of the coat. What I wore beneath was hardly what I would have called spectacular: slim jeans and a form-fitting top. But the look on Michael's face told me he definitely approved.

"I hope you don't think it's hokey, but I ordered some champagne." He gestured to where a bottle sat in its sweating ice bucket.

"Champagne is only hokey if it's cheap," I replied.

He laughed and drew me to him. "I like you," he said. "I didn't expect that, somehow."

"What the hell is that supposed to mean?" I asked.

He made a face, and I saw his cheekbones color. "Come on, you know. Just because we're compatible one way doesn't mean we are in others. And it was a totally lame statement and the sooner you forget I made it, the better. Let me pour you a glass of this seriously nonhokey champagne. You can drink it while I get my foot out of my mouth."

He knew his way around a champagne bottle, I couldn't help but notice. No cork flying across the room, just a quick twist, then a slow ease out of the bottle. I felt a slow trickle of heat pool low in my body. Michael Pressman was definitely good with his hands.

He filled two flutes, handed one to me.

I held up my glass. "To luck in the coming rounds!"

He tapped his glass against mine. "To meeting you," he said. We drank at the same time. I felt the icy slide of the champagne meet the heat in my body.

"Are you superstitious?" Michael asked, taking me by surprise.

"Not usually, no," I said.

"Me, neither." I caught a gleam of mischief in his eyes. "But there's one superstition I've always wondered about. You know that thing about a kiss for luck?"

I took a second sip of champagne but kept my eyes on his.

"Mmm hmm. What about it?"

"I was just wondering whether there was any truth to it, that's all. We poker players are a very superstitious bunch."

I set my glass down on one of the side tables with a sharp *click*. "Why don't we perform an experiment and find out?"

"I was hoping you might feel that way," Michael said. He set his champagne glass down next to mine.

He drew me to him, cupping my face with his hands. Very slowly, with the same care he had used to ease the champagne cork from the bottle, he pressed his lips to mine. I let him set the pace. For the moment. It was his experiment after all. He traced his tongue around the contours of my mouth, then coaxed them open to move inside. I pulled it deeper, a promise of passion to come, and felt him shudder, ever so slightly. Slowly, the tip of his tongue stroking against the roof of my mouth, Michael eased back.

"That felt pretty lucky."

"It did, didn't it?" I said.

I stepped back, reaching for my champagne. We both knew why I had come here, where this was going. But we'd gone fast the first time. I didn't want to rush things now. Just because I had decided to indulge in a little holiday fling didn't mean I had to behave like some slut. At least not right off. And not that there was anything little about Michael Pressman.

I took a sip of champagne. "So how do you like living like the other half? Or do you live like this all the time, Mr. Big-Time Stockbroker?"

"I wish," Michael remarked. He sipped his own champagne, watching me over the rim of the glass. "My place in Chicago could fit in the bathroom here and have room left over," he went on. "That's why I intend to enjoy this while I can."

"Good choice."

He smiled and tilted back his glass. The music stopped, and he reached for a remote on the table in front of us. He aimed it toward the dining room and pushed a button. Ella Fitzgerald's voice filled the room. Sensual and sultry, Ella's voice felt like an invitation, the opening of a doorway into something rich and delightful.

Another good choice, I thought.

"I hope you don't mind the oldies," he said.

"Not when it's Ella. She's still the best."

"I agree." He set his champagne down. "Would you like to dance with me, Candace?"

Would I like to press my body against yours and slide my hands beneath that robe? I wondered. *Oh, yes. I think so.*

"I thought you'd never ask."

He took the champagne glass from my hand and set it on a table beside his own. Then he drew me to him, linking my arms around his neck so that my breasts pressed against his chest. I moved in close, shifting against him till we both felt the way my nipples hardened. Michael eased one leg between mine.

"About that experiment for luck," I said. "I'm thinking we should try it at least one more time."

Michael bent his head to mine at once. I could taste the urgency in him now. I let my own tongue go exploring, enjoying the contours of his mouth. His hands dropped to either side of my hips, tugging my pelvis toward him with each sway of our dance. I ran my hands down his arms to his waist, found the knot of the robe's sash, tugged it apart. And then my hands were on his skin, sliding around to cup his ass. I felt his cock go stiff as it pressed against my hip.

"You're wearing too many clothes," he said.

I leaned back, feeling his hands at the bottom of my shirt. "Bet you know how to fix that."

"I do."

I grinned. "Just my luck."

Michael drew the shirt up over my head in a motion that was fierce and fluid all at once. His mouth was hungry on my breast even before I could lower my arms. I linked one around his neck, arching up so that his mouth could explore, and felt his hands move to the fastening of my jeans, deftly flicking the buttons open.

You do have good hands, I thought.

"Hold on to me, Candace," I heard him say. "Hold on." And for one dizzying moment, I was back in my dream of Ash.

No! I thought. *That is not what I want!*

Not the past. Not even the future, but precisely what Michael Pressman offered: the flash and heat of the here and now. I wrapped my arms tightly around his neck, my mouth seeking his as he lifted me from my feet to pull the jeans down. The second he set me on my feet, I shoved the robe from his shoulders. It dropped to the floor.

"The bed," he managed.

"Later," I answered. I put my own hands to the front clasp of my bra, snicked it open. I shrugged my shoulders, pushing my breasts forward and the lace away. "Right here, Michael. Right now."

We never would have made it to the bedroom anyhow. Arms banded around one another, mouths fused, we tumbled together onto the couch. Michael reared up to draw the panties down my legs. With a sudden, playful smile, I slid down to the floor. I wanted to feel that thick carpet against my skin. If I was going to break the rules, I was going to go all-in. Michael followed, his mouth feasting on my breasts like a starving man, even as his hands stroked down. I parted my legs, then squeezed together tightly as I felt his probing fingers slip inside.

My upper body arched against his questing mouth even as I let my lower body begin to rock in the rhythm as old as time. I heard a deep sound of passion and realized I had made the sound myself. Michael murmured in reaction, and suddenly his lips were back on mine. He reached to stretch both my arms above my head and my body protested the loss of him inside me even as it thrilled to be so exposed.

"You," I panted around our kisses. "Inside me. Now."

He released my hands to pull my legs onto his shoulders, reared back, then filled me in one long, slow stroke. I lifted my body up to meet his, felt him inside me, deep and hard.

"God, Candace," I heard him say. And then we were moving in tandem once more. Bodies pulling back only to drive together. Michael's hands were tight on my ass now, holding me still as he plunged. I felt his body straining, reaching for the brink, knew the very second that he toppled over. His body, one long arch of passion straight into mine. I tightened myself around him and felt myself begin to fly. As my own climax took me, Michael began to move once more, his mouth on my breasts. I gave myself up to the white-hot fire.

"I think I may have rug burns," I said, some time later.

Michael gave a spurt of laughter. "Don't blame me," he replied. "You're the one who insisted on the floor."

"I insisted on you," I corrected, and saw the way his eyes blazed with new possibilities.

"I stand corrected," he said.

"Okay, you win. I can't stand at all."

I did manage to roll to one side, lever myself up onto one elbow to watch him sit up and retrieve our champagne glasses.

"How long before your next round?"

Michael downed a slug of champagne. "About an hour, I think," he replied. "I'm not actually sure what time it is, in fact. I'd have to check my watch."

"And where would that be?" I inquired.

"In the bedroom."

"Remarkable coincidence," I said. "I hear there's this really amazing bed in there."

He cocked an eyebrow. "How are you going to see it if you can't walk?"

"You can get that thought right out of your mind, Michael Pressman," I said. "I am not the sort of woman who crawls."

He threw back his head and laughed. I watched the way it moved along his throat. "In that case, I suppose I'll just have to give you a hand," he said. He stood, reached down a hand for mine. His cock was already jutting from his body again, not at full attention, but definitely starting to rise.

Good hands and stamina. Now there was a combination a girl could really wrap herself around, I thought. Michael Pressman was exactly what I needed. We were two bodies, ready and willing to come together. Nothing less, nothing more. No promises about the future. No lies.

I reached to take his hand, then gave a startled shriek as he pulled me all the way up and onto his shoulder. As he strode toward the bedroom, his hands stroked my ass. By the time he gave me a toss that had me bouncing on the bed, I was breathing hard.

The bed truly was amazing, a gigantic four-poster. Its gauzy hangings were pulled back. There was a second bottle of champagne beside it. I propped myself up on the cushions while Michael dealt with the cork. He poured a single glass this time. Coming down beside me on the bed, he held it to my lips. I drank deeply, but the angle was slightly off. Some of the frothy liquid dripped from the corners of my mouth. It ran down my chin to slide across my breasts.

"Looks like you made a mess," I said.

Before I quite realized what he intended, Michael tilted the glass over my belly. I gasped as the cool liquid slid straight down between my legs.

"Guess I'm just going to have to clean you up, aren't I?"

When we got out of the shower, the phone was ringing.

"That's my heads-up," Michael said, as he sprinted for the phone. He lifted the receiver, acknowledged the message. I shrugged into my scattered clothes.

"Sorry about this," he said, when he realized what I was doing.

"What for? You came to play—to win," I corrected quickly. "If you weren't in the tournament, you wouldn't be here at all. I can hardly get upset when you go off to do the thing that brought you here in the first place."

He crossed the room, gave me a quick, hard kiss.

"How come you don't live in Chicago?"

"Because I live in Vegas," I said. *Besides,* I thought, *this wouldn't be the same if we lived in the same city. Part of the reason people come to Vegas in the first place is to do things they would never do at home.*

"I was thinking we should do the town when I get my next break," he said. I trailed him to the bedroom, watched as he began to tug on his own clothes. "Or at least some of it. As long as you don't mind it being kind of spur of the moment."

"I don't mind," I said. "In fact . . ." Before I could complete the thought, my cell phone buzzed. I had clipped it back onto my waistband as I'd dressed. I glanced down and read the number. Bibi.

"You're sure?" Michael said as I reached for the phone.

"Absolutely," I said. "But I've got to take this call."

"Sure thing," Michael said at once. "I'll just check my e-mail before I head on down." He walked back into the living room, to give me some privacy.

I flipped open the phone. "Hi," I said. "What's up?"

"I need you to come stop me from killing Randolph," Bibi's voice rasped into the phone.

"Why would I want to do an idiotic thing like that?" I inquired. I had never been wild about the Bibi/Randolph relationship, which Bibi knew quite well.

"I mean it, Candace," she said. "I really need your help."

All of a sudden, I heard the tears behind her voice.

"Where are you?" I asked.

"In the Sand Bar."

I gave a silent groan. Bibi hates the Sand Bar. She goes there only when she's seriously depressed.

"I'm on my way," I said, closing the phone.

Going out into the suite's main room, I saw Michael staring at the screen on his laptop. I went over to kiss him good-bye.

"You really are obsessed," I said, pointing to a sticker of a miniature royal flush that he had stuck on the edge of his keyboard.

"Yet another good luck experiment," he said, standing up to draw me into his arms. He gave me a kiss that made me want to linger.

"Michael," I sighed. "I have to go. You have to go triumph in the next round, and I have to go rescue a friend who's down."

"This isn't some prearranged kiss-off, is it?" he asked.

I shook my head. "Absolutely not. I'd really like to see you for as long as you're in Vegas. What do you say to that?"

"Now I know I'm lucky."

Other than Louie, the bartender, Bibi was the only occupant of the Sand Bar. Not even the tourists like to come here. Louie glanced at me as I walked in, but I shook my head. I didn't want anything to drink. He picked up some damp cloths and went through a swinging door into the kitchen behind the bar.

For a second, light spilled past the door, bringing the dreary space to life. The walls became a vibrant red, and the fake gemstones pasted to the wooden beams sparkled. Then the door swung closed and all was bleak once more.

Bibi was sitting on a high stool with a diet soda in front of her. She was staring off into the distance, lost in thought. Her long legs, clad in pink practice tights, were crossed, the heel of her left shoe balanced on the lowest rung. Bibi Schwartz is one of those women who is . . . *more.* Her black hair has more highlights in it, and it's far more manageable than mine. Her breasts are more lush. Her legs have more length than any one woman's should. And she feels emotions with more depth than anyone I know.

We met in a dance class in San Francisco and clicked right away. But our friendship was signed, sealed, and delivered when she came to my rescue after Ash had taken his too-big bite out of me. An event we always refer to as the "elevator incident." It was Bibi who found me and who got me to a doctor before I bled to death. It was Bibi who stayed by my side while my body healed, who held me while I wept and stormed and raged, while I struggled to heal emotionally. I literally owe Bibi Schwartz my life.

"So I take it Randolph is still alive?" I said as I slipped onto the stool next to her. "Why do you want to kill him, by the way?"

"Katherine is coming to Vegas for New Year's Eve. The slimy sonofabitch has known for months. He didn't tell me until tonight."

Katherine is Mrs. Randolph Glass, aka the boss's wife. Bibi and Randolph hooked up not long after Bibi moved to Vegas. It would have been a happily ever-after if there wasn't also a Mrs. Glass involved.

"I'm sorry," I said.

"She's supposed to stay on the East Coast," Bibi said now. "Katherine plays society lady in Boston and Martha's Vineyard. Randolph lives here, three time zones away, and invests her money in the casino. That's the way things are."

"Sounds like a plan," I said, loyally. I knew Bibi wanted only sympathy. Otherwise, she wouldn't be telling me what we were both perfectly well aware I already knew.

"It *was* a plan," she said. "It *is* a plan. A damn good one. They see each other at Christmas and for a week in the summer when Randolph flies back East. But New Year's Eve is *our* special night. Randolph's and mine." Fury flashed in her dark eyes. "Then, just an hour ago, he springs it on me. Katherine's coming for the big party he's planning to hold on New Year's Eve!"

"Well, that completely sucks. Did he at least give you a reason?" I asked.

Bibi gave a weary sigh. "Of course. When you own a casino, you always need money, approval, and goodwill. Which is why we've got this charity tournament taking over half the Sher. The fact that Senator Hamlyn—who's got friends on the gaming commission by the way—has agreed to play in the tournament is Randolph's dream come true. It gives him real cachet with the power brokers.

"Well, guess whose family and the senator's have been friends since the dawn of time?" Bibi finished her soda with a slurpy flourish.

"Uh-oh," I replied.

"Damn straight, uh-oh," Bibi snarled. "If Katherine doesn't show up for at least the tournament's finale, it won't look right. Even *I* can see that much."

"Bibi, I'm so sorry."

She patted my hand as if I were the one needing consolation. "Thanks, kiddo. I knew I could count on you to let me enjoy a good whine. You know I'm not really mad at Randolph. I'm mad at myself for putting up with his shit for so long. And I am *not* crawling back after Katherine leaves. I can tell you that much. I deserve better, and I am going out to look for it."

"Here, here!" I gave her a round of applause.

"And you're coming with me," she said. "You could use a little something new yourself, Candace."

"Actually . . . ," I said. Instantly, Bibi's eyes grew wide.

"You've got a guy. Who is he?" she pounced.

"His name is Michael."

"Is it serious?"

"No—but it's fun."

"How much fun? Is he good in bed?"

"What makes you think I've slept with him?"

She gave a snort. "Give me a break, Steele," she said. "You've got that big-O look in your eyes. But do you think you can give me one night on the town?"

"Absolutely," I said. "What else are friends for?"

"Outstanding," Bibi said. She leaned forward, gave me a hug. "Let's both go home, get fancied up. Meet me in front of the Bellagio in about an hour. Then we can decide where we want to go."

All of a sudden, she grinned, her eyes dancing wickedly. "You know, I might just go pick up my things from Randolph's penthouse. Katherine usually stays out at the lake house, but you never know . . . I would hate for her to think the diamond bracelet Randolph bought me to soften the blow was hers."

"You are one mean and avaricious bitch, Bibi," I said, delighted when she crowed with laughter.

"Oh, honey. You know it." Bibi hoisted her

soda. I raised one of the votive candles lining the bar. We clinked them together.

"To moving on," Bibi declared.

Now there was an outstanding sentiment if ever I heard one.

"To moving on."

Six

I met Bibi an hour later by the lagoon in front of the Bellagio. The wall along the lagoon's edge was crowded with tourists watching the spectacular fountains spurt water in the air in time with music. I knew when Bibi was approaching. Male heads snapped around as if she had them all on a leash. Her turquoise leather skirt was so short there was at least a mile of legs between the hem and her rhinestone Jimmy Choos. A leather jacket of the same color was open to reveal a lacy top and a black silk scarf edged with fringe.

"You look great!" she said as she gave me a hug. "Where did you get those jeans? They're fabulous!"

I looked down at the jeans that had cost me a month's tips. The right leg was plain denim, but the left leg had been slit up the side. Black lace had been sewn in to reveal a hint of leg from ankle to hip. I was wearing a lacy black camisole and a cashmere shrug that tied over my breasts. My hair was up and my silver stakes at the ready, though I was hoping I wouldn't need them tonight.

"So where to?" I asked.

Before Bibi could answer, a shadow moved behind her, and I heard a deep voice ask, "Are you ready to go?"

Bibi gave me an apologetic smile then turned to a guy dressed in jeans, black T-shirt, and black jacket. He had that dark, steamy, Mediterranean look that makes some women melt. I'm not one of them.

"I don't know if you two have ever run in to each other," Bibi went on brightly. "Candace, this is Theo. Theo, my friend, Candace. Theo's dancing in the New Year's Eve show. Candace is . . ."

"All over the place," I said. "I work the floor."

"Nice to meet you," Theo said, eyeing me with a broadening smile. "Sorry I didn't recognize you without the harem outfit."

"That's all right," I said pleasantly. "I didn't recognize you at all."

"Theo's been telling me about a new club off the Strip he went to last week. He's offered to take us there."

Theo lifted Bibi's hand and kissed it with a suave European flair. "I can take you wherever you want to go."

"Come on, Candace. Theo says this place is

where the action is *really* happening. It's called Taste."

"Taste?" I repeated even as I thought, *Uh-oh*.

Uh-oh turned out to be right on the money. Taste was dimly lit, filled to the brim with high fashion and loud music. People dancing and drinking and reveling in the thrill of hard bodies in close contact.

It was also filled with vampires.

The second the bouncer let us through the velvet rope, I felt my body temperature plummeting toward absolute zero. The trouble was, there were so many vamps I couldn't figure out who might pose a true danger and who might not. My vampire-detection system had shot from zero to a hundred in less than sixty seconds. One thing was for certain, I did *not* want to be here, and I didn't want Bibi here, either.

Bibi and Theo had already hit the bar. Each was holding a cocktail. I grabbed Bibi by the elbow. "Wrong place, wrong time," I said. "Let's go get some Mexican food. I'm craving quesadillas now."

She yanked away. "What is the matter with you tonight?" She pouted. "I thought you were on my side. That you were going to help me have fun." She downed this drink as rapidly as she had her first, then turned to Theo. "I'll bet Theo will help me, won't you?" she asked. "You'll help me have fun."

By way of answer, he set his drink down on the bar and pulled Bibi out onto the packed dance floor.

Shit, shit, shit, I thought. Now all I could do was wait. I was not about to leave Bibi at a place like Taste all on her own. The worst part was, I felt partly to blame. The simple truth was that I had let myself step away from the vampire scene in the last six months since Ash had walked out. Wounded by our most recent encounter, not to mention my run-in with ultra-strong vampire Temptation McCoy, I had been more than willing to give the vampires of Vegas a wide berth. If I had kept more current, I might have known the sort of place Taste was ahead of time.

At least I could check it out now. The place really was spectacular. The walls were suede, a dove gray color that shimmered as clever lighting effects projected colors on the surface. The dance floor was small and intimate, but in reality the club was huge, with a honeycomb of lounges and private spaces. With Bibi and Theo occupied for the moment, I decided to explore, edging my way around the dance floor. The lounges that ringed it had deep banquettes with sides high enough to give the patrons enough privacy to do whatever they had in mind.

I saw a man approach. He was dressed in expensive but casual clothes and walked with such an imperious air that I was surprised when he asked if he could take my drink order. I declined and turned another corner to face a three-story waterfall that cascaded into a pool filled with floating candles. I couldn't understand how the candles stayed lit until I realized that the fountain was actually contained within a glass column. Another turn brought me to a room that was totally dark except for a light on the far wall that illuminated a huge red velvet mouth. The mouth was actually a door that led to another dark room, but I had seen enough. Gorgeous and unusual as it was, the longer I spent in Taste, the colder I got.

I turned around, trying to retrace my steps, but the mazelike rooms, the darkness, and the pounding music were disorienting. Each room I passed through looked just like the one before it. And each one sent a shiver through my body. There were so many vampires here, my senses were on overload. I managed to lurch back to the main room where the dance floor was, but there was no comfort there. The music was louder, the dance floor was teeming with dancers. I was getting dizzy now. With all these bodies crammed together I had no idea who was human, and who was a vampire.

Find Bibi and get out now, I commanded myself.

Then, all of a sudden, Theo was there. Over his shoulder, I could see Bibi, out on the dance floor. Dancing with abandon, her body gyrating, hands over her head. Even in that packed space, the other dancers had fallen back a little, to give her room to move.

They're watching her, I thought. I might not be able to tell the humans from the vamps, but I was dead certain the vampires did not have the same problem.

"What's the matter, Candace?" Theo asked, moving his body closer to mine. "Don't you like to dance?"

"Bibi and I have a deal when we go out together. We always keep each other in sight." Kind of a lame answer, but it happened to be the truth. It also happened to be true that Bibi wasn't abiding by the rule.

"Bibi's just fine," Theo commented. He laughed, and the sound grated in my ears. "Just look at her. She's having the time of her life." He pulled me out onto the dance floor and began to move his hips against mine. "Surely you don't want her to have all the fun."

I don't want her to have any fun at all in a place like this, I thought. But being on the dance floor did get me closer to her. I let my hips begin to move in time to Theo's and felt his hand move down my back to cup my ass. He urged me toward him, sliding one hip against my crotch, then turned me so that my back was against his chest. He wrapped his arms tightly around my waist, his hands sliding down my belly. I pushed my hair out of my eyes and came face-to-face with . . . myself.

Dancing right across from me was a woman with wild and curly dark brown hair the same length as mine. She had a tight, athletic build. The dress slicking down her body, hugging her every curve, almost an exact match of one I had in my own closet. A vibrant bronze silk that clung close and plunged low. She smiled, showing gorgeous white teeth, ran her tongue along the bottom of them in a slow, seductive gesture. And in that moment, beyond a shadow of a doubt, I knew the truth.

My look-alike was a vampire.

Bile rose in my throat. If I didn't get off the dance floor right now, this second, I was going to be sick all over it.

I jerked away from Theo, began to push through the crowd, ignoring the sharp words snarled in my wake. I didn't give a damn. I had to get out. Get away. Now.

I have literally no idea how I found the ladies' room. I kept heading away from the center of the coldness until I hit a door that opened. It closed behind me, and the pounding of the music abruptly ceased. It wasn't piped in, thank God. The ladies' room was even darker than the dance floor, illuminated only by a cluster of votive candles on the sink counters. I didn't give a damn. I could see enough to stumble to one of the empty stalls. I rushed in, shut the door that reached all the way to the floor, and locked it behind me, then leaned against it.

Breathe, just breathe, Candace, I thought.

I closed my eyes and rested the back of my head on the door. The clatter of the silver spikes in my hair was both reassuring and frightening. I had a weapon, but of course I couldn't use it in the crowded club.

Come on now, get a hold of yourself, I thought.

Yes, coming face-to-face with my doppelgänger was extremely creepy, but it was nothing to have a panic attack about. They say everyone has a double. It was just my sick, twisted luck that mine was a vampire. Coming to Taste was teaching me an important lesson. I now knew that my vampire-sensing skills could actually go on overload. I had experienced this once before, when I had sought out Ash at a vampire meeting place called the Majestic. But that experience had been nowhere near this disorienting, or this strong.

Congratulations. You're a fast learner, I told myself sarcastically. *Now find Bibi and get out.*

I turned, reached for the lock on the door, then stiffened. Male voices. Several of them. Coming from high up. I squinted through the dark and saw dim light glinting off an open transom window near the ceiling. I heard water splashing. *The window must be between the two restrooms,* I thought.

". . . see those legs?" I heard one guy ask.

"Jesus, Dino," a second voice said. "We don't have time for that now. New Year's Eve is right around the corner. We've got plans to finalize."

Then the words hit me: *Dino. We. New Year's Eve,* I thought. Could I possibly be eavesdropping on the Bat Pack? But surely that didn't make any sense. Blanchard had claimed they were low-level losers, and he had never steered me wrong. Someone else was speaking now, but I couldn't catch his words. Blanchard might not deliberately *steer* me wrong. That wasn't the same as saying he couldn't *be* wrong. *I need to get closer to that window,* I thought.

The toilet. Grabbing the top of the marble walls of the stall, I set one shoe on the seat, then hoisted myself up. I balanced precariously, straining my ears to listen.

". . . when we finish at the Sher" came through, clear as a bell.

"Why does it have to be the Sher?" a voice I

hadn't heard before complained. "Why can't it be New York–New York? I like that one better."

"Because it's not up to you, buddy boy. And if you want to be a player in this town, you'll do things *his* way, or pretty soon you won't be doing them at all."

"After what goes down at the Sher, things are going to go *our* way," the guy who had wanted New York–New York gloated. "You watch. The power in this town is gonna change. We're gonna count down to midnight in style."

I felt sick. The vamp at the Sher had been telling the truth. Al's instincts had been right, and mine wrong. The rumors were more than rumors. They were fact. There was a major con set to go down at the Sher on New Year's Eve, and vampires were very definitely involved.

Something moved in the faint reflection on the transom. Acting purely on instinct, I ducked. I knew it was the wrong move the second I made it. My heel slid off the seat, banging into porcelain.

The voices stopped at once. There was a beat of silence.

"Check the ladies' room." One of them gave the order.

Shit! Now I'd done it.

I slipped out of the stall and inched open the outer door, peering out as the music thudded in, wondering if I could simply make a run for it. The trouble was, I didn't know which direction to go. There was no way out except along a narrow corridor that led to both bathrooms. How in hell did I find my way here in the first place? If I had been thinking, I would have noticed how easily I could be trapped.

But I hadn't been thinking, I had been reacting, and now I was just plain fucked. I heard the sound of a door—it had to be the door to the men's room— swinging open. I couldn't pass them without being seen. That left just one option: bluff. If I could make them think I was just a dumb human who had wandered into Taste by mistake, I might still get out of this alive.

I slid the silver stakes from my hair, allowing my curls to tumble down around my shoulders. I palmed the stakes in my right hand. I didn't want to fight in such a restricted space, but I would if forced to make that choice. On sudden inspiration, I eased the door closed silently, took two steps to the closest sink and turned the water on. My one bit of luck was that it wasn't the kind controlled by a motion detector. Just a good old-fashioned faucet. I hoped it would prove a good omen. I needed one.

Taking a deep breath, praying it wouldn't be among my last, I pushed open the door. I knew what was waiting for me on the other side—or I hoped I did.

There were four of them waiting in the hallway. All male. All dressed like refugees from the old Sands Hotel. Frank Sinatra, Sammy Davis Jr., Peter Lawford, Dean Martin.

"Cool chick," the one who looked like Sinatra said. He leered at me, casually flicking ashes off his cigarette. If the situation hadn't been so desperate, I might have laughed. These guys really got into their roles.

"What are you doing back here all by yourself, doll face?" the Sammy Davis clone inquired.

"Waiting for my friend," I replied. "She's in the ladies' room." I leaned back against the door, cracking it ever so slightly to make sure they could hear the water running. "You know the rule, don't you? No woman can go to the restroom alone." I was babbling like an idiot, not that I cared. The stupider they thought I was, the better my chance of outsmarting them.

"So you were in there?" The Peter Lawford clone stepped closer. They all followed suit.

"Isn't that a little personal to ask someone you don't know?"

"That all depends," said the one who looked like Dean Martin.

"On what?"

"On how much better we can get to know you."

They laughed then, all four, in unison, and I knew I was in really, really big trouble. These guys were pack animals, and they were having a good time. The Dean Martin Bat Packer—he even held a martini in one hand—swayed toward me. I tried to make myself small against the wall, but it was pretty clear these guys weren't going to let me go. Not yet. They were having too much fun.

"Hey, baby!" Dean tilted his glass as if he were going to take a sip, then grabbed my arm.

I twisted out of his grip and shoved him back in the same motion. His drink splattered into my face and dripped down the front of my shrug, soaking through to the lace camisole.

"What is your problem?" I let my voice rise in an outraged whine. "Do you have any idea what liquor will do to cashmere?" I adjusted the stakes in my hand. I didn't want to use them. There were too many vampires in the club, and I was too far from the door.

"How clumsy of me," he crooned in a perfect Dino drawl. "Let me help you clean that off."

"No thanks."

"I insist." He grabbed me by the shoulders and ran his tongue along where the drink had splashed on my cheek.

"Get off me!" I gave the Dino a shove. He

rocked back and laughed. Could vampires get drunk? He sure was acting that way. Then I remembered that appearing slightly sloshed had been Dean Martin's act.

In the next moment, he abandoned staying in character. He was all vampire now. Leaping toward me, pressing me back against the wall. Not with his hands this time, but his whole body. Low level or not, his cock was high and hard. Even in the dim light, I could see the fiery glow of anticipation in his eyes.

Wait for it, Candace, I thought, even as my skin crawled, the voice in my head an echo of every self-defense class I had ever taken, and there had been a lot. *Give your foe a chance to reveal what he intends before you act. Then you'll know which way to move to block him. And if you're outnumbered, wait for a chance to take your best shot.*

Dino's thumb came up to brush against my wet camisole. He found my breast, then my nipple. He squeezed. Hard. I didn't want to cry out, give him what he wanted, but I knew it was my safest course of action.

"Please . . . please don't hurt me," I gasped out.

"Then stop making me, baby," he crooned, in character again now. "Relax. You might like it."

He bent toward me once more. He ran his tongue along my neck, licking off the martini. Disgust welled up in me as his tongue slid lower, over the curve of my breast, then back up toward my throat. I felt the smooth enamel of his teeth against my neck. Cold sweat broke out across my skin. Unable to stop myself, I put my left hand to his chest and pushed back, hard. He fell into his buddies. They laughed. The Dean Martin vampire narrowed his eyes. He took a step, but the Sammy Davis Jr. clone cut him off.

"My turn," Sammy said. "Watch this technique, cats. Let me show you how it's done."

Entirely without warning, the vampire pretending to be Frank Sinatra made a disparaging sound.

"You boys stay and play if you want to," he said. "I got better things to do with my time."

There was a moment of humming silence. Then, the vampire dressed as Dean Martin shrugged and straightened his shirt cuffs. "I'm with you," he said.

Without another word, they turned and walked off. I sagged against the wall, hardly able to believe my good luck. If they had wanted to scare the hell out of me, they had succeeded. They'd also shown me which way was out.

Bursting back into the club, I skirted the dance floor once, then a second time. I wanted to go home and take a shower and wash away all memory of those undead fingers and lips and teeth on me. But not until I found Bibi. I was seriously considering a foray onto the dance floor itself, when I spotted a familiar figure over by the bar.

"Theo, where's Bibi?" I demanded. He gave a shrug.

"Gone. She thought you left, so she went home, too."

"Are you sure?"

He gave another shrug. "That's what she said," he replied. "She was a little pissed off, if you want to know. She thought you'd cut out on her so she said she was going to call it a night. That's all I know."

As if to make clear he considered our conversation over, he turned away from me and melted back into the crowd of dancers. *Okay. Well, that's that,* I thought. Bibi was on her way home. Time to cut my losses and get out of Dodge. I made for the front door.

It was cold outside Taste, but I was warmer with every step I put between me and the vampire club. I pulled out my cell and pressed speed-dial for Bibi. She didn't pick up. I left her a message apologizing for the misunderstanding. Then hit the button to call for my voice mail. Sure enough, there was a message from Bibi, left almost an hour ago. I hadn't realized my encounter with the Bat Pack had taken so long. I had to play Bibi's message several times, the club noise in the background was so loud. It was garbled, but I could clearly make out the words "Going home."

No doubt that's where she was, sleeping off the excesses of the night. There was no sense swinging by her place to make sure she was all right. I would only wake her up, piss her off even more.

Walking toward the Strip where I could find a cab wasn't fun in high heels. I slipped my shoes off and kept going. When I saw the lights of the Rio casino coming up, I hurried toward it, knowing I could get a cab there. Fifteen minutes later, I was in a taxi that smelled of old cigars. For once the smell didn't bother me. All that mattered was that the cab was taking me home.

My house was dark when I stepped out of the cab. I never leave lights on. What I worry about could be waiting in light just as easily as in shadows. I didn't bother to turn on the lights as I locked the door behind me, staggered down the hall to the bathroom, stripped off my clothes, showered quickly, then reached for the soft flannel nightshirt that hung on the inside of the bathroom door. I was cleaner, definitely a plus, but my head still ached, as if the music had followed me home from the club.

I made the quick trip to my bedroom, pushed back the bedcovers, and fell into bed, facedown. Too tired to even pull the covers around me, I had one final thought: With any luck, I wouldn't dream at all this time.

Seven

"There's the bad news, and then there's the bad news," I said the following day. Al Manelli and I were in his private office. I had slept late, but once I was up and going I had headed straight for the Sher and Al. He needed to be told what I had discovered. I had also tried to reach Bibi. No answer. Just as soon as I'd shared what I had overheard with Al, finding Bibi was my top priority.

"Just tell me what you know," Al said now.

"To tell you the truth, it's not much," I said. "But it looks as if you were right to follow up on rumors of a con. Something is definitely set for New Year's Eve. The guys I overheard discussing this were vamps, so we also have to figure vampires are involved somehow."

Al was silent for a moment, worrying his lower lip. "Do you know who they are?"

"Yes, and no," I replied. Quickly, I filled him in on what I knew about the Bat Pack. Al's eyebrows rose sky high.

"Now, I've heard everything," he said. "Still . . ." He drummed his fingers against the top of his desk. "It's not much to go on."

"I'll go back to my sources, see if they can find out more," I offered. "I may have to step back just a little here, Al." I didn't like saying this, but it was the truth and he had a right to know. "I've had one encounter with these guys already and it was pretty memorable. I don't want to press my luck."

I was not going to tell Al how close I had come to getting roughed up.

"Do what you think is best," Al said at once. "Meantime, I guess we just have to sit tight, see if they make a move."

"Not my favorite choice for a plan," I said sourly. "I'll let you know what I find out."

Leaving Al's office, I checked my watch. It was one p.m. Bibi should be at dance rehearsal by now. She's the featured dancer in the New Year's Eve show. I turned my steps toward the dance studios. Like everything else in the employee area of the Sher, the hallways in the back of the house all look pretty much alike. Narrow corridors, painted off-white, they were well-marked with abbreviations that corresponded to use. Convention storage. Casino machine storage. Laundry. I turned into the hall that led to the back of the theater. And I realized I wasn't alone.

Instantly, my senses went on full alert. There was someone else down here, someone deliberately trailing along behind. Somebody human, at least. I didn't feel any vampire cold. I turned down an intersecting hallway. The footsteps stayed with me, a little closer now. I glanced back, but still didn't see anyone. I stopped. The footsteps stopped. I started walking again and I heard the footsteps once more. Then, as if from nowhere, I felt a hand on my right shoulder. I reacted with all the adrenaline that had been building up. Stepping back, I stomped hard on my attacker's instep. I heard a grunt of pain as he released me. I grabbed his arm, ducked under it, and twisted it at the same time as I slammed him against the wall.

Sunglasses popped off his head. A bunch of credit cards clattered onto the tile floor. A single poker chip bounced, then rolled to a stop next to my foot. I ignored them, staring at my prisoner.

"Michael!" I choked out.

"Is this some sort of Vegas greeting?" he asked in a strained voice. "Couldn't I learn the secret handshake instead?"

"What are you doing down here? This is supposed to be employees only."

"Take your fist out of my gut, and I'll tell you."

I stepped back, lowering my hands to my sides.

"You didn't mention that you were a black belt," Michael muttered, gingerly straightening up.

"I'm not," I said, backpedaling like mad. "The Sher gives all their cocktail waitresses basic classes in self-defense. I really am sorry, Michael. You startled me, is all."

"Want to try it again? I can take you two out of three, I'm sure." He eased away from the wall and bent down to collect his things.

"Let me help," I said, kneeling down and picking up the poker chip. It wasn't from the Sher; it didn't have the genie's lamp logo.

"Thanks," he said, pocketing it. "That's my lucky chip. Someday, if you're a good girl, I'll tell you where I got it."

"You like it better when I'm a bad girl," I answered, reaching for his sunglasses and glanced quickly at the opaque lenses. "They don't look broken."

"Good thing. I need them for the game—to keep my tells to a minimum." He smiled, and I breathed a silent sigh of relief. "A pro poker player can guess by an eyebrow's motion or eyes widening what cards someone else has. So we all do what we can to hide 'tells'—those little body reactions. You know how my face shows everything when I'm feeling good," Michael added.

"I've noticed," I said with a smile. On impulse, I

slid the glasses onto my own face, surprised how much heavier they were than my own shades. But, unlike my barely there wire frames, these were broader, made of a thick, black plastic.

He lifted the glasses off and settled them on his own face. "See?"

"I can't see your eyes at all."

"Precisely. I look inscrutable. I'll bet not even you can tell what I'm thinking."

"Oh, I have some idea what you're thinking," I teased. "But I really *am* sorry," I repeated.

"Now what do you mean?" Michael said as he began to gather up the plastic cards still lying on the floor.

They weren't credit cards, I realized, when I saw the hole punched near one corner. Emblazoned with the Sher's name and genie's lamp logo, they were what the marketing department called Magic Carpet Cards. Like all casinos along the Strip, the Sher wanted to make it as enticing to gamble as possible. The cards are for frequent bettors. The longer someone played and the more he or she bet, the more points were added onto the card. The points could then be traded in for comps at shops or at restaurants in the casino.

"Why do you have so many Magic Carpet Cards?" I inquired.

"I got them to hand out to my friends," Michael said happily. "While I'm playing poker, they're going to hit the slots and tables. With the points they get, I plan to take you out for a special dinner on New Year's Eve." He paused. "If you don't have other plans."

I gave an inward wince. "I have to work New Year's Eve. Everyone in the casino pulls long shifts that night."

"I can wait. When I win the tournament, I'll bribe your boss to give you the rest of the night off."

We both stood up. "My boss can't be bribed."

"Five million bucks can buy a lot of goodwill."

I smoothed the front of his shirt. "And you really believe you'll win it all?"

"Why not? I told you, I'm a lucky guy." He grinned at me. "Lucky you didn't break half my ribs. But I've learned my lesson. Next time, I'll scream my name whenever I get within ten feet of you."

"I told you I'd make you scream." I smiled. "Are you going back to the tournament now?"

"Mmm hmm." He nodded. "I played all night. That's why I haven't called."

I ran a hand through his hair. "That's all right. But we can't have you all mussed up in front of the cameras." I slid my hand down his chest, all the way to his belt, pretending to straighten his shirt. "Think about the effect on your TV audience."

He drew in a quick breath. Cupping my chin, he kissed me, hard. A kiss that told me the same thought was flashing through his mind: Could we? Right here? Not a good idea, I pulled away from him and tried to get myself under control.

"I better go. I don't want to miss my chance to get the five million to bribe your boss." He slid one hand down my back to caress my butt.

"You know how to get where you need to go?" I asked.

He gave a spurt of laughter as he stepped back. "Oh, yeah. I think so."

The door to the dance studio stood ajar, and music filtered out into the hall. One thing I could count on, Bibi never missed rehearsal. Dancing is her life. Several dancers waved to me as I entered. They were in the middle of a sequence of impossibly high kicks. I watched and checked out the line.

No Bibi. I felt a trickle of unease snake down my spine.

She usually danced between Jennifer and Jennifer. Actually there were four Jennifers among the twenty dancers, all from the Midwest. No wonder

Bibi claimed the title of premiere Jewish showgirl in Vegas. Everyone else was from the Corn Belt. I looked around the room, using the mirrored wall to help me. The director, the rehearsal pianist, the dancers.

No Bibi. Not anywhere.

Before I could go after information myself, Jennifer—the one who danced on Bibi's left—came over.

"Did Bibi tell you that she wouldn't be here today?" she asked before I could say anything.

I shook my head. "No. She didn't show up? Not at all?"

Jennifer wiped her face with a towel and shrugged. "Nope. Anybody else, I'd say she got lucky, but you know Bibi . . ." Her voice trailed off.

"Thanks, Jennifer," I said. "Let me give her a call," I said, struggling to keep my voice even. "Maybe she overslept."

"Until now?"

Hurrying back out into the hall, I opened my phone. Not enough signal. If I went up to the ground floor and . . .

Stop kidding yourself, Candace, I thought. Bibi wasn't answering because she wasn't there. She never made it home from the vampire club.

*   *   *

Moments later, I was walking through the casino, the incessant ringing of the slots battering my eardrums. I had to find Bibi, and I didn't have the faintest idea where to start. There wasn't any point in going to Taste. Not at this hour. The club would be shut up tighter than a drum.

The thought of Bibi taken by vampires literally made me ill. I could only pray that she was still alive. If not for me, she would never have been drawn into their world in the first place. *This is all your fault, Candace,* I thought.

There's a coffee bar at the back of the casino. I knew I could sit there, get my head on straight, without being hassled. I made for it. I was halfway there when my cell phone vibrated. I snatched it off my hip, not even bothering to check the number.

"Bibi, is that you?" I said into the phone. "Where are you? Are you all right?"

"Turn around."

The voice wasn't Bibi's, but it was one I knew almost as well. Slowly, I did as the voice requested. I turned around. Desperately trying to keep my breathing steady, my face from betraying emotion of any kind. Even though the blood was singing in my veins, pounding inside my head.

And there he was. His always slightly too long hair sweeping low across his forehead, but not quite low enough to conceal his starlit eyes. Eyes that had won me with their very first look.

Ash. The vampire I both hated and loved with all my heart.

He came to me, I thought. Just the way he had in my dream. Gone back on his promise to make me come to him, to make me crawl. And then I realized what he was holding in his hands, sliding it through his fingers as if he were shaping it with his touch: a black silk scarf. Bibi's scarf.

I was across the casino as if fired from a gun.

"You bastard," I said. "What have you done?"

His eyes kindled with emotion then, something I couldn't quite identify. "Lovely to see you, too," Ash said, and I felt the way his voice seemed to skim along every inch of my body, stroking it to life, and hated myself.

"Thanks for the benefit of the doubt. For your information, I am your friend's savior, not her persecutor." He passed the scarf from one hand to the other once again. "The situation could still be considered fluid, of course."

"Stop playing games, Ash," I said. "Just tell me if she's all right."

"Your friend Bibi," Ash said, as the scarf played through his fingers, "is just fine. No thanks to you, I might add. A true friend would never have taken her to a place like Taste at all."

Precisely what I had just been telling myself. Which didn't make hearing it from him one bit easier.

"I tried," I said, but even I could hear how pathetic I sounded. "I tried."

"Try harder next time," Ash suggested, and his voice had steel inside it now. "If it hadn't been for me, Bibi would be dead."

I felt the world swoop. I closed my eyes. When I opened them again, Ash's own were on me, his expression utterly unreadable now.

"Don't tell me," I said. "And now I owe you one."

"Yes, as a matter of fact, you do," he said. "A simple *thank-you* might have sufficed, but I think we've gone beyond that now. You clearly expect me to extract some sort of payment in order for me to return her to you, safe and sound. Very well. I'm happy to oblige."

"I hate you," I said.

"No. You don't. You want me, Candace, just as I want you. Your friend Bibi has provided us with an opportunity to address that fact, that's all."

"What sort of opportunity?" I asked, though I thought I knew.

"An exchange," Ash said, calmly. "Your friend, for your time. Give me a night with you, Candace.

Give us a night together. I'll return your friend the following morning."

This cannot be happening, I thought. I had dreamed of Ash coming back to me, of one night together with no strings, and no holds barred. And now he was here, proposing the very thing I had imagined.

"What happened to making me crawl?" I taunted, and saw him smile.

"Perhaps you will, before our night is out."

"Don't count on it."

"So we have a deal then?" Ash asked.

There was really only one answer, and we both knew it.

"I want Bibi returned right now," I said. "Or we don't deal at all."

"Done," Ash said at once. Without another word, he turned and walked toward the Sher's entrance and out onto the street. I trailed behind.

An enormous white stretch limo was pulled up beneath the awning that covered the drive. Ash stepped to the back door, opened it, held out a hand. At once, a slender arm reached out. The fingers grasped his, and Ash gently drew forth the occupant of the car. It was Bibi. Her eyes, unfocused and wide. She swayed on her feet, and I rushed forward to enfold her in a tight embrace.

"Bibi! Thank God."

"Candace?" Bibi's voice was shaky, but other than that, she seemed all right. Appearances could be deceiving, however. I knew that well enough.

"You should go on inside," I instructed. "Go back to the coffee bar, have Denise pull you an espresso. I'll be there just as soon as I can." I took her face between my hands, gazed down into her dazzled eyes. "You stay there until I get there, Bibi. You hear me?"

She blinked, and her eyes began to clear. "Of course I do," she said. "There's no need to treat me like a child." She moved inside the Sher without looking back. I don't think she realized Ash was there at all.

His doing, I realized suddenly. For my benefit, as much as Bibi's own. He knows how much she hates him.

"Our bargain," Ash said quietly. "Tomorrow night. I'll send the car."

I should have known, I thought, even as I battled back surprise. Ash wouldn't want to cash in right away. He would want to make me wait, to wonder and to suffer as I had made him suffer. Anticipation. It was the oldest aphrodisiac in the book.

"We'll see who crawls first," I said.

Ash smiled. "Yes, we will. Won't we?"

* * *

Bibi had no memory of the past twelve hours, for which I was profoundly grateful, and for which I owed Ash, no doubt. Just as I had no doubt he would seek to extract his own form of payment when we met the following night.

I got Bibi home, put her to bed, then sat by her bedside until I knew she was well and truly asleep. Much as I hated the thought of vampire mojo messing with her brain, I sincerely hoped she never regained her memory of last night. Never knew how close she had come to disaster.

Never knew how close I had let her come.

When I had watched her quiet breathing for almost half an hour, I got up and let myself out of the house. It was only when I went to drive away that I realized her silk scarf was still on the front seat of my car. I reached for it, and Ash's scent rose up. Unable to help myself, I pressed the silk to my face, inhaled deeply.

He wants me, I thought. Enough to use any means at his disposal just to have me for one night. I was so accustomed to thinking of Ash as the one with all the power, the control. But in spite of the way he had trapped me within it, I wasn't the one who had been compelled to drive this devil's bargain. Perhaps he was more vulnerable than he appeared. In which case, I would have to be stronger.

I folded the scarf and tucked it into the glove compartment. Starting now, I was not going to spend the next twenty-four hours brooding over Ash. He could wait until tomorrow.

Eight

The moon was a silver disc, floating in a cloud-less sky. When I looked up, I could see it through the skylight in the study of my house. In just a few moments the Board would summon me to the Nigredo, the test of the dark. And on this night, as I had one month ago, I would triumph.

There could be no other option.

I had not been idle in the month since the meeting with the Board. As the Chairman himself had suggested, I had done my best to use my time well. And so, or so it seemed, had my competitor, my fellow supplicant, Sloane. The inquiries he had been making about me had reached my ears. *If he hoped I would feel threatened, he was doomed to disappointment,* I thought. If anything, I was flattered. I hadn't bothered with Sloane. But the fact that he felt obliged to dig into my background confirmed what I already knew: I was the stronger.

Keep digging, I thought. I have nothing to hide. I had even continued and deepened my relationship, with the human woman I had met on the same night as my first encounter with the Board. I delved into the history of the Board hoping to find any advantage that would help me triumph. And as I studied and thought about the Chairman, and his absolute authority and power, I began to feel that I belonged on the Board. My entire past, my fascination with antiquities, my long, isolated years as a vampire, and now my relationship with this woman—all had been building to this moment. Yes, the woman was somehow a part of it. The fact that she and the Board and I had all come together on the same night could not be coincidence.

I stood for a moment, gazing up at the moon. *What are you doing right now, my sweet?* I wondered. And then there was no more time for questions, no more time for reflection. I saw a single wisp of blood-red cloud move across the moon and knew the summons from the Board had come.

Moments later, I stood in the Board's great chamber, clad in the simple linen garment I had worn before. Once more, Sloane was at my side.

"You are about to undergo the first of three trials,"

the Chairman informed us. "Three, to correspond with the objects that comprise our great quest: the Emblems of Thoth. For centuries we have sought them. Only when the Emblems are once again united can the god's curse upon us be undone.

"The first is already in our possession. The second, very close. The third remains to be discovered, but its time cannot be far off. Soon, the true spell for immortality will be spoken. Then we will no longer be merely undead, dependent upon the living blood of others. We will be immortal, invincible, incapable of being destroyed. All this will be bestowed by the third trial, the Rubedo, the test of blood.

"But the time for that has not yet come. First, we must reestablish the sacred number, the seven who are the Board. Tonight, we will begin to see which of you is worthiest to join our great quest, to earn our great reward."

The Chairman paused, gazing at Sloane and me, each in turn.

"Tonight's trial is the Nigredo. To pass it, you must surrender to the darkness. Think on this, and let the trial begin."

He raised his hand, and darkness was precisely what engulfed us.

* * *

When my senses functioned once again, I was in a room out of time. An ancient Egyptian burial chamber. There were no windows, no source of light, only a faint glow that seemed to come from the very air itself. Every wall was covered with figures and symbols I recognized from my research on the Board. The gods of ancient Egypt: the jackal-headed Anubis; the falcon god Horus; the lion-headed war goddess Sekhmet; Bastet, with the body of a woman and head of a cat. And, of course, there was Thoth, himself. *Fitting imagery for vampires,* I suddenly thought. For we have human bodies but are human no longer. Alchemical symbols danced across the ceiling. Planets, elements, processes for turning base metals into gold.

I was chained to the wall.

I gave a slight tug to the manacles, testing their strength. As the metal made greater contact with my flesh, pain flashed along my arms. I strained upward to gaze at them more closely. They were lined with silver, the metal lethal to vampires.

Interesting choice, I thought. There were no sharp edges, nothing that could cut me. The restraint was not designed to put an end to my existence. Only, depending on the circumstances and how I reacted to them of course, to make it very, very uncomfortable.

Without warning, I heard a low rumbling sound.

The floor beneath my feet began to tremble, then shifted abruptly. One sudden motion that had my wrists pulling against the silver in agony before I could right myself. But in that painful moment, I was sure I understood. Had Edgar Allan Poe been a human servant of the Board? For surely the floor was going to drop away, little by little, inch by inch, until all my weight was on my arms, a process that could take hours or days. There was absolutely no way to tell. Only one thing was certain. I would be in agony before the end.

Think, Ash, I commanded myself, even as I felt the floor shift once more. *Use your mind to get you out of this. It is a test of the dark. A test of will over matter.*

The floor slipped again, and I shifted up to my toes. The seconds ticked by. I put my feet flat up against the wall at my back, desperately trying to keep myself upright. It simply could not be done. With a second great groan, the floor dropped away entirely. My feet slid down. The manacles tightened against my wrists, searing like acid, as my arms took my full weight. Pain screamed up my arms, spread throughout my body like wildfire. I fought to subdue it, to force my mind away from the pain even as my body thrashed like a fish on a line.

My vision went gray around the edges. Spots

danced before my eyes. *Don't black out,* I chanted to myself. *You are strong enough to hold on. Don't black out. Don't give in to the dark.*

And in that moment I understood. I was getting it all wrong. I had provided the clue myself: not surrender of will, but conscious dedication to a greater cause. This was what the Board demanded. This was the true test of the dark. To surrender not my will, but my ego. To give it over to the pain and the dark.

I let my body go completely limp. Screaming in agony as the silver slid along skin already scraped raw. *Surrender is a voluntary act,* I thought. An act of will that seems like defeat but, in the end, brings its own kind of triumph.

And at that moment, the manacles snapped free and I felt myself begin an endless fall through what I had just chosen of my own free will: the darkness.

Nine

Early the next evening I was back at the Scherazade. After an entire day of getting nowhere with my con investigations, I had decided to come into work for two reasons. First, if I got as familiar with the overall tournament setup as I could, maybe it would be easier, come New Year's Eve, to spot where something was going wrong. And second—a far less noble reason—was that I wanted a distraction against further thoughts of Ash, even if that distraction meant wearing the *I Dream of Jeannie* uniform.

I walked toward the poker area. I saw Michael sitting at one of the tables. I didn't think he noticed me, but it was hard to tell for sure. He had his sunglasses on and seemed to be staring at the center of the table where the dealer was putting out the flop, three cards faceup that all the players used to make their best hand.

Then I saw another familiar man standing a dozen feet from the area marked off for the tournament. Senator Cabot Hamlyn. It was impossible to pick up a newspaper without reading about the brilliant New England senator who appeared destined to be the Democratic presidential nominee.

He was even better looking in person, tall with an Ivy League polish. I watched him walking past the tournament tables, chatting with the players, seeming engaged and interested in what each player had to say.

Randolph Glass was just a few steps behind him, a chic blond woman on his arm. I hadn't ever given Katherine Glass much thought. I just assumed—based on comments from Bibi and a few from Randolph—that she was an unappealing bitch. In fact, Mrs. Glass was Grace Kelly–gorgeous. She appeared gracious and had a friendly word for everyone at the tournament. She laughed at something her husband said, her hand on his arm.

They were the perfect image of a power couple. Worse, a power couple who shared intimate jokes and looked comfortable together. Bibi wasn't going to be happy.

I walked into the tournament area and went

over to Michael. He had a huge stack of chips in front of him and looked relaxed. Things were obviously going well.

"Would you like something, sir?" I asked.

"I would." He wasn't playing that hand, but he was watching the other players, looking for anything that might help him the next time he bet.

"And what would that be?"

"What would *you* recommend? I need something on the rocks to ease the heat here." His smile made it clear that I was the cause of the heat. It was the first time he had seen me in my costume. "Can you get me an All Night Long?"

I gave him a wide-eyed innocent smile. "Let me check with the bartender, sir."

"I was hoping *you* could answer that."

I returned to the bar with my drink orders, my thoughts circling back to Ash once more. *You have to hold him at arm's length, Candace,* I thought. I knew how persuasive Ash could be. Getting too close to him again was a risk I was not prepared to take. I had already been down that road.

I gave my drink order to the bartender and turned to watch the activity in the casino. Everything seemed normal. The calm before the storm?

One of my favorite coworkers appeared at the bar. Marlene has been a cocktail waitress at the Sher ever since Randolph took it over. She dropped a folded napkin on my tray. "For you." She nodded toward the tournament area. "From the guy at the middle table with the dark glasses."

I opened it. Michael's note was to the point.

Dinner? After this round. Choose the place.

Picking up another napkin, I scribbled a message.

Can't tonight. Previous plans. Sorry.

I folded it and gave it to Marlene to return to Michael. If I took it over myself, he would have questions I wouldn't want to answer.

"And it's all about the children. Nothing's too good for them," I heard Senator Hamlyn saying as he walked past with the Glasses and the rest of his entourage in tow. I could pick out the bodyguards, because they were looking everywhere *but* at the senator.

All of a sudden, I just felt depressed. I was getting nowhere on every front. I was no closer to figuring out how the con would go down, and I had just turned down a date with a very attractive living, breathing male to keep one with a vampire.

"I'm packing it in," I told Marlene, as she swung back by. Thanks to Al, I wasn't officially on the schedule anyhow.

"Go on ahead," she said at once. She sent me a wink, clearly thinking I was ditching out to be with the guy at the poker table. "Have fun."

*   *   *

After changing into my streets, I headed for the rehearsal halls. Classical music filtered out of one of the smaller rooms. I opened the door and saw Bibi, dressed in a pale pink leotard with a ratty gray sweatshirt over it, working at the barre in front of the mirrored wall. Her motions were slow and graceful. She was in her zone, the place she went when she couldn't endure what was going on around her.

"Hey," she called as she caught sight of me. Grabbing a water bottle, she turned off the music and walked over to me. "How's it going? What are you doing around?"

"I came to see you," I said. "Things are kind of weird out on the floor, what with the press and all." At the mention of press, Bibi's face grew taut. *Nice, Candace,* I thought. *Way to go. Rub her nose in the fact that Katherine's in the casino, why don't you . . .*

"It's okay," she said with a strained smile. "I know what's going on with the meet-and-greet. So, have you seen her?" she asked.

I didn't have to ask who "her" was. "Uh-huh," I nodded.

"Gorgeous, isn't she?" Bibi asked, her tone glum. "Not to mention blond."

"You could be a blonde if you wanted to be," I said loyally. "And your legs are longer.

"So how are you, really?" I asked.

"Actually," she said, "I'm fine. It's amazing how a good night's sleep, even one with the strangest dreams, can take the edge off a hangover."

"Still don't remember much?"

Bibi's forehead creased. "Nope. I remember talking to you, meeting at the Bellagio. There was some guy."

"Theo."

"Oh, yeah, Theo. That's right." All of a sudden, her eyes widened. "I didn't go home with him, did I?"

"No way," I said. "You were never that far gone. We went to a club, Taste." I hesitated, then said, "Taste turned out to be a vampire club."

Bibi's eyes widened. "Omigod. Candace, are you okay?"

"Fine," I said, completely taken by surprise.

"Ash wasn't around?"

"No," I said firmly, as I understood her concern. She thought I had been in danger, when it was actually the other way around. "We did not run into Ash last night." Sometimes, sticking to a half-truth is better than no truth at all.

"Maybe he's left Vegas," Bibi suggested.

"No."

"You don't know that."

"Yes, I do."

"How?"

"Ash and I are . . . connected, Bibi," I said. "If he left Vegas, I would know."

"New Year's is coming," she said with an attempt at a smile. "I propose we make some serious kick-ass resolutions."

"I second the motion."

"Here's mine: I'm going to do a serious reassessment of my relationship with Randolph. I didn't come to Vegas for him, after all. I came here to dance. I'm a good dancer. A really good dancer. I know it, and so does everybody else in town. If Randolph doesn't want me at the Sher, so be it. There are other jobs, not to mention other men."

"Good for you." Grinning like idiots, we high-fived.

"And what's your resolution?" Bibi asked.

I considered for a moment. "To find balance in my life."

She choked halfway through a swallow of water. "To hell with that New Age crap," she snorted. "You need a man in your life. A man who'll make you laugh at breakfast and scream with passion anywhere you like. What about Michael? Would he fit the bill?"

"Michael's just in town for the tournament," I

explained. "I'm his 'what happens in Vegas, stays in Vegas' fling. He's fun, and he's good for my equilibrium."

"Your balance."

"Exactly."

"Huh," she made an unconvinced sound, then grabbed her water bottle and stood up. "I'm sorry to cut this short. Rehearsals start in ten minutes."

I stood, gave her a hug. "In that case, I'll see you tomorrow."

"You going out tonight?" she asked.

I nodded, not specifying.

She shot me a wink.

"Try not to lose your balance."

Good advice, I thought.

A huge black box tied with a glorious white ribbon was leaning against the door when I arrived home. Even as I was getting out of the car, I saw the unmistakable Chanel logo embossed across the top. Briefly, I considered leaving the box where it was, but couldn't quite bring myself to do that. No woman in her right mind disses Chanel.

I took it inside and set it on the sofa. The eclectic furniture in my living room looked even funkier than usual surrounding that fancy box. But my home was *me*. The box wasn't. It was what Ash was tempting me to become.

Of course I opened it anyway. I'm only human . . .
I slid off the white satin ribbon. Drawing back the
tissue paper, I saw a little black dress gone wild. It
was strapless with a black bow at the top of the
bodice. The skirt puffed out from the waist with
layers of black lace, each exquisitely embroidered.
I reached for another item wrapped in tissue. It was
a black quilted evening bag. Understated, but with
the unmistakable Chanel logo on the front. There
was one more tissue-wrapped package. I opened it
and stared at black lace underwear. Panties, strapless corset, and a delicate garter belt.

I simply could not help myself. Instantly, my
body reacted to the idea of Ash seeing me in these
sexy garments. *Anticipation,* I thought once more.
All part of Ash's careful orchestration. He had
known how looking at these would make me feel,
known I would find it all too easy to conjure up
how he felt, himself.

I threw the garments in the box. Then I walked
into my bedroom. I wasn't Ash's doll to dress up as
he pleased. I opened my closet. I would wear what
pleased me. I would not do what Ash wanted.

I chose a simple slip dress in a vibrant red, a
power color to propel me through the night, left
my hair down. I'd had a cobbler remake a pair of
red high heels for me. The double line of silver
down the heel appeared to match the trim, but a

careful incision had been cut into each heel to allow me to insert a folded silver spike. If there was trouble, I could snap the spikes out in seconds.

My *formal* vampire-hunting outfit.

An hour later, as I was finishing my makeup, there was a knock at the front door. Picking up the shoes by the heels, I peeked out a front window. The white stretch limo was parked in front.

"Miss Steele?" asked the driver when I opened the door. "Whenever you're ready . . ."

"To go where?"

"I'm afraid I was instructed not to say, Miss Steele." He backed away to stand by his car, which was already drawing the neighbors' stares.

Shrugging on the short red jacket that matched my dress, I stepped into my heels and picked up my clutch.

I was as ready as I was going to be. I could only hope it was ready enough.

Ten

There's definitely something to be said for traveling in style. As the limo pulled up before the poshest hotel on the Strip, it was hard not to fantasize about this sort of life all the time. There's a reason the story of Cinderella has such staying power. We all dream of being transformed.

The place Ash had chosen for our assignation was the Beijing, the most exclusive and elegant place in town. The Beijing experience, as the ads called it, began the moment you turned off the Strip and into the hotel's curved drive. It was lined with plantings and statues that looked as if they might have come from the Forbidden City. The main entrance was through a building with a pagoda-style roof. The casino, with its eaves slanting upward and decorated with gilded columns and enormous stone temple lions, was visible behind it. Like a swooping dragon, the hotel rose with its two great curved wings. Graceful and ele-

gant, the entire complex seemed to have materialized straight out of ancient China.

The driver drew the limo up to the largest arch in
the red wall, and a valet in a gold-trimmed coat
rushed to open the door. I offered the driver a tip,
but he said, "Already taken care of, Miss Steele. I
hope you have a pleasant evening."

"Thank you. I hope so, too." I slid out of the
limo, remembering how celebrities did it. Swing
out one leg then ease out by standing up slowly.
That was my plan for the whole evening. Ease out
and go slowly.

A second man in an elegant valet uniform
opened a door shadowed by the arch. He tipped his
hat, and I guessed he thought I was a high roller.
My breath caught again when I stepped through
the door and into a grand courtyard lit by golden
lanterns.

"Miss Steele?" asked a young man who was
dressed in a green silk robe that reached to the
turned up toes of his slippers.

"Yes."

He gave a bow. "The gentleman has requested
that I escort you to the restaurant."

I followed him up a flight of stairs that spanned
what appeared to be a moat and then entered a
building on the far side of the courtyard. I heard
the familiar *ching* of slots and with a slight shock

realized I was in the casino. For a second I felt absurdly disappointed. And then I was glad. Even here the decor was grand, but that couldn't disguise the essence: same old games, same old bored faces staring at the lights. I was not in some enchanted dreamland. This was Vegas, and even Ash couldn't keep reality at bay for long.

"Is this your first visit to the Beijing, Miss Steele?" my escort inquired.

"Yes," I said.

"The restaurant where you'll be dining is down these stairs," he said, sweeping his hand toward a gilded staircase that wouldn't have been out of place in Versailles. "Have a pleasant evening."

"Thank you."

I walked down the curving staircase, my hand sliding along the gold banister. *Don't be too impressed,* I told myself. *Forget all the damn gilding and remember who, and what, you're really dealing with . . .*

I never finished the thought. I reached the bottom of the stairs where the soft lighting seemed to focus on a spot by a fountain decorated with orchids. I barely noticed the fountain. My eyes locked on the man who stood beside it.

Ash always looked good, but in a tuxedo with understated gold-and-diamond cuff links matching the studs on his shirt, he was gorgeous. His tawny hair fell forward, as if trying to conceal his amazing eyes. He had that nonchalance that had made Sean Connery the consummate James Bond, dashing and dangerous at the same time. And he was standing there, waiting just for *me*.

He turned as I walked toward him. His eyes widened when he saw what I was wearing, but he didn't comment. He drew me to him, gave me a demure kiss on the cheek. Even that touch sent my senses humming.

"You look lovely, Candace," he said, his voice rich and resonant.

"You don't look so bad yourself," I said, trying to match his casual tone.

He smiled, and I knew my own voice had revealed more than I intended. "Did you have a nice ride?"

I decided to give that double entendre a very wide berth. "Very nice. Thank you."

"I reserved a table for us at The Soaring Crane."

It was the Beijing's signature restaurant. The Soaring Crane was the kind of place that made food critics cry with rapture and search for superlatives. Asian fusion in an environment of exquisite beauty with impeccable service. The review in the paper had blazed with stars and a warning that it could take months to get a reservation.

Ash had really gone all out. And much as I hated

to admit it, it was working. He had chosen amazing surroundings and arranged things to make me feel like the most important person to ever enter the Beijing.

"I can't believe you got reservations here," I said. "I've heard it can take months."

"It does. But there are certain perks offered to residents of the Beijing."

That brought me up short. "You're living here at the hotel?"

"In one of the residential condos attached to the hotel," Ash amended. "Buying one enabled me to get a number of my favorite antique pieces out of storage, so I can enjoy them."

I couldn't help but be curious. I had only seen a small part of Ash's precious collection in San Francisco, but what I saw was impressive, every item museum-quality.

"Which pieces?" I asked now.

"A few of the Chinese vases, as well as the Egyptian statues and the Rembrandt." His mouth twitched as he fought not to smile. "The etching."

I smiled in spite of myself. "So you really can invite women to come up and see your etching?"

He laughed. It was that wondrous, free sound. When Ash laughed, I could almost believe, just for a moment, that we could have the future together I once dreamed of.

"I see I'm going to have to do more to impress you, Candace."

"Oh, you've made an impression," I assured him.

He smiled, and I felt myself smiling back.

"I would like to show you my place sometime."

I let that one go. Ash hadn't specified what would happen when we were together tonight. I could only assume he thought matters would see to themselves. But I had no intention of being swept away by Ash again. He wanted to wine and dine me? Fine. I'd be more than happy to oblige, then bring the evening to a close.

"Shall we go in?" he inquired.

The restaurant was as magnificent as the ads promised. The waiters were dressed in spotless black trousers and vests over white shirts. The only concession to the Asian atmosphere was the yin and yang symbols on their red band ties. We were escorted to a private room. Gauzy curtains gave a view of the rest of the restaurant but shielded us from the curious.

"May I?" Ash asked, and put his hands on my shoulders to draw off my jacket. The gesture, so ordinary, so familiar, nearly undid me. How many times had he undressed me as I stood before him trembling with need? That, in a nutshell, was the problem. Ash's every gesture set off some sort of erotic reaction in me, as if I had been hardwired to desire him.

The table was low, surrounded by red and gold cushions. I sat down, and immediately some sort of silent internal mechanism in the cushions adjusted them to provide perfect support. "I want one of these in my car," I said.

The waiter poured a sample of white wine into Ash's glass. Ash picked it up and sniffed it as he swirled the wine in the glass. Taking a sip, he held it in his mouth a long moment. Then, swallowing, he nodded.

"I took the liberty of ordering," Ash said, after the wine was poured and the waiter departed. "I hope you don't mind."

I leaned back against the cushions, my eyes challenging his. "You always like to be in charge, don't you, Ash?"

Somewhat to my surprise, he nodded. "I often find it best, yes. Being out of control can lead to . . . unfortunate results."

I felt my mind tilt, sliding straight toward the elevator where I had come so close to losing my life, to being made a vampire. *No!* I thought. *Do not go there.* Ash and I had both lost control that night. The consequences would haunt me forever.

"I promised myself I wasn't going to say this," Ash's quiet voice broke into my troubled thoughts.

"But the truth is, I've missed you, Candace. Very much."

"Have you?" I asked. I took a sip of the wine, to prevent myself from making a similar confession. Not a day went by that I didn't miss him. Very, very much.

"I need to thank you," I said instead. "For what you did for Bibi. She seems fine. Doesn't remember a thing."

"Need to, or want to?" Ash asked at once.

I blew out a breath. "Both. You have to know how much she means to me, and I . . . thank you, Ash."

"That wasn't so hard, was it?" he asked with a smile.

"Don't be an idiot," I said. "Of course it was. You saved her and I'm grateful, but you used her, as well. You're using me, right this minute."

"You enjoyed that once."

"No," I said with a vigorous shake of my head. "No, I didn't, Ash. I enjoyed . . . I *loved* what I thought we had *together*. I never wanted to be your puppet."

"Loved," Ash said. "Past tense."

"How can it be anything else? Go ahead, Ash. Try and tell me: How? I don't see any way to go forward and I know we can't go back."

He didn't answer, fingers slowly tracing the rim of his wineglass. *You did it, Candace,* I thought. I held my ground, made my point. I had won. So why was I suddenly feeling as if I'd lost instead?

"So how is it living here in the hotel?" I asked, in a deliberate change of subject. I forced myself to relax, lean back against the cushions. My legs were folded beneath me. Ash's were stretched out, long. It would be so easy to slide mine alongside his.

"It's comfortable," he said. "I'm staying here until the paperwork on the house is finalized."

"You're buying a house? Relocating to Vegas permanently?" I asked, surprised.

He nodded and sipped his wine reflectively. "I had been thinking about expanding my business even before I met you. Vegas is the perfect town. Filled with high rollers looking to spend money on the finest things. Like my antiques."

He refilled his glass as our meal arrived. Ash and I ate in companionable silence, one broken by easy, simple conversation, as the rhythms of our relationship began to restore themselves. *How many times had we done this?* I thought. My first date with Ash had been out for dinner. When we became a couple, I often cooked for him in my tiny apartment. Afterward, we would make love. Feasting on one another more voraciously than we ever did on food and drink. Even now, not once, had I ever had enough.

By the time the fortune cookies arrived, I could barely swallow past the lump in my throat. Of all the things I had expected tonight, this had surely been the last one: That simply being with Ash again would show me how deeply, how irrevocably I was still in love.

"What does yours say?" Ash asked as I pulled the slip of paper from a fortune cookie.

"The obstacle is the path." I arched a single brow at him. "How about yours?"

"To follow the path, look to the master, follow the master, walk with the master, see through the master, become the master," he said in a grave tone.

I gave a choke of laughter. "It does not! They couldn't fit that many words on there." I grabbed his hand and tilted the slip of paper. With a laugh, I read, "You like Chinese food." I laughed again. "I should have known. You are such a liar."

"I was only trying to make it sound more mysterious."

"Sometimes ordinary is better."

Ash shook his head. "No. You don't believe that. How can you, when you are so far from ordinary yourself?"

All of a sudden I realized I was still holding his hand, that he was holding mine.

"Ash," I said, my voice no more than a thread of sound. "You have got to let me go."

His mouth twisted then, into something that was almost, but not quite, a smile.

"The time for that has passed, Candace," he said. "It moved by us both a long time ago."

I went absolutely still, then, gazing straight into those starlit eyes, asked, "So what happens now?

"Now? Now I will ask you for a favor, I think. Kiss me, Candace. Just once."

I couldn't have said no even if I'd wanted to. With my free hand, I reached up and brought his lips to mine.

Ash's lips were firm and smooth. Trailing magic, trailing fire. I parted mine beneath them, deepened our simple embrace, and saw the world explode with color. Only Ash had ever possessed this power, to make my heart believe in our impossible love even as my mind denied it.

"I love you, Candace," he murmured against my mouth. "Sweet God, I love you so much."

And then the kiss was over and I found myself in the one place I had promised myself I would never go again: cradled in Ash's arms.

"It doesn't matter," I whispered back. "It can't matter."

I saw the muscle in his jaw work as he released me. "You are such a terrible liar. Do it for your own benefit if you must, but don't trot it out for mine."

He stood, and I understood suddenly. I had hurt him. I hadn't known I had the power.

"You disappoint me, Candace," Ash said. "I thought you had more guts."

I stood up myself then, pretending I didn't notice the way my knees were shaking.

"I'm done here, Ash," I said. "We're done. I want to go home now."

"And you think I'm going to try and stop you, don't you? You think I can't survive without you. You have no idea how wrong you are."

I'll never know what made me say it. Guardian angel or inner devil-child. But it was the truth, either way. A truth that was never going to set either of us free.

"I love you, too, Ash," I said. "Now call the damned limo."

The short trip from the restaurant to the curb was accomplished in total silence. Ash and I were both infinitely careful to avoid so much as brushing together, as if equally uncertain of the consequences. He let the limo driver hand me into the backseat.

"Thank you for the meal, and for helping Bibi," I said.

"You're welcome."

For one split second, I thought he would say something more. Instead, Ash stepped back, and the driver shut the door. The last thing I saw as the limousine pulled away from the curb were Ash's hands, curling into tight fists at his sides.

"Where to?" the driver asked, after several blocks had gone by. That was the moment I realized how very much I did not want to go home. Home to peace and quiet and far too many memories of Ash.

"Just drive along the Strip, will you?"

"Sure thing," the driver replied.

I need light, I thought. Light and color and sound. All the things that make Vegas so enticing. That make it so alive.

"Here, let me out here," I suddenly called.

I caught the driver's startled gaze in the rearview mirror. "You sure?" he inquired. We were nowhere near my house.

"I'm sure," I replied. Obediently, he edged the limo over to the sidewalk. "Thanks," I said as I climbed out.

"Don't mention it," he said. "Have a nice night, now."

That's just what I intend to do, I thought. *Starting now.*

I flipped open my cell, paged through the recent incoming calls. *There it is,* I thought. My evening out with Ash had done something to me, something I didn't like much. It had opened up an empty space inside me, a space that was cold and empty and dark. I intended to fill it with what I wanted there instead, something funny, vibrant, and alive.

Praying he would still be free, that he hadn't opted for some other form of Vegas entertainment, I punched in Michael Pressman's number.

Eleven

"Hey, Candace." Michael's warm voice came through my cell, despite the noise of the traffic all around me. "You've got the best timing in the world."

"I've heard that line before."

His laugh came through the phone, and I felt my tension ease a little. It was going to be all right. *Fun,* I thought. Fun is precisely how I had described Michael to Bibi. Precisely what I wanted right now.

"Well, it's not a line this time," Michael went on. "They just called an extended break because they want to rearrange the cameras for taping the next rounds."

"How long do you have?" I asked.

"A couple of hours minimum. They'll call us when everything's ready." He paused. "I thought you were busy this evening."

"I was," I said simply. "Now, I'm done. I'd really like to see you, Michael. If you're still interested."

"Just tell me where you are."

"Why don't we meet at the Venetian?" I proposed. I looked at its brightly lit sign towering above the Strip. I went toward one of the pedestrian bridges that kept tourists from ending up as traffic statistics. "It's about halfway between where I am and the Sher."

"Sounds great. Where should I meet you?"

"I'll be in the loggia there," I told him as I crossed over the eight lanes of traffic on the Strip.

"Okay, I'll find it. Wait for me, and don't run off with someone else, okay?"

"Okay." I could make that promise wholeheartedly. I closed my cell and stuck it in my purse, then went to the steps leading to street level and headed toward the Strip.

Almost at once, I sensed I was being followed. *Okay, Candace. Do NOT panic this time,* I thought. I was on the Strip. There were people everywhere. Last time I hit the panic button, I had all but decked Michael. That's when I felt it. The chill from inside me, *the* chill down my spine. The one that reminded, and warned, that not everyone on the street was alive.

I picked up my pace, hurrying down the crowded sidewalk, past the hawkers passing out cards with photos of naked women and phone numbers. Being careful not to let my narrow heels slide on the discarded cards scattered on the sidewalk. Out of the corner of my eye, I saw one of the card guys turn and point to something behind me. Risking a quick glance over my shoulder as I reached the corner, I saw them.

Frank. Peter. Sammy. Dino. The Bat Packers who had taunted me at Taste. Right behind me, staring at me openly. My first instinct was to run like hell. Instead, I kept a steady pace as I turned onto the Strip in front of the Treasure Island casino. Beneath my feet, the concrete gave way to the boards that were the Vegas version of a pier. A crowd was gathering in front of Treasure Island to watch the pirate ship show. On the clogged sidewalk, the Bat Pack wouldn't have any trouble cornering me again, cutting me off, even in the midst of the crowd.

So much for safety in numbers, I thought.

Going forward was dangerous. Going back was stupid. I couldn't walk across the lagoon where the pirate ship would be sailing in just a couple of minutes. That left only one direction. Back across the Strip.

But I couldn't just step off the sidewalk here and cross the Strip. Instead of the steel railings or plantings that other hotels used, Treasure Island had protected pedestrians from the traffic by stringing thick "nautical" rope netting from waist-high wooden posts. Which was fine if you were into the casino's motif, but it left me without a way to get past the crowd and away from the Bat Packers. Unless . . .

I pulled off my heels. Sticking my toes into the rope net, I clambered over it, then onto the street. Horns sounded as I raced across the lanes of traffic, weaving in and out of the cars stopped for a red light. I reached the median and kept running. Brakes squealed, and a cabbie shouted out his window as the light turned green. I glanced behind me quickly. The Bat Packers were pinned on the median as traffic whizzed by. They were definitely chasing me. No two ways about it.

Pushing my feet into my heels, I hurried toward the Venetian. An icy chill swept over me, and I knew the vampires were right behind. I ducked into the Venetian's closest entrance. Beyond the arch, people were milling by an elevator that would take them either to the shops in the Venetian or the pedestrian bridge across to Treasure Island and the Mirage. I edged into the center of the crowd and watched the arched doorway.

The Bat Pack approached the arch and stopped there. That surprised me. I was sure they would follow me. What made them stop? I would have figured the Venetian for home turf, if only for nostalgia's sake. It was built on the site of the old Sands, the late, great hotel where the real Frank and company had held court. But the vampire versions of the Rat Pack stayed in the entry until I got into the elevator. As the door closed, I caught sight of them turning away.

Wrapping my arms around myself, I tried to control my trembling. I forced a smile when a woman said something about Vegas nights being much colder than she expected. *You have no idea,* I thought.

Michael was waiting when I reached the loggia, gazing down into the canal built to resemble the ones in Venice. I had never been so happy to see another human in my life. I threw my arms around his neck, indulged myself in a serious deep kiss. Then, hooking my arm through his, I led him inside so fast he barely got to say two words. Ahead of us the Grand Canal Shoppes were shutting for the night, but we took the escalator down to the casino, which never closed.

"Wow!" he said as we started through the casino.

"Spectacular, isn't it?" I agreed.

"I wasn't talking about the casino. I was talking about you." Michael stepped away and let his gaze roam up and down me. "You look fabulous."

"I clean up nicely." I eyed him the same way, wanting to get caught up again in the sexy fun of a flirtation that meant no more than the frothy bubbles in a drink. "You don't look half bad yourself."

He turned slowly, showing off the simple navy jacket that he wore over khakis. The preppy look wasn't one I usually cared for, but on Michael it worked just fine.

A restaurant with walls of cascading water was directly in front of us as we passed a few shops. We turned left and walked into the bar across from the theater. I glanced over my shoulder, but there was no sign of the Bat Packers. *Safe,* I thought.

The bar had a curved wall of frosted glass divided by black strips of wood. It was ultra-modern and retro at the same time. The seats were like giant ottomans, the floor the glossy black of patent leather, and the wall behind the bar a deep orange. It was bright and brassy, a place to see and be seen.

"What do you want to drink?" Michael asked.

"Whatever's on tap."

"You got it."

He set off for the bar, and I found a section of empty settee where I could have a view of the door. Just in case. Michael returned with the beers and the news that he had once again won his round.

"The level of competition has definitely amped up," he explained. "The next round I'll be playing Donny de Leon." Even I knew Donny was a pro and a favorite in the televised tournaments. "Think my luck can hold?"

"Absolutely," I said.

He smiled and kissed me. "It's all up to you, you know. Remember the experiment?"

"You won before you met me," I reminded him, but I moved closer and put my hand on his thigh.

"But I've been doing so much better since we—" He halted midword. He was staring at something—someone?—behind me.

"Is something wrong?" I asked, hoping he wasn't about to tell me that Frank Sinatra and Sammy Davis Jr. look-alikes had just walked into the bar. I risked a quick look past two heavyset guys blocking my view. No Bat Pack in sight.

"No, no." He wavered between a frown and a smile, as if he wasn't sure which expression to wear.

"What's wrong, Michael?"

"Sorry," he said, looking back at me. "It's just so weird."

"What?"

"That woman over there . . ." He gestured with his drink. "She could be your twin."

I swung around to look at the bar. The cold struck me as if I had run into a wall of ice.

Sitting on a stool at the bar was the female vampire from Taste. The woman who was a dead ringer for me. First the Bat Pack and now my double. Seeing them so close together twice was weird, no two ways about it. It could have been pure chance, but I had been in Vegas long enough to discount that option. Someone has always got the odds. Before this moment, I hadn't even considered the possibility that this female look-alike might be connected to the con. Now my instinct was telling me she was.

Michael and I watched as she rose and walked out of the bar, her hips swaying easily beneath the silk of her dress. Sapphire blue silk, precisely in the shade I would have chosen.

"I'll be right back," I said sliding away from Michael.

"Are you okay?" he asked. "Do you want me to go with you?"

"I'm fine. And I think I can go to the ladies' room by myself." I fought down the shiver climbing up my spine. My last visit to a public restroom had been at Taste; I didn't want to get into a confrontation like that again.

But I needed answers, and maybe following my vampire double would be the route to getting them.

I had never been in the Grand Canal Shoppes area after the stores were closed. But the security guy at the bottom of the escalator told me that "my sister in the blue dress" had gone this way, so I didn't have much choice.

I stepped off the escalator and went toward the

shopping center. The lights were still on in the roof high above the Venetian square, but the shops were dim. The street performers had vanished. The gondolas were stored away, their singing gondoliers gone. The food courts were empty, and the chairs tilted against the tables. I heard a vacuum somewhere but couldn't pinpoint it. The canal snaking through the shops distorted all the sounds.

I stood in the middle of the square and listened, straining to hear something, *feel* something, that would tell me where the female vampire was.

I climbed over a bridge that seemed to be dropping right into some fancy jewelry store, paused, and listened again. The water lapped against the sides of the narrow canal. A white-and-gold gondola was moored near the bridge. It swayed lightly on the surface of the water. The lights from the ceiling reflected in the canal like candles burning in its depths. It was so eerie and beautiful, the whole scene could have come from *The Phantom of the Opera.*

A motion past the next bridge caught my eye. There she was! Locked in an embrace with a tall man who was holding her between his body and a wall on the far side of the canal. Their passion so fierce it was almost brutal, I watched as his hand moved down the front of the sapphire-blue dress to seize her breast, then begin to stroke. She arched against him in response. Without warning, he lifted his head, took his mouth from hers, as if he had sensed my presence, somehow. I saw his profile, and felt a vicious kick, straight in my gut.

It was Ash. And in his arms, my vampire double.

Twelve

You bastard, I thought as rage and jealousy seared through me. Heedless of the consequences, I let it carry me toward them.

The female saw me first. She was the one facing my direction, after all. She hissed a word, and Ash spun around. I let my momentum move me to just outside his arm's reach, then stopped short.

"I may be a terrible liar, Ash," I said, "but you're a first-class one."

He shifted his weight slightly, as if to protect the female vampire. I had wanted to do many things to Ash, and with him, but I had never wanted to truly end him until this moment.

"Does he tell you that he loves you, too?" I asked her, looking over Ash's shoulder straight into her eyes. Up close the differences between us were immediately apparent to me. Her eyes had a different slant. Her skin was paler. Not better not worse. Just not me. "What was it you said earlier tonight,

Ash?" I switched my attention back to him. " 'I love you, Candace. Sweet God, how I love you'?"

"What's between us has no business here," Ash spoke at last, and I laughed out loud.

"You believe that," I said, "and I'd love to sell you some beachfront property in Iowa. You know better." I pointed. "She knows better, and so do I." I took a step forward, reckless in my fury. "Let me see your neck," I demanded of the female vampire.

Her eyes went from furious to confused, uncertain.

"What? Why?"

"Just lift your hair up," I said. "Go on. Do it."

At a nod from Ash, she complied. Her neck was bare. There was no cross-shaped tattoo, no "x" marks the spot. The spot where Ash had tried, and failed, to drain the blood from my body to make me what he was: a vampire.

I lifted my own, revealed the tattoo, the scars.

"Close," I said, my voice cheerful. "But no cigar. She's just a cheap imitation and you know it, Ash. But hey, at least she's a vampire."

"That's enough, Candace," Ash said, his voice like a whip.

"Like hell it is," I snarled. As long as I kept talking, stayed on the offensive, there was a chance I could drown out the sound of my breaking heart.

"How did you do it?" I asked now. "Did she just

happen along? Or did you *create* her? Make her
over in my image like the bride of Frankenstein?"

With a cry of rage, the female lunged forward,
nails first, like the beast she was. But Ash was too
quick. He drew her back against him, pinning her
arms down with his own.

"Stop it, Dune," he said. "Leave her alone."

She struggled for a moment before subsiding.
"Why? You don't need her, Ash. She was too stupid to know when she had a good thing going."

"I *know* I have a good thing going," I retorted.
"I'm still alive!"

Abruptly, she changed tactics, turning sideways
and wrapping her arms around Ash's torso. She
slid one bent knee up to brush against his crotch.

"Then you don't know what you're missing. All
this could have been yours. Now it's mine."

I laughed then, and saw the fury leap into her
eyes.

"Don't kid yourself," I said. "Ash doesn't belong
to anyone but himself."

"This is pointless," Ash broke in. "Dune, go
wait for me over by the gondolas."

Her expression fell at once. "Ash, no, please!
Don't send me away."

Bad choice, I thought. He really hates to hear
anyone whine. When he didn't countermand his in-
struction, she took a reluctant step away.

"I am going to end you, you bitch," my look-alike, Dune, said in a low and vicious voice. "Some moment when you think you're safe and warm. I am going to take you so far out of this world no one will even remember you were in it."

"No, you won't," I said. "But I'll look forward to seeing you try."

"Do as I tell you, right now, Dune," Ash snapped, and at the naked power in his voice, I felt a finger of pure ice shoot straight down my spine. With a last look of frustrated rage, Dune moved off.

Ash and I faced each other.

"I'm sorry you had to see all this, Candace," he said.

"No," I said. "I don't think you are. I think I've done precisely what you wanted, Ash. Learned what you wanted me to learn. What I don't understand is why. *What do you want?*"

"The same thing I've always wanted," he said simply. "You with me, in my world, for all time. Dune is simply an attempt to satisfy one part of that need, nothing more."

"She's only a body, Ash," I said. "She's not me. She doesn't have my soul or my mind. Those things belong to me. They always have. They always will."

Then I turned and walked away from him for the second time that night.

Going back across the bridge, I walked through the empty square. My steps echoed oddly in the silence. After about ten paces, I was horrified to realize I was blinking back tears. *I would* not *cry over Ash*, I thought. Or over the vampire created in my image who was utterly pathetic in her eagerness to deny it. I would not even weep for myself. The whole situation was painful and twisted, a maze with no hope of getting out.

Bad analogy, Candace. Somehow I had missed the arch that led to the bar where Michael was waiting. By now he was probably wondering if I had skipped town. Before me was a bank of escalators I had never seen before. I wasn't sure where they would take me, but I sure as hell wasn't returning to the canal. I got on, going in the only direction there was: down.

I reached the bottom of the escalator and looked around me. I had wandered into a huge meeting space, the kind of area they give to convention groups. I found a broad hallway and walked in what I thought was the direction of the casino. Rows of closed doors seemed slightly surreal, as they repeated toward the distant end of the hall. The place was eerie. I could have been the only person on the planet, roaming in a maze of halls and doors that opened into some *Twilight Zone* episode. Knowing there were hundreds of people nearby in the casino made it feel even more deserted.

But it wasn't deserted.

I was cold.

Was it Dune, following me, already making good on her promise? I quickened my pace. The cold deepened, grinding into my bones. *Not Dune, then,* I thought. She was simply not this strong. That meant someone new, or . . . I took two few steps into the intersection between two corridors and I saw them.

The Bat Pack. Coming straight toward me.

What in the hell was going on? Except for that night at Taste, I had always been able to depend on my senses. Now they were completely out of sync. The Bat Pack were jerks, and they definitely outnumbered me, but even together they weren't strong enough to send out this sort of cold. Then I remembered. When I had overheard them at Taste, the Bat Packers had talked about *gaining* power. But how. Was that even possible?

To hell with staying and fighting. Instead, I propelled myself through the intersection of the corridors, then kept on running, their footsteps pounding behind me. I followed a zigzagging path through the corridors, hoping to throw them off. I knew there was no chance that anyone would hear my screams over the noise of the casino. I was praying the hallway didn't dead-end on me. All that mattered was that I keep running.

Without warning, the floor beneath my feet changed to marble. I was running up the ramp by the theater. People stared at me. People! I slowed to a walk and dared to glance over my shoulder. Even as I watched, the Bat Pack faded into the shadows. I thought I heard one say "Not this chick." It might have been Rat Pack–ese, but it was the truth, right enough. Not this chick. And not here. Too many of the living around me. And there was Michael! Standing by the curved wall of the bar and looking in the opposite direction.

"Michael!" I called, waving like an out-of-towner on her first visit to Sin City.

He turned and grinned. "Didn't you go the other way? I was beginning to think you got lost." He put an arm around my waist, drawing me close.

"I did." I laid my hand over the center of his chest. His heart skipped at my touch, but it beat. He couldn't have guessed how much that meant to me now. "Took the scenic route when I missed a turn. I'm sorry."

"That's okay. These places are made to lure you in and never let you find your way out."

I forced a smile, wishing I wasn't getting so good

at it. "Do you want to go back and finish our drinks?"

"Are you sure you're okay? You look pale."

"No, I'm fine. It's just . . ." I didn't want to lie. He was honest with me. That was one of the things I liked best about being with him.

His hand at my waist, Michael turned me toward the casino. "It's all right. No need to explain. I thought guys were the only ones who didn't ask for directions."

I laughed because he expected me to. And because he had saved me from having to lie. That was a privilege it seemed I would reserve for myself.

Michael suggested we go back to his room, and I wasn't about to argue. I wanted to feel his warm skin on mine, to lose myself in his arms. But when Michael opened the door to his suite, we both got a shock. A chorus of voices shouted out, "Surprise!"

The living room and dining room were filled with a mix of twenty- and thirty-somethings, most of them holding beer cans. Michael made a sheepish grimace.

"I guess maybe I should have mentioned it's my birthday, huh?"

"I guess maybe you should have," I said.

"Well it wasn't, not until about ten minutes ago."

"And you thought we'd forget?" A guy with bright-red hair and glasses that had gone out of style twenty years ago handed Michael a beer, then leered at me. "If we'd known about you, we would have ordered a cake for you to jump out of."

Michael gave him an elbow in the stomach. "Ignore him. Josh is used to being around computers. He rates low on people skills. Candace, this idiot is Josh Doyle. Josh, this is Candace Steele. Jumping out of cakes is not her style."

"So you're the guy who dared Michael to enter the tournament," I said, deciding the best way to get around the fact that Michael's sponsor had thought I was a hooker was to ignore it. This was Vegas, after all. "You must be proud of how well he's doing."

"It's gonna cost me a hundred bucks more if he wins."

Michael grinned. "Now you can see why I'm determined to win. It's not the five million. It's Josh's hundred bucks. C'mon. I'll get you a beer, Candace."

Michael introduced me to a few of the others then led me into the sleek galley kitchen where he took beers from the fridge.

"I didn't know you knew so many people in Vegas," I said.

"None of them are from Vegas," he explained with a sigh. "These are my friends, mostly from Chicago, who came to watch me play. Now they're making themselves at home, as you can see."

He drew me close.

"I really am sorry about all this," he said. "I had no idea they were going to show up tonight. I'll figure out some way to make it up to you," he whispered as he slid his leg between my thighs, sending spikes of pleasure through my body.

I smiled at him. "Don't apologize. It's good that your friends turned out to support you in the tournament."

He gave a sigh. "Too bad they don't have your sense of timing. I thought they wouldn't be here until tomorrow. But they did come a long way. I should probably go socialize. Do you mind?"

"No, of course not. I should be getting home anyhow." Now that the adrenaline of the strange evening was wearing off, I was beginning to realize how exhausted I was. "Go be with your friends. We can connect tomorrow."

I gave Michael a good-bye kiss, lingering just one moment to run my thumb into the adorable cleft in his chin. I saw myself out, then grabbed a cab for home.

* * *

My house is unique. When I renovated it with my own two hands and the skills my father taught me, I literally built in a safety net, a vampire-free zone. Some houses have storm shelters deep in their centers. Others have panic rooms. I have my office, which contains everything I know about vampires and how to fight them.

If there's a book printed about vampires, I have it: from medieval texts to *Dracula* to modern science and pseudoscience. Weapons, traditional ones, like stakes and holy water, and some far more exotic. Then there's my desk, complete with state-of-the-art laptop. A small fridge with emergency supplies in case I'm ever under siege. A corkboard on the wall.

A situation board, just like in the cop shows. This is where I problem solve, writing facts, names, and places on three-by-five cards, then pinning them to the board. If I'm lucky, sooner or later a pattern will emerge.

I was hoping for some luck tonight.

It didn't take long to write out cards with the scanty information I already possessed. But putting them on the board only made one thing crystal clear: I didn't have much to go on.

"Okay, there's the Bat Pack," I said out loud. The sound of my own voice helped me focus my thoughts sometimes. "Rude bastards, but that's not a crime."

I had put the card for them beside one that read "Con at Sher."

"A rumored threat of a con at the Sher with a high-tech aspect." I still didn't have the first idea of what that might be, and realized I had failed to follow up on Al's suggestion that I check in with the Sher's own IT department. *Top of tomorrow's to-do list,* I thought.

"Could anything high tech be connected to the Bat Pack?" I wondered aloud, then sighed. This was part of the problem. High tech and vampires don't usually mix.

I looked at the Bat Pack's card once more. There was their assumption that they would be more powerful *after* New Year's Eve. Was that related to the con, or just something that would happen at the same time?

Then there was Dune, who mostly seemed connected to Ash. I put up a Dune card, pulled it down at once, then ripped it to shreds. Not very useful, but highly satisfying.

I moved the remaining cards around a bit then groaned. Moving them around wasn't going to make a single bit of difference. All I did was create bigger holes. All I had were impressions. I could see no pattern.

I reached into my desk drawer, fished around for some more cards, and came to a sudden halt as my fingers encountered something I had forgotten. Lying in the drawer was a charcoal drawing of Ash. It once sat in a silver frame on top of the desk. When the frame broke, I had taken that as the perfect excuse to shut the picture away.

I gazed at it now. It was a remarkable likeness. The artist had captured Ash's strong, clear features in no more than a few strokes. His eyes seemed to be staring straight into mine. Annoyed with myself, I turned the drawing facedown.

I looked once again at the strange red mark I had noticed when the frame broke. The first time I had seen it I thought it was a drop of blood. Now, tilting the mark toward the light, I examined it once more. The tiny figure of a man with the head of a bird. A bloodred headdress—a disc nestled in a crescent—topped his head. He held a scale in one hand and a rolled papyrus in the other. The figure's two-dimensional, stiff profile made me think the image was Egyptian.

I fished a magnifying glass out of the drawer and looked at the image on the paper again. There were even tinier marks beneath the figure. Letters? Hieroglyphics? One of these days, I was going to have to see if I could decode them. I didn't have that kind of time now.

I turned my attention back to the cards on the corkboard. It was as if I were looking at pieces of two different puzzles instead of one. Nothing added up, and the clock was ticking down to New Year's Eve.

There is at least one pattern. Whatever was going to happen at the Sher could spell disaster. Just like the terrible love I still harbored in my heart.

Thirteen

"Then it's a deal," I said, "you drove a hard bargain."

Listening to the satisfied laugh coming through my cell, I clicked it closed. I was sitting in the lobby lounge at the St. Francis Hotel on Union Square. I reached for the glass of merlot on the small table in front of me and smiled. For more than a year I had been trying to convince a retired movie star to sell a certain Grecian bowl that a wealthy client of mine wanted enough to pay me several thousand dollars more than I would have to pay.

Leaning back, I took a sip, then reopened my cell and dialed a number I knew by heart.

"Hello?" I heard as I put the glass down again.

"I got it."

She understood at once. "He's willing to sell the bowl?"

"Yes. Let's go out and celebrate."

There was a moment of hesitation, then she said, "Oh, Ash. I'm sorry. Don't you remember I have that big deadline tomorrow? I have to stay in and work, but you could come over here. I can fix us something."

"That sounds like *more* work for you," I protested, and heard her warm chuckle.

"For such a smooth-talker, you sure don't know much about women."

"And you're going to teach me?"

"I guess I'll have to. Lesson number one: The more often I cook for you, the more you won't be able to live without me. Especially after you've tasted my pasta."

"Lesson learned," I said. "What time do you want me?"

"Lesson number two," she said. "Never ask questions you know the answers to yourself. I always want you."

I smiled as I closed the cell and slipped it into my pocket. Stretching forward to pick up my drink, I saw a familiar figure standing beside the wide stairs that led to one of the restaurants.

He walked toward me as if he already had laid claim to the Board and the whole universe.

"Hello, Sloane. To what do I owe the pleasure?"

"I heard you passed the Nigredo, too," Sloane

said, the emphasis on the final word. I was aware that Sloane had also been successful. Otherwise, there would be no need for the second trial. The Albedo, the test of purity.

"Are you here for some pointers about the next test?" I inquired.

He flushed, but sat down. He leaned his portfolio on the table between us. "They're playing us, you know."

Now there was a news flash, I thought.

"Their game. Their rules. If you don't like it, take your ball and go home. What the hell do you want, Sloane?" It was a pretty sure bet the Board was keeping tabs on us. I didn't want to risk any action that smacked of conspiring with Sloane. "Speak up, or come to the point. Your choice."

He sat back, his gaze assessing. "You've bought into their mumbo-jumbo, haven't you?" he asked. "All that ancient crap. It's bullshit."

"And your point?"

"My point is, if that's a load of crap, then maybe the Chairman's so-called power is also. If we work together, we might be able to take him. Then *we'd* run the Board."

Was this some sort of test in and of itself? I wondered. The point of the Nigredo was to prove I could surrender to the darkness, subvert my ego for a greater cause. Joining Sloane to take on the

Chairman ran counter to everything the first test stood for.

"I don't have time for this," I said. "I want you to go."

"Why won't you even listen?" Sloane exclaimed. His eyes blazing with passion, he struck his fist against the table and the portfolio toppled over. Papers spilled out onto the table, cascaded onto the floor. With a curse, he began to gather them up. I scooted my chair back to help.

"I'll get them," he growled. "Leave them alone."

"Have it your way," I said. I sat back down. Resting on the tabletop was a single sheet of paper, smaller than the others. It had slipped out from between several larger pages as Sloane had hurried to turn his attention to the ones on the floor. Keeping my movement slow and simple, I slid it toward me, then slipped it into the inside breast pocket of my jacket just as Sloane straightened up. The color in his face was high. His eyes, alarmed and wide. He looked like someone afraid he'd just been caught in the act.

What have you done, Sloane? I thought.

He stuffed the pages back into the portfolio, zipped it closed. "I tell you, we need an exit strategy," he insisted.

"Wrong. I don't need one and you've already been given one."

"So you are going to accept being destroyed?"

"I'm not planning on being destroyed."

"You *should* be," Sloane's superior smile returned.

"That's not your decision to make," I said.

"Not yours either."

"So what's the point of continuing this conversation?" I held up my glass. "I'd like to enjoy this . . . alone."

His jaw worked in fury. "You think you're so safe, so smart. They know about her. I'll bet you didn't know that, did you? I told them myself."

I felt fury tear through me then. It took all the strength I had not to let it show. Nothing was going to interfere with what I was trying to accomplish. Certainly not a junkyard dog like Sloane.

"Thank you for sharing," I said. "Anything else before you go?"

"Damn you, Donahue," he said. "I am going to take you down."

"You're going to try," I said. "But first you're going to leave. Right now."

He turned on his heel, strode out of the bar and toward the main lobby. For the first time, I wondered if I had underestimated Sloane. I hadn't bothered to conceal my relationship with a human woman. I hadn't seen the point. Now, I wondered whether I had made a mistake. A costly one.

Finishing the wine, I reached for my wallet. My fingers encountered the piece of paper I had rescued from Sloane's portfolio. Curious now, I drew it out, examined it more closely.

This is old, I thought. Heavy linen, the edges rough. I was about to return it to my pocket when a bright spot of red caught my eye. I leaned down. It was a miniature image of Thoth. There was the human body, the ibis head. One hand held a scale, the other, a rolled papyrus. The ibis head was crowned by a full moon rising from a crescent. Beneath the god, a line of hieroglyphics I couldn't decipher.

Where did Sloane get this? I wondered.

The answer came to me immediately: He had stolen it from the Board. No wonder he wouldn't let me help him pick up the papers. He was afraid I would see *this.*

Was it a deliberate setup? Was he seeking to defeat me by any means, at any cost?

I left the restaurant, went out onto the street. I was just debating which way to go when I spotted Sloane standing on a nearby street corner, anxiously searching through his portfolio. *Not a setup, then,* I thought. If it was, Sloane wouldn't look so desperate. He had stolen something from the Board, and now he'd lost it. Now it was mine.

I crossed Powell on my way to Union Square.

The streets were crowded, busy with people heading for the BART station on Market Street. The palm trees were rocking gently in the breeze carrying the fog over the city. I was almost across the square when I heard the sound of someone running behind me. It didn't take an ounce of vampire's rapport to figure out it was Sloane.

On the stairs to the left of me, I saw a street artist closing up his art box. Samples of his charcoal portraits were set on a board next to his easel. I moved toward him.

"I need a portrait done," I said. "Right now."

The artist looked up, annoyed. "It's too dark, man," he said. "Come back tomorrow."

I held out a hundred-dollar bill. "Perhaps this will help you see the light."

He gave a sudden laugh. "Sure," he said. "Why not?"

I reached past him, clipped the linen page to the sketchpad on his easel, turning the page so the image of Thoth was concealed. "Use this."

"Whatever you want."

He dug out a fresh piece of charcoal. Began to move it across the paper in swift, practiced strokes. I was standing perfectly relaxed and still when Sloane approached.

"What did you do with it, Donahue?" he asked.

"I don't know what you're talking about."

He swore creatively. "The page."

"What page?" I glanced around the square where vagrant pieces of paper bounced along on the breeze. "Did you drop your portfolio again? You seriously need to keep that thing zipped, Sloane."

Sloane opened his mouth then closed it again. *Busted, aren't you?* I thought. He couldn't tell me precisely what he was looking for because that would also no doubt reveal the fact that he had stolen it.

"I won't forget this," he said.

"Neither will I. Since you've been so kind as to share with me, let me offer you a piece of advice, Sloane. Stay out of my affairs, and I'll stay out of yours."

I let my eyes hold his until I saw he understood. He wasn't the only one who could take information to the Board. He turned on one heel, moved off down the street. The artist finished the portrait, unclipped it from the easel.

"Aren't you going to look at it?" he asked as I took the sketch from him.

Until that moment, I hadn't even considered it. The sketch had been a means to an end, nothing more. But now I studied it, my curiosity piqued. It had been a long time since I had seen myself through someone else's eyes.

The artist had captured a man in his early thirties with pale eyes and an expression that was both open and knowing at the same time. With a shock, I realized he had made me look entirely human.

Carefully, I rolled up the drawing and slipped it beneath my coat. Tomorrow I would have to do some research and figure out how to turn Sloane's larceny to my advantage. Tonight . . . I glanced at my watch.

Damn! I was going to be late. The smart choice might be to call off my date altogether. But that would feel too much like giving in to Sloane. He had upped the ante, but he wasn't the only one who could do that.

No, that's not the reason I couldn't break my date. She was the reason. I wanted her long wild brown hair tangled in my fingers. I craved the scent of her skin, her touch. I wanted to feel the weight of her body pressed against mine. I wanted to love her tonight and all the other nights.

Perhaps the time had come to tell Candace what I truly was.

Fourteen

Before I could leave my office, my cell phone rang. I recognized the number and the name: Gray Skies. Gray for Blanchard Gray. *Finally,* I thought. Maybe I was about to get a break at last.

"Talk to me, Blanchard," I said, as I picked up.

He didn't bother with a hello, but then neither had I. "I need to see you, Candace. We need to talk right now."

I have heard Blanchard's voice do many things. Beg. Laugh. Cry. But I had never heard it this close to panic.

"Where?"

"My office."

It was almost two a.m.

"I'm on my way," I said. And rang off.

* * *

Blanchard works at the medical examiner's office. At this hour, it was deserted except for the people who work the night shift and, of course, the corpses. Instantly, as I walked in, my heels loud against the tile floor, I was assaulted by the harsh smell of chemicals. I smell dead people. Or not. I hate coming here. It always means trouble.

I knocked on Blanchard's office door. It swung open, and I saw him throwing papers into a box.

"What's up?" I asked. "Are you quitting? What the hell is going on?"

"Leave of absence," he answered shortly. He yanked another drawer open.

"Wait a minute," I protested. "For how long?"

"For as long as it takes," he replied. "If you had an ounce of sense, you'd leave town, too."

"Blanchard, wait. Stop." I picked up the box he was packing and moved it out of reach. "What do you mean leaving town?"

"Leaving town as in scramming. Cutting my losses. Running like hell. There's trouble brewing, sweetheart. A big power struggle . . ." He held up a hand when I would have spoken. "I know, I know. There's been vampire infighting before, someone trying to grab someone else's power to move up the ladder, but nothing like what's about to go down. This is like a war."

"Who's behind it?"

"Uh-uh," he said. "Not until you give me back my box."

I could feel my temper start to slip. It was two a.m., after all, I was tired and frustrated, and all he was doing was putting me off.

"Blanchard, will you please cut the crap and tell me what you know right now?"

"There's a power play about to go down."

"I know that much!" I all but shouted. "You said that before. Who's behind it? Who's involved?"

"I don't know for sure. It's all just rumors."

"Of course it is," I sighed. "But rumors have names that go with them, Blanchard. I may be just a dumb human, but even I know that much."

"It's the Bat Pack," he suddenly burst out. "The rumors are saying it's the Bat Pack. Can I please have my box back now?"

"Well, shit," I said.

"That's exactly right. We're paddling up shit creek, and I'm getting out before my canoe capsizes."

"But you told me the Bat Packers were low-level wannabes."

"So sue me! I was wrong." He made a sudden lunge and snatched back the box. "Apparently, they're not as stupid or as powerless as advertised."

"Apparently," I said. But some things did make more sense, now. Such as my reaction to them at the Venetian. "Anything else I should know?"

"It's about a power shift. I know I keep saying that, but it's really all I know. I think it's bigger than Vegas, but I don't know for sure."

"So the Bat Pack is trying to get more power."

"More than that. They're after someone, someone up the hierarchy."

"Someone high on the vampire hierarchy? Who?"

"How would I know? I'm not exactly up there myself. But listen! If you tell anyone I told you this, my existence won't be worth a damn, Candace."

"For crying out loud, Blanchard," I said. "Who the hell do you think I'm going to tell?"

"I don't know who you'll tell," Blanchard exploded. "I never know what you do with the information I pass on. That's the way you like it, and the way I like it. I'm just trying to maintain some semblance of the status quo."

"By leaving town."

"You are so right. I'm getting out of Vegas till the whole thing blows over." He tossed one last folder into the box, hefted it, and walked to the door. "Do you want to come?"

I opened my mouth, then closed it again. *Things must be bad,* I thought. Blanchard was breaking our number-one rule: no personal involvement.

"Thanks for the invitation," I said. "I really mean that. But I think I'd better stick around."

"They've seen us together. The Bat Pack."

"I know that," I said. I didn't add that I had already had additional run-ins with the Bat Pack on my own. Fear pumped through me. I had played these games before. I hoped that experience would be enough to prepare me for what had scared Blanchard this much. "Don't worry. I'll be careful."

"See you when I get back, then," he said. "I hope."

"I hope so, too," I replied, but he was already gone.

My phone rang. Again. I rolled over and stared at the clock. Nine a.m. Shit! I overslept. After my chat with Blanchard, I had trouble drifting off into a peaceful sleep. The last time I looked at the clock it was six a.m. Now I felt as if I had been run over by a convoy of tourist buses. I reached out, picked up the phone.

"Yeah?" I croaked.

"Wake up, Steele," Al's voice barked into the phone. "I need you down here, pronto."

I pushed myself upright. "What is it? Did you catch whoever's running the con?"

Al gave a short, unamused laugh. "I wish," he said.

"Then what's going on?"

"Did you see the morning news on *Sunrise Las Vegas*?"

"Do I sound like I saw it?"

Al ignored my tone. "They did a stand-up in front of the Sher. Lance Weatherly reporting on the No-Limits tournament."

"And you're going to tell me why this free publicity is not a good thing any little minute now."

"Because the free publicity included the fact that the tournament may be the target of a con."

This time, I sat bolt upright. "He did what?"

"You heard me," Al said grimly. "The information got left on an anonymous tip line."

"That's incredibly unreliable, Al. Any legitimate reporter would have . . ."

"No one ever said Lance Weatherly was legitimate." Al cut me off. "He's a pretty boy who likes digging up dirt, and he doesn't particularly care if what he digs up is true or false. So Weatherly made the most of the opportunity to ask some leading questions about whether anyone should trust the casino. I don't suppose I have to tell you that Randolph Glass is fit to be tied."

I'll just bet he is, I thought.

"And he came straight to you, didn't he?" I said, as my sleep-deprived mind finally came up with the real reason for Al's call. "To ask who else knew about the possibility of the con."

"Bingo," Al said. "Do I need to tell you whose name tops the list?"

"I'm on my way, Al," I said.

We both knew it was mine.

By the time I got to Al's office, Randolph Glass was in prime form. Storming from one side to another like a drill sergeant dressing down new recruits. Al sat behind his desk, saying nothing. I sat in the chair in front of it, saying more of the same.

"How did this happen?" Randolph demanded. He wore a black suit with a gray silk tie, pretty damned slick for an internal morning meeting. I couldn't help wondering if he had already arranged a press conference to refute the report. "I'm not going to rest till I know."

"Why don't you just accuse me and be done with it?" I snapped. "Then you can fire me and we can all go home."

"*You* can go home any time you like," Randolph said. "But with or without you, *I* have a casino to run."

"Candace did not leak the rumors to the press," Al put in quietly.

Randolph swung toward him. "You can't be sure of that."

"Of course I can," Al said, evenly. "Randolph, you have got to calm down. Your reaction is only making things worse. Candace is a key member of my staff and I trust her."

"She knows people at Weatherly's station."

"I know reporters at every TV station in Vegas," I answered for myself, shooting a quick, grateful look at Al. The fact that I had lost my temper so easily hadn't helped the situation either.

"A fact that has worked to the Sher's advantage more than once," I went on. "Human-interest angles or stand-ups in front of our sign when they need a Strip backdrop. The shots aren't always in front of the dancing waters at the Bellagio anymore, or haven't you noticed?"

"Actually, I have noticed that," Randolph said shortly. "You're saying it's you and not the marketing department."

"I'm saying it's both," I replied. "I'm also saying I know enough to know that Lance Weatherly could have been listening to the buzz on the streets. There's absolutely no reason to think his information is accurate, or that it came from inside. You said it yourself, Al," I said, switching my attention to him. "There are always rumors of a big con."

"I did say that," Al acknowledged. "I said it and I meant it."

"We can't do anything about Weatherly," I said. "That damage is done. Instead of going after his source, maybe we should be mounting a media event of our own. Give meaning to the notion there's no such thing as bad publicity."

"She's got a point," Al said.

And you just hate that little fact, don't you Mr. Randolph Glass?

"Call my secretary, Al," Randolph suddenly barked. "Better yet, go get her yourself." Which was just his charming way of saying he wanted a moment alone with me, even if it meant kicking Al out of his own office.

"Sure thing," Al said. He got up and left the room without making eye contact with me. Good choice.

"I suppose you think I owe you an apology," Randolph Glass said, when we were alone.

I decided it was time to stand on my own two feet, literally, as well as verbally. I got up.

"Except for a paycheck, I don't think you owe me anything at all."

"I've worked hard for what I've established here," Randolph Glass continued. "And I'm hoping to expand soon, to grow." He shot me a look. "I don't know whether Bibi's mentioned that or not."

"Bibi does not discuss your business affairs and neither do I."

So that's what this little tête-à-tête is really all about, I thought.

"Have you spoken to her? How is she?" Randolph asked.

"Bibi," I said, "is just fine. If you have any other questions for her, I suggest you ask them yourself."

I walked out the door.

I stomped back through the casino, my mind a seething cauldron of Randolph's bad behavior and Blanchard's dire predictions of what he called a war. The more I thought about it, the more it scared me. People were going to get hurt, and it looked more and more as if I wouldn't be able to stop it. There are always innocent bystanders when it comes to war. What was the official term? "Collateral damage." I could only hope the damage wouldn't be restricted to humans only.

As I walked past the slots that circled the perimeter of the casino, I caught sight of some of Michael's friends from last night's party happily putting their Magic Carpet Cards into the slots. *You guys sure aren't wasting any time,* I thought. At the rate they'd been going when I left the suite, I would have said they intended to party all night. Maybe they'd done just that, then come downstairs for some casino action. They were only here for a short period of time, after all. I passed by a woman whose name I'd forgotten two seconds after I'd been introduced. She was moving from machine to machine, not playing more than a dollar at each. I wondered if I should tell her that the odds are better if you stick with one machine, but I didn't really feel like talking to her.

I walked toward the poker tournament. Only six tables remained, roped off from the rest of the casino by brass stanchions with purple velvet ropes. The crowd watching the games had grown; it was at least six people deep on every side. I thought I remembered Michael had expected an early call, but I couldn't see him over the crowd in front of me.

A man with a camera on his shoulder muttered an apology as he pushed past me.

I saw Michael's friend Josh Doyle. He was talking with two cameramen who weren't taping. I could tell, even from where I stood, that he was asking questions and listening closely to their answers. I inched closer, keeping a rotund man with a fragrant cigar between Josh and me.

"So how often do you switch cameras?" Josh was asking.

"Whenever the director decides." One cameraman motioned with his elbow. "See that skinny blonde in black by the tables? She's the director."

Josh kept asking questions about the type of cameras the men were using to shoot the tournament and the lighting and the director's controls and using a lot of technical terms that I wasn't familiar with.

I watched Josh walk away, stopping at the slot machines where Michael's friends were playing. He paused to talk with each one. I followed him at a distance, growing more and more curious.

"Candace!" I heard Michael call.

Turning, I saw him a few paces away. I didn't have to ask how he was doing. He looked like a winner. I turned my face so he kissed my cheek instead of my mouth.

"Something wrong?" he asked.

"I'm not supposed to fraternize with the guests, remember?"

"You're not working."

"Well, I'm not playing." I glanced at the cameramen who were fiddling with their equipment. "Josh was certainly interested in those guys."

"I'm not surprised." Michael turned to watch the men adjusting the cameras for the next round of play. "Now that he's sold his company, Josh has been thinking about what he wants to do next.

Near as I can tell, it's something to do with TV production and high def."

He went on, but, as with the cameramen and Josh, too many of the terms were gibberish to me. I needed a quick course, and I didn't feel comfortable asking Michael to explain.

"I'm exhausted," I said when he paused to take a breath.

"I've got the perfect solution," he said, capturing my hand. "Come rest upstairs."

"Michael," I protested, even as I let him pull me along. "We don't rest upstairs."

"So we'll do other things, then," he said. "C'mon, Candace. I need a break, too." He waggled his eyebrows at me. "I'll order up some coffee."

"Coffee? Okay," I said. "You're on."

Five minutes later Michael led me through the suite. The living room was a maze of overnight bags and briefcases. Josh was sitting at the dining table, talking into a cell phone. He lifted a hand in greeting, then turned to the table and began to scribble furiously on a yellow pad. I would have stopped short if Michael hadn't maintained his grip on my hand. Quietly but purposefully, he steered me toward the bedroom, urged me through the door, followed me inside, then closed the door behind us. I heard the lock catch with a *click*.

"Michael, for crying out loud," I whispered. "Josh is right outside the door."

Michael made a face. "Josh is working," he said. "The television could explode right next to him and he wouldn't notice. Besides, I promised you a rest, remember? Now be a good girl and lie down on the bed."

I put my hands on my hips, though I could feel the first stirrings of excitement. "You're getting awfully bossy all of a sudden, don't you think?" I asked.

Michael smiled. "Candace," he said softly. "Will you please lie down on the bed?"

I could feel the laughter start to ripple through me, and pressed my lips together to hold it back. "Facedown or faceup?" I asked.

"Facedown," Michael said. "Though that position is subject to revision, of course."

"Naturally," I said.

I sat down on the bed, scooted backward, then rolled over onto my stomach, nestling my face in my arms. I felt the bed give as Michael joined me. He eased off my shoes and socks, then knelt, his knees on either side of my body, just below my ass.

"You seem a little tense to me, Candace," he

said. "Fortunately for you, I know just the way to fix that. Did I ever mention I went to massage school?"

"Why, no," I said, my voice slightly muffled. "Somehow I think you neglected to mention that. You're just full of talents, aren't you?"

I heard him laugh beneath his breath. His hands moved against my shoulders in a series of firm squeezes, then swept down my back in slow, easy strokes. The only sounds in the room were Michael's hands moving across the fabric of my clothing, and our quiet breathing. In the other room, I could hear Josh raise his voice.

"Are all your friends staying with you?" I murmured.

"Most of them," Michael sighed, his voice resigned. His hands were sweeping lower now, gently stroking across my ass. I felt a fine tingling begin to seep slowly through my body. "Fortunately, they're here to do some serious gambling, so they're not around most of the time."

His hands moved up once more. They were in my hair now. Massaging my scalp with the tips of his fingers. I felt his weight shift, then come back down. I could feel his erection, pressing against my ass. The tingling in my body became a low, hot throb. His hands still busy in my hair, Michael leaned forward. I felt his breath on my neck, then his tongue. Slowly circling my earlobe, then sliding down my neck. Ever so slightly, I began to move my ass from side to side.

Without warning, he fisted his fingers in my hair, bringing my head back even as he brought his down. He turned my head, urged my mouth to his for an openmouthed kiss, his tongue thrusting deep. I sucked it in, holding it prisoner with my teeth and heard him make a quickly cutoff sound. He released me and, as I dropped my head forward, back onto my arms, I pressed my ass more firmly against his cock. His hands slid beneath me, seeking my breasts. Still pressing back against him, I raised myself up onto my elbows.

He filled his hands with my breasts, kneading, caressing, stroking, even as he began to rock against me from behind. His fingers danced down my body, seeking the fastening of my pants. He undid the buttons, then gave the tight material a quick tug. It slid over my hips, down across my ass, its tight slide only adding to my arousal. The silk of the panties I wore went along for the ride. I felt Michael's weight withdraw as he drew the pants down my legs and off. Then the soft *slump* of fabric as they hit the floor. A moment later I heard the sound of his belt hissing through its loops, the high whine of a zipper. My back still to him, I got to my knees, pulled the shirt I wore over my head. But when I went to unfasten the front clasp of the bra, I felt the return of Michael's weight on the bed. He put his hands over mine, then pulled me back against him, filling his hands with my silk-clad breasts.

I could feel his shirt as it pressed against my back. But his cock was naked, pulsing against my rump. Slowly, his hands still at my breasts, he eased me forward until I rested on my elbows once more. With one hand, he reached to pull several pillows down from the head of the bed, tucking them beneath me for support. His fingers stroked the length of my naked ass, broadening my stance, tilting me up. And then he was gripping my ass tightly with both hands, drawing his breath in one long inhalation as he pushed his cock slowly, slowly inside me.

I pressed my face down against my hands, tilting my pelvis up still higher. *Deep, go deeper, Michael,* I thought. I felt one of his hands release my hip, move around to stroke my clit. And then he began to ride.

I felt the world narrow to the sensations in that room. Nothing else existed. Nothing else at all. The feel of my face, pressed against my own hands. The soft slap our bodies made as Michael moved inside me. His hand at my clit, a wild spiral of sensations, coiling tighter and tighter. I heard him make just one guttural sound, and then his body went rigid, arcing forward. Deep inside me, I felt him come. I held myself still, muscles clenched around him. Felt the way he pulsed and shuddered. His head dropped forward, forehead resting on the back of my neck, even as his hand continued to stroke.

And then, almost before I realized what he was doing, he was pulling back, turning me around. Sliding me toward the edge of the bed, parting my legs, even as he knelt on the floor. He put his mouth on me then, stroking down, hard with his tongue. Across my clit, then thrusting deep inside me, just as he had thrust his cock. I felt my body spasm up. He held me there, pelvis raised above the bed, while his tongue continued to delve and stroke. As if my body was a feast and he could not get enough.

On a choked-back cry, I came, hands grasping at the bedspread, even as Michael continued to use his mouth. I dragged in great, burning lungfuls of air, as my body seemed to tumble through space, and still he did not stop. I felt the second orgasm rip through me. My body, a wordless arc of pleasure, literally incapable of sound.

The second my body relaxed, Michael released me, joined me on the bed, pulling me up to its head to take me in his arms. I let him move me, limp as a rag doll, utterly sated. He pressed a deep kiss to my mouth and I tasted my own flavor.

"Well," I murmured when I could finally speak. "I don't think I'm nearly as tense as I was."

I felt the laughter quiver through his belly, knew he was fighting to hold back the sound.

"I'm so pleased to hear you say that," he whispered.

"I'll just bet you are."

Without warning, a strange buzzing filled the room.

"Damn," Michael exclaimed aloud as he sat up. "That's my cell. It's probably my call to go back down."

"It's either great timing or lousy," I said, as I watched him slide from the bed to retrieve the phone from his pants' pocket. "Depending on what else you had in mind."

"Just hold that thought," he said, as he flipped open the cell. "Pressman." He listened, briefly. "Thank you," he said. "I'll be right down." He snapped the phone shut, began to pull on his scattered clothing. "I'm sorry," he said. "That really is my call."

"What's to be sorry about?" I asked, as I scooted off the bed and began to dress. "We knew you didn't have much time. Outstanding use of it, by the way. I forgot all about Josh."

Michael caught me to him then, for a quick, hard kiss. "You know what?" he said quietly. "In addition to your many other sterling attributes, you are pretty damned understanding."

"Just so you appreciate me," I said.

He kissed me again. "You know it. In fact, I have a little something for you."

"Not *that* again," I said, and made him laugh out loud.

He dug in his back pants' pocket, pulled out a key card. "Actually, it's this," he said. "It will give you access to any door in the suite." He gave a nod at the far corner of the room. "In particular, that one. It opens directly onto the hall. You can come and go whenever you like without having to worry about the menagerie out there. Everybody knows this room is strictly off limits. It's mine and mine alone."

He took a step closer when I hesitated. "I'd really like to keep seeing you, Candace, but it's going to be tough with all my friends around. If I had known I was going to meet you, I never would have agreed to them camping out in my suite. As it is, this is the best that I can offer. I'm really hoping you'll say yes. I know you could get into trouble."

"I think it's a little late for that," I said. "So, yes, thanks. I'd like to keep seeing you, too."

I took the card.

"Excellent," Michael said. "I promise I'll make it worth your while. I should probably go down first, don't you think?"

"I do think," I said. "I should do one more work-related thing anyhow. You'll let me know when you get a break?"

"Absolutely," he nodded. He gave me one last, swift kiss, his eyes grinning down into mine. "For luck."

Then he let himself out into the hall. I gave him a couple of minutes, then left the suite myself. As long as I was still in the casino, it was high time I handled the item that should have been number one on my to-do list: a trip to the IT department.

A buzzer sounded the second I stepped through the door of the IT center. I held up my ID badge, and a guard nodded at me to sign in at the counter. The place was as sterile as an operating room. Everything that wasn't white was glass or steel. A coffeepot was half-full. I picked it up and sniffed. The coffee smelled a bit overcooked; I filled a Styrofoam cup and added a generous hit of sugar.

"Can I help you?" The voice was so deep that I

looked up, expecting to see someone the size of a linebacker behind the counter.

Instead, the man standing there brought Deputy Barney Fife to mind. He was thin, and not much taller than I am. He wore a long white coat, the pockets of which bulged with wires. An upper pocket held a pocket protector with several expensive-looking gold and silver pens. Behind dark-rimmed glasses, his eyes were intelligent and anxious. The classic geek.

"Are you Chet McGuire?" I asked, even though I could read his ID tag with his name and title of IT SECURITY SUPERVISOR.

"I am," he nodded. "How can I help you?"

I stuck out my hand. "Candace Steele, security," I said.

"Candace Steele," he mused. "Employee number 65-9857, hired—"

"Hey, that's information I don't usually share until at least the second date."

He stared at me for a moment, then said, "Oh, you're joking." A buzz came near my right ear. A fly? Then I realized the high-pitched sound was in both ears.

"Do you hear a buzz?"

He cocked his head. "No."

Either he was used to the annoying sound or couldn't hear it.

"Do you mind answering a few questions?" I

asked after taking a sip of the coffee. It tasted like sludge, but it was sludge with caffeine and sugar, and I needed both.

"I'll answer what I can." He glanced at the glass window that showed the computer servers being taken care of by other white-coated attendants. "Al told me a couple of days ago that you might stop in."

I nodded. "I need to know about the kind of surveillance we do in the casino. High Tech 101. No buzzwords. Just the basic facts."

"Okay, the basics." He folded his arms on the counter. "As you know, almost every inch of the Sher is under surveillance. There are cameras in all the public spaces, and they're monitored 24/7. The people who work the monitoring room have a minimum of two years' experience on the casino floor overseeing games, so they've learned what the usual scams are. It's the unusual ones that make them earn their pay."

"And these computers?" I hooked a thumb toward the glass.

"They're used for everything from directing the cameras in random patterns to gathering information and crunching it to detect any aberrations."

"Such as a table where the house loses more than the averages show."

"Exactly. When we see something like that, the croupier will be monitored—discreetly—until we learn if it's the laws of chance throwing us a curve or if there's something funny going on."

"So if someone tries to pull a con—"

"We'll be on him right away." He smiled. "Under normal conditions."

"What do you mean?" I took another sip from my cup.

"These cameras for the tournament—"

"How can they be a problem? There're only a few guys, and they're carrying the cameras on their shoulders."

"Not those cameras. The ones in the tables."

"I didn't know there were cameras in the tables."

He poured himself the rest of the sludge and pulled a box of doughnuts out from under the counter and opened it. "Have you ever watched poker shows on TV? They have little eyeball cameras set into the tables. That allows the viewers and the commentators to see what hole cards each player has, the cards they've got that the other players can't see."

"I don't see how those can be a problem either." I picked out a glazed doughnut.

"Those small cameras require special wiring and

monitoring. A pain in the butt when we're busy with the holiday crowds."

"Does that mean it's easier for someone to pull a scam now?"

"Not exactly, there's just more that we have to keep track of."

I thought of Josh and his interest in the cameras.

"And the cameras themselves, the TV and news cameras, couldn't be used to somehow affect the outcome of the game?"

Chet munched thoughtfully on his doughnut. "I don't see how."

I had one more question. "If someone like you, someone who knows the technology, were going to pull a scam connected with the tournament, any ideas on how he might go about it?"

"That's the kind of question we ask ourselves day in and day out," Chet said. "Truthfully, anything that's worked in the past, any new angle we can imagine—we've already taken steps to prevent it. Any con that works is going to have to be pretty darn original."

"Thanks," I said, not at all comforted.

I signed out of the computer center and went straight to the garage. I sat in my car but didn't turn the ignition key. Crossing my arms on the steering wheel, I leaned forward and rested my head. I obviously wasn't going to get anywhere by trying to chase down high-tech answers. The clock was ticking down to the final round of the tournament and New Year's Eve—and, if what Blanchard said was even partially true, to a war in the vampire world. If the two events were connected, I couldn't figure out how.

Focus, Candace. I had to think about what I could do and forget about what I couldn't. What I could do was concentrate on what Blanchard had told me before he skipped town. The Bat Pack had found a way to amp up their powers. They were going to make a move against someone high up in the hierarchy. Their action could cause a big power shift and enough disturbance that it could result in what he called a vampire war. What would it take to start a vampire war? Had it already started? Without Blanchard, who the hell could I ask?

The answer was so obvious. Someone high up in the vampire hierarchy. Someone with power. I groaned. Ash. Ash would know if anything big was going down in the vampire world. As much as I wanted to avoid him, I needed to find out what was going on even more. Sometimes you have to do more than think outside the box; you have to think outside yourself. Ash. A new thought flicked across my mind. Could Ash be the Bat Pack's target?

Could he be the high-up vampire whose power they were after?

Collateral damage, I thought once more. To avoid it, I was going to have to do the one thing I wanted least: ask for Ash's help.

Fifteen

The sun had set behind the mountains ringing Las Vegas. A faint reddish glow outlined the peaks but was overpowered by the neon extravagance of the Strip. Each hotel and casino vied for attention. Loud music, flashy signs, hints of sex and cash, suggestions of the good life.

Even the Beijing with its understated elegance wasn't immune. As I walked from the closest parking garage toward the casino, I was greeted by loud advertisements for its shows and restaurants. The music was glorious—a mixture of western and Asian influences—but it was way too loud.

Or was it my ears? I was turned up on every frequency for any sign that I was being watched. As far as I knew, there was nothing to connect me to Ash, but I couldn't be sure the Bat Pack hadn't seen the two of us together at the Beijing or the Venetian.

Walking through the casino, I followed the discreet signs to the residential tower. The long hallway was as formal as the areas surrounding the casino. Rich, dark woods covered the lower half of the walls, and exquisite wallpapers in soothing shades of gold and cream reached toward the high barrel ceiling. Great brass chandeliers were set every ten feet along the corridor.

The carpet muffled my steps, but as I emerged from the corridor, a woman looked up from her desk with a practiced smile. The space was a perfect circle. Several elevator doors decorated with bas relief images of Chinese landscapes broke the walls. Between them were gilded chairs that looked as if nobody had ever sat on them. In the center beneath a smaller version of the grand chandeliers was a gilded desk ornately carved with birds and vines. The computer monitor sitting on top offered a single bit of practicality.

The beautiful, young Asian woman sitting at the desk had the poise and *sang-froid* of royalty. I could almost feel her assessing me in my faded jeans and striped sweater. Her suit was a pristine ivory with sateen lapels. A subtle nameplate on her left breast identified her as Su Li.

"Good evening," Su Li said in a carefully modulated voice. "Welcome to the Beijing, ma'am. How may I help you?"

"I need to see Ash Donahue."

Su Li glanced down, as if consulting some sort of

guest log or appointment book. "Is he expecting you?"

"No," I said. "But there must be some way you can let him know I'm here."

"Of course," Su Li replied. "If I might have your name?"

"Candace," I said. "Candace Steele."

"Thank you, Miss Steele. One moment." She tapped her keyboard, then said, "I am sorry, Miss Steele, but Mr. Donahue has left instructions that he not be disturbed tonight."

Instantly, my head was filled with an image of Ash and Dune wrapped together in an embrace even more passionate than what I had witnessed at the Venetian. I pushed it from my mind. Tonight wasn't about emotion. It was about getting information and letting Ash know what I had learned in case he was the Bat Pack's target.

"This is an emergency," I said. "I'm afraid I must insist I be allowed to speak with Mr. Donahue at once."

Her gaze swept over me, assessing. "Perhaps, if I might know the nature of the emergency?"

"Now look, I said it was an emergency," I could feel myself losing control.

"Thank you, Su Li. I'll take it from here," Ash's voice suddenly sounded. He had come down in the elevator without either of us noticing him. He wore a black cotton shirt and those well-worn jeans.

"If you're quite certain, Mr. Donahue," Su Li said.

"Quite certain, thank you," Ash replied. He turned to me, made a gesture toward the elevator. "Well, Candace. Shall we go?"

I crossed to the elevator. As if motion sensitive, it slid open at our approach. And I discovered to my horror that I simply could not make my body move. I could not make myself get into an elevator alone with Ash. Last time I did I had almost lost my life.

"Actually, if you'll excuse me for a moment," Ash said. "There is one last item of business I should attend to while I'm downstairs." He leaned into the elevator, punched in a code. "This will take you straight up. I have the whole floor. I'll join you in a moment."

He stepped back and I managed to propel my body forward. I let the elevator lift me, my mind high and blank. When the doors slid open again, I was in Ash's condo. Before me was an enormous wall of glass.

I stepped out of the elevator, moving forward to admire the view, and heard the doors whisper closed behind me. The floors were smooth, polished wood beneath my feet. Vegas at night before me, in all its glory.

Looking south, I could see most of the Strip. The Wynn, its arc of floors rising from the pools surrounding it. The Venetian's canals were silvery fingers, calm compared to the pirates' pyrotechnic battle of fireworks at Treasure Island. Caesar's Palace and the Bellagio fought for the brightest lights, but were dwarfed by the rise of the Eiffel Tower above the Paris casino. At the far end, beyond the bright green MGM Grand and the gaudy Vegas versions of the Chrysler and the Empire State buildings of New York–New York was the unmistakable blue-white light coming from the apex of the Luxor's black glass pyramid. And connecting them all were moving streams of white headlights and red taillights.

"It's dazzling." Only when Ash spoke behind me did I realize I had spoken aloud.

"I've always thought so." Ash came to stand beside me. He didn't touch me, but every inch of my skin was aware of him. "I bought this place after seeing this view. I didn't give a damn what the rest of the apartment was like."

I turned my back against the cool glass wall, and my gaze took in the rest of the living room—a vast space broken by a low sofa and a number of Greek and Egyptian carvings, each on a pedestal illuminated by a recessed spotlight. Ash continued to gaze out the window, his profile lit by the reflected lights rising up from the Strip.

"Why are you here, Candace?" he asked.

Because I couldn't stay away, I thought. *Because the plain and simple truth is that I do not want to live without you.*

But I said neither of those things. If I did, everything I had fought so hard for would go up in smoke. The fact that I couldn't always remember just why I was fighting was part of the reason I had to keep on doing so.

"To ask for your help," I finally replied. "And to offer it, if I can. I came to warn you. It's possible you may be in danger, Ash."

He took a step closer then, so suddenly I didn't even have time to step back, even if I had wanted to. Gently, he caught my chin in one hand, tilting my face up.

"I believe that you are genuinely concerned about me," he said, and I thought I heard something in his voice that sounded remarkably like wonder. "Would you be sorry if something happened to me, Candace?"

It never occurred to me to lie. Never even occurred to me I could. "Of course I would, Ash," I said. "I love you. The fact that I don't always want to hasn't managed to change that yet."

His fingers tightened, involuntarily, I thought. Because, in the next instant, they were gentle once more.

"No, it hasn't, has it?" he asked softly. He brought his own face closer. All I would have to do was rise to my toes for our lips to meet. "Doesn't that tell you something?"

"Ash," I said, my voice no more than a whisper. "Please. Don't."

For a moment, I thought he would protest. Then, he released me, stepped back, and turned away.

"If you say so."

"Ash, please, you have to listen to me," I said. I grasped his arm and turned him back to face me. "I didn't come here to argue about us. I came here to talk to you. There's a group of vampires calling themselves the Bat Pack."

He made a derisive sound. "Sounds appropriate for Vegas."

"I know it sounds idiotic," I said. "But they're attempting some sort of power grab. I know the Sher is one of their targets. The other one could be you. You've got to tell me what you know."

"So that's what this is really about," Ash said as he pulled away, and now I could hear anger in his voice. "You're here because of the casino."

"Yes," I said at once. "No. Both. Shit!" I suddenly exploded. "Shit. Shit. Shit. Why must you always make everything so impossible? This was a mistake. I should never have come."

"No," Ash said. And, as abruptly as it had come, the anger seemed to go out of him. "No, I'm glad you came, Candace. And I appreciate the warning. I shouldn't have taunted you. I apologize."

"Okay, that does it," I said. "Now I *know* there's something wrong." Ash lifted a brow and I answered his unspoken question. "You just apologized. You never do that."

He laughed, and the sound was rich and warm. "Why is it," he asked, "that I sometimes find you so surprising? I suppose I shouldn't question it, as it's one of the things I love best about you."

"And Dune," I said, despising the words even as I spoke them. Despising myself. "Does she surprise you?"

Ash sobered at once. "Dune was . . . a mistake," he said quietly. "One I am trying to find a way to rectify, and that's all I'm going to say about her."

"I suppose you think I should apologize now," I said.

"No," Ash said simply. "Not unless you want to."

"Ash," I said. "Something bad is coming. You have to help me stop it."

"No, Candace," he said. "As a matter of fact, I

don't. But if it makes you feel any better, I have heard rumors. I'm taking steps to protect myself."

"And the Scheherazade?"

Ash made an impatient gesture. "I don't give a damn about Randolph Glass's toy. I will protect myself. Do my best to make sure innocent people don't get hurt. And I will protect what I love. Don't ask for more than that."

"So that's it," I said. "You won't help me."

"On the contrary," Ash said. "I am helping, more than you know. I don't want you in this, Candace."

"I'm already in it," I said.

"Then step away."

"No. You won't do it. Why should I?"

"How about because I asked you to, Candace?" Ash said. "How about, because it's important to me? But wait a minute, I'm forgetting, aren't I? It's what you want that's important, even if it means all you're doing is running away. If you ever find the courage to stop, you might want to ask yourself why you're in such a hurry to escape from the only thing you truly desire."

"Meaning you," I said.

"Meaning *us*," Ash came right back. "Tell me something Candace: If this coup you suspect were to succeed, if I were no longer in the world, would you mourn for me?"

I opened my mouth, then shut it with a snap. I had imagined being free of Ash so many times. But never had I envisioned a world where he did not exist. That's how deeply Ash was a part of me. I felt the sudden spill of tears across my cheeks, knew I had given us both an answer. If Ash were gone, I would survive, but I would never truly live without him. No wonder I was running away.

"I'm sorry," Ash said at once. He came to me swiftly, drew me into his arms. "So sorry, Candace. I truly didn't know."

"I can't," I said. "I won't." And we both knew I wasn't denying our passion, our impossible love. I was denying the possibility of Ash's demise. "And I can't believe you didn't know. You always know everything, you sonofabitch."

I felt a tremor move through him. I thought it might be laughter. "No. If I did, you couldn't surprise me." I lifted my head. He placed his fingers on the tracks of my tears. "Candace, Candace," he whispered. "How I wish you would surprise me now."

"How can I, when we both know what you want?"

"By giving it to me."

I sank into the kiss, letting Ash's need, his hunger, fill up every empty place inside. Until I could no longer tell where he ended and I began.

Until I no longer wanted to tell. He lifted his head and I met his eyes. The expression in them was enough to strike me blind.

Before I could give myself time to think, I pulled back, out of his arms. One step, then another as Ash began to reach for me.

"No. Don't." With one fluid motion, I pulled the sweater I had worn over my head. Beneath it was the black lace corset, the one he had sent with the dress I'd refused to wear for him.

"Well," Ash said, and now both laughter and delight were clear in his voice. "This *is* a surprise."

I closed one of the spaces I had put between us, stopped. "Ash," I said his name like a prayer, like a promise. "Tell me that you want me."

"I want you," he said. "Give me tonight, Candace. I won't ask for more. Just tonight."

"Yes," I answered. "Yes, Ash. Just for tonight, love me."

"I will always love you, Candace," Ash said.

Then he closed the final step between us and pulled me into his arms. His mouth slanted over mine savagely, then gentled until I feared that I would weep with the sweetness of it. Weep with the joy of once more feeling Ash's lips on mine. I could feel the way his body trembled as he held himself back. Knew how fiercely he wanted to possess me, not just for tonight, but for all time.

"You are mine, do you hear me?" he said. "You. Are. Mine."

His lips trailed fire across my face, then moved down across my collarbone to my breast. He pulled both skin and lace into his mouth and I arched up.

"Yes! Yes!" I panted, as his tongue slid beneath the lace to find my bare nipple. "I want you now."

"Slow, my love. If it's only tonight, let's make it last."

He put his hands between my breasts, flicked open the clasp that held the lace together. My breasts spilled out, and Ash gathered them into his hands. I swayed on my feet as pleasure speared through me. "Hold on to me, Candace," he urged. "Hold on."

I put my arms around his neck and felt him lift me up. I wrapped my legs around his waist, even as I sought his mouth with my own. Arms banded around my back, Ash turned, then walked across the living room and through an open door beyond. I felt the air change, becoming thick with heat, damp with moisture. Slowly, Ash slid me down his body to set me on my feet. I opened my eyes to see we were in an elegant room with granite tiles on the wall, a tile mosaic on the floor. In one corner, an enormous whirlpool bath shushed and murmured softly to itself. Across from it, more windows revealed the night sky, the Vegas skyline. Candles seemed to float there, on glass shelves so cunningly made they were practically invisible. In the dark, there were only the colors of the Strip, the flickering of the candles, the glow of passion in Ash's eyes.

He reached beyond me to press a button, and the whirlpool came to life, bubbling and whirring. The scent of jasmine rose in the damp air. Eyes on his, I unfastened the slacks I wore. Shimmied them and my panties down my hips, then let them drop to the floor.

This is my dream, I thought. My dream one better. For I was really here with my lover, my love.

Ash lifted me gently, set me on my feet in the tub. I let myself slide along his body, my hands slowly exploring its contours as I sank down. Now. Now! I wanted to scream, but I followed Ash's lead— slowly savoring each moment. I slipped back, submerging myself up to my chin. The tub was deep and luxurious. I lay in the steaming scented water and watched as Ash undressed himself. Broad chest, narrow hips, those long legs that I had wanted entwined with mine from the first moment I saw him. His cock was erect and proud. And suddenly I wanted it, wanted him, more than anything I had ever desired in my life. I scooted forward, reached up to take his cock between my soapy hands, and felt the power of my own touch.

"You are so beautiful," I said. "I want you so much, even though it pisses me off."

Ash laughed then, the force of it moving his cock as I grasped it between my hands, then he stepped into the tub. He lowered himself beside me, mouth seeking mine. *Hungry. We were both so hungry for each other.*

His mouth left mine to dance across my face in quick, nipping kisses until I gave a breathless, joyful laugh. I felt his hands move down to tangle with my legs. Entirely without warning, he gave them a tug. With a shriek, I slipped down deeper into the water. Only a quick grab for the bars on the side of the tub kept my head from going under. I leaned forward to see Ash disappear below the bubbles; then gasped as I felt his tongue slide up my right thigh. I felt his hands gently grasp my hips, turning my body ever so slightly so that the bubbles from the jet danced across my clit even as his tongue slid inside me. He thrust it powerfully, in and out.

Advantages of a vampire lover, I suddenly thought. Ash didn't have to worry about coming up for air.

How many women have dreamed of this sort of seduction? I wondered. Dreamed of feeling their lover's caress join with the caress of the water. I leaned my head back, completely giving myself over to the sensations. In the glossy black tiles above my head, I saw a reflection of Ash's body and mine. My legs were splayed, Ash between them. I tightened my grip on the handrails as I felt my passion climb.

Without warning, Ash shifted position, tilting and lifting me so that the bubbles pounded into my body now. I gave a shocked cry of pleasure, my fingers writhing around the bars. Ash's tongue moved across my clit. His hands grasped my ass, easing my body out of the water, then back down. The change from water to air was absolutely exquisite, the pressure of his tongue the only constant. I pressed myself up against his mouth.

"Ash," I gasped out. "*Ash.*"

"Come for me, Candace," I heard him say, his mouth never leaving my body. And, almost impossibly, the feel of his lips forming my name drove me even higher. My body bowed upward, as I pulled on one last, ragged breath.

"Come for me, my sweet love," I heard Ash say, and felt the power of it carry me up and over. "If you love me, show me."

On a great, wild surge of pleasure, I came, the small room echoing with my cries. Before they had died out, Ash rose from the water like some ancient god. Pulling me up to meet him, my legs still open, wide. Dazed with passion, dazed with love, I gazed down at my own body, watched as Ash slid his cock deep inside. I tightened myself around him, heard his own hoarse cry of pleasure. I wrapped my legs around his waist and began to ride.

"Again," I panted. "Again, Ash. Don't stop. Don't ever stop."

Wanting me. Loving me. Filling every empty space inside. In all the world, there was nothing I wanted more than this: myself in Ash's arms.

"Candace," I heard him say.

And then the climax took us both. I felt Ash's arms band around me, tight. Understood that, if he could have had anything he wanted in that moment, it would be to never let me go.

"Stay with me," I thought I heard him say. "Stay with me, Candace."

And then there was nothing at all but the surprise of our love.

In silence, Ash watched me dress. I could not, would not, stay the whole night. I knew the truth. I thought we both did. If I fell asleep in his arms, it would all be over and done. If I let him hold me through the darkest hours of the night, I would never be able to leave him, or to let him go.

"Take care of yourself, Ash," I said. "Don't forget. I warned you."

"I won't forget," he said. He walked me to the elevator doors. "I'll even trade you for it, with some advice for you. Don't deny yourself forever, Candace. You don't have that long."

"That's the price I pay for staying human, isn't it?" I asked.

I drove myself home in the cold hour just before the dawn.

Sixteen

The night of the Albedo had come. This time, I
was ushered before the Chairman, alone. One-on-
one, his power was almost overwhelming. How
Sloane could believe it was anything but potent
and real was utterly beyond me.

Steady, I cautioned myself. Part of any vampire's
power rests in the minds of those he seeks to overcome. The more power I gave to the Chairman, the
more he possessed.

"Please be seated," the Chairman said, when
my silent vampire guide had departed. There had
been no sign of Simmons since that first night.

I took the chair I had occupied then, at the center of the base of the great triangular table that
symbolized the power of the Board. Again, the Chairman sat opposite. This time, though, it wasn't his

face that riveted my attention but the necklace he wore. Hanging from a thick gold chain around his neck was an ancient Egyptian image, also made of gold. An upturned crescent with a disc in its very center. It was precisely like that of the headdress always depicted in images of Thoth.

The first Emblem, I thought. For surely it could be nothing else. So the Chairman's claims that the Board had obtained the first Emblem of Thoth were true. I felt my excitement kick up a notch.

In the days since acquiring the piece of paper from Sloane, I had done my best to translate the hieroglyphics upon it. It was beyond even my skill. It was almost as if they had been scrambled somehow. Deliberately distorted. In any other circumstances, I would have dismissed the entire paper as a hoax. Sloane's behavior had made me reluctant to do that.

"The test you are about to undergo is called the Albedo," the Chairman spoke in his strange and melodic voice. "White, for purity. Before any vampire can become a member of the Board, he must first purge himself of all lingering human emotion. Only in this way can he exist only for the Board and for its quest."

Related to, yet not quite the same as the Nigredo, I thought. The first was a test of opening up to power. This, a test to see if a supplicant could expel from himself that which was no longer important. Human emotion. Human ties.

"I understand," I replied.

"Do you?" the Chairman countered, swiftly. "I wonder." He moved then, leaning forward to place his hands upon the sole object before him, a manila folder. He slid it across the table toward me. "Open it."

I did so. It was filled with pictures of Candace. The top one showed the two of us together, her hand in mine. She was laughing, her head tilted back so her curls cascaded along my arm. Something fierce and ugly twisted in my gut. *Sloane*, I thought.

"The Board has learned of your involvement with this woman," the Chairman said. "A *human* woman."

"She is a willing woman with an empty place in her bed," I said, my tone calm.

"That's a lie and you know it," the Chairman said, his voice like the crack of a whip. And my body jerked, as if he had given me an actual blow. Fire danced along every nerve ending in my body.

Oh, yes. This power is very, very real, I thought.

"You disappoint me, Ash, and I do not care to be disappointed. Your relationship with this woman is

far more complex than that, and far more important. She is a tie to the human world."

"Yes, Chairman," I acknowledged, and thought
I knew where he was going.

"Your test, therefore, is a simple one. Make this
woman one of us, undead, or end her life. Which
can be your choice. For doing either will serve the
Albedo. Either will prove you are willing to eradi-
cate every passion, sever all human ties. You are allowed no passions of your own, Ash, only the ones
of the Board."

"I understand," I said again.

"Yes," the Chairman said. "I think you do, this
time. Go now, and return when your task is complete. I advise you not to disappoint me in this. If
you fail, you will be destroyed."

I stood, and bowed low. Then I left the room, my
mind spinning in a thousand different directions.
Was Sloane out there somewhere, already thinking
that he had won? If so, he would gloat too soon,
for I was ready for him. I had already revealed myself to Candace, had done so weeks ago. Slowly,
carefully, I had prepared her for the next step, the
inevitable step. The moment she gave herself to me
fully and became a vampire.

I had been right to take as a sign the fact that
Candace and the Board had come into my life on
the same night. A sign that I would have both love

and power. Never would I have to choose between them. They would be joined together for all time.

I will give Candace the picture, I thought. My face on one side, on the other, the Mark of Thoth. A lover's gift, a token of what was about to come.

Seventeen

The next afternoon, I was dressed in one of the few corporate-type suits I own and was on my way to St. Peter's Children's Hospital with Al. Randolph had decided to take me up on my suggestion and counter Lance Weatherly's attempt at frightening patrons away from the Sher by staging a media event of his own. One that put the spotlight on someone only Randolph and the Sher could deliver: Senator Hamlyn. St. Peter's Children's Hospital had been built with funds from the No-Limits Foundation, so the tie-in was perfect.

The hospital is only five miles from the Strip, so it was about fifteen minutes from when we stepped into Al's car until we stepped off the elevator to the fourth floor of the hospital. A nurse directed us toward a dayroom. The walls were covered with photos of animals and pictures enthusiastically colored and drawn. Low tables held art supplies, and big colorful boxes were filled with toys. There were about a dozen kids in the room, some attached to IVs, others sporting bandages, slings, or crutches.

I noticed a trio of men edging around the room, scanning every corner of it. I didn't need Al's whisper to tell me that these guys were the senator's private security detail.

Senator Hamlyn stood to one side with Randolph. They both had rolled up the sleeves of their white shirts. It was that "going to get to work to solve your problems" look that public figures often affect when there are photographers around. Al went over to talk with them. I stayed by the door.

I watched Lance Weatherly, my least-favorite TV news reporter, aim a mic at a little girl who was hooked to an IV.

"And how are you today?" he asked with patently false cheer.

"Okay," she said. I figured she was about five.

"Why are you here?" he went on. "Do you have a boo-boo?"

"I have cancer," she said matter-of-factly.

Take that, you s.o.b., I thought.

Senator Hamlyn, with a politician's unerring instinct for good PR, was suddenly kneeling beside the girl. "You know, a lot of people want to help you," he told her. "We're doing everything we can—"

"Let me get a shot of them," said a voice behind me.

I looked over my shoulder. Diane Fernandez, whom I often saw taping on the Strip, elbowed Lance aside to aim her camera at Hamlyn and the girl. From her new position, she was standing right beside me.

"So, do you think he's actually going to do it?" she murmured. She was film only, the sound on the camera was off.

"Do what?" I inquired.

"You mean you don't know?" She lowered her voice, as a second cameraman got in on the action. "Word on the street is that Hamlyn's ready to announce that he's officially running for president. It could be any time. That's what we're really all here for.

"That guy's new," Diane said suddenly pointing to a man who stood in the crowd of reporters.

I looked at the man she had indicated, who was even now pushing his way toward the front of the press of reporters. He did not look healthy. His skin was a funny yellow color, as if he had jaundice.

"Definitely not," I said. "Don't you know him?"

"Not really," Diane replied. "I think his name is

Simmons, but whether that's first or last . . . Uh-oh. I'm getting the 'get over here now' signal. Sorry. Gotta go."

The senator went over to a podium that had the hospital's logo prominently displayed across its front. Randolph was already standing on one edge of the podium, looking thrilled to be in the reflected glow of a prepresidential moment.

I stood to the left of the podium close to the door. Al remained at the far side of the room, his arms folded, his face expressionless, his eyes in constant motion as they scanned the room. On either side of him was the senator's security detail.

Senator Hamlyn stood in front of the forest of mics on the podium, giving the cameras a calculated, megawatt smile.

"Good afternoon, my friends," Hamlyn began. "I'm delighted to have the opportunity to be here today in St. Peter's Children's Hospital, proof of the extraordinary work being done every day by the No-Limits Foundation. It's an example of what can be done when good people join together. It's time for . . ."

My mind wandered as he went into his standard stump speech, though it did snap back when I heard a reporter ask about his presidential bid.

"No," Hamlyn was saying now with that smile.

"I won't make an announcement about running for president of the United States *this* year."

There was polite laughter at the senator's joke: The year was going to end in almost exactly thirty-six hours. I didn't laugh. Thirty-six hours until New Year's. Not a particularly happy thought. As another reporter asked the same question in a slightly different way, a motion caught my eye. Someone was pushing up through the crowd toward the podium.

Simmons, I realized.

Before anyone could move, he jumped up and grabbed one of the microphones off the podium. "You've got to listen to me!" he shouted. "Hamlyn must be stopped! He's not what you think he is. He wants to get into all our heads and control us!"

I had heard enough. As the senator's detail began to close in, I leaped toward Simmons, grabbed him by the arm, and twisted it in back of him as I pulled him away from the microphones. I locked my other arm around his neck. A quick tug, and he was off the podium.

He didn't go quietly. He jammed an elbow toward my stomach. I moved to the side, avoiding the jab, but didn't release him.

"Ladies and gentleman," the senator said, as his security team attempted to pull him away from the microphones and I planted one knee on Simmons's back to pin him to the floor. "I'm sure it's just a small difference of opinion. He must be a Republican."

My blood was roaring in my ears. There was something wrong here. Very, very wrong. The moment I had touched Simmons, I had gone cold. He wasn't human. He was a vampire. But so low level I hadn't been able to detect him from across the room. That had never happened before.

Simmons's eyes were glazed, wide open but lifeless. He looked like a sleepwalker. Then, with a strength that shocked me, caught me off-guard, he rolled out from under me, jumped to his feet, and pulled a knife.

I focused on the metal blade. All around me people were screaming. Lights from cameras flashed in my eyes, nearly blinding me. I was aware of the senator's detail, finally hustling their man to safety. I kept my eyes focused on the desperate figure in front of me. I grabbed Simmons's wrist and took a step to the left, forcing his arm away from me. At the same time, I rammed my knee into his hand. The knife flew out of his fingers. A quick step forward, jabbing my hip into his side, and he toppled, hitting the floor hard.

He lay there, groaning softly. I knelt beside him, one knee on his side to make sure he didn't pull another slick move. Al and one of the senator's security team were attempting to herd the reporters out of the room. All of a sudden, the head of the senator's security was kneeling at my side.

"I'll take it from here," he said.

But as I was about to get up, Simmons grasped my hand. "They've got to be stopped!" he whispered, his eyes wild. "They've got to be stopped! You've got to stop them."

"Stop who?" I asked.

"The Board."

As if just speaking the name had brought on some sort of fit, Simmons's body spasmed, his mouth stretching wide. Then the light of fear in his eyes went out, snuffed like a candle flame.

"Get back!" Senator Hamlyn's guard snapped. "Give me some room."

He tore Simmons's shirt open, getting ready for CPR, then fell back with a gasp. The surface of Simmons's chest was a mass of festering sores, as if he had once been badly burned and the tissue had simply refused to heal. *Incredibly, badly burned,* I thought. Simmons hadn't been a man. He had been a vampire, an animated corpse. Now, a corpse was all he was. But as to what had ended him, I had no idea.

I put my fingertips on his carotid artery, already knowing what I would find.

"He's gone."

The hospital mechanism took over then. Gurneys. Technicians in lab coats. *The Board needs to be stopped,* Simmons had said. Who on earth was he talking about? What Board?

Al came up to me, his eyes concerned. "So I guess we're all glad you came along. What the hell happened?"

"Who the hell knows? All of a sudden, he just had a knife."

"Candace! Candace, can you tell us how it feels to have saved Senator Hamlyn's life?"

All of a sudden, I realized Al and I were surrounded by TV cameras.

"It feels great," I answered honestly. "But I just did what anyone would have done."

A barrage of questions rolled over me like a wave, and suddenly Randolph Glass was at my side.

"Ms. Steele has no further comment at this time. Naturally, as her employer, the Scheherazade will issue a full press statement, commending her for her actions. Now, if you'll excuse us." He took my arm in a grip of iron, hustled me out the door.

As soon as I was through it, Senator Hamlyn stepped toward me at once, flanked by his security guards.

"Thank you. I appreciate your taking action the way you did."

He offered me his hand and as I clasped it I realized he was trembling. I wondered how he'd feel if he realized what I had really just prevented.

A vampire had just tried to kill a United States senator. What the hell was going on?

Al and I returned to the Sher. Al spent the entire ride back talking on his cell phone. I didn't even try to decipher his half of the conversations. I kept replaying the fight with Simmons in my mind. Even though he was the one who pulled a knife, I couldn't help feeling that Simmons hadn't been the real threat in that room. That blank, wild look in Simmons's eyes told me something else was going on, something I had missed. Something that had to do with the Board—whatever that is.

The second we got to the casino, we went straight to Al's office. He sat behind the desk. I sat in front of it.

"You go first," I said, and won a tight smile.

"According to the senator's press secretary, the guy in the bad suit is, was, a nutcase who's been stalking the senator for months. Somehow he came up with press credentials from some tabloid."

"Then why didn't Hamlyn's guys take him down before he got so close?"

"Up until now he's behaved himself."

"Give me a break," I groaned. "So they figured what? Better the devil they could keep an eye on?"

Al gave an expressive shrug. "Who the hell knows? That's their story, and they're sticking with it."

"Covering their asses. So what was Simmons's beef with Hamlyn?"

Al rested one elbow on his desk. "Are you ready for this? He claims the senator takes his marching orders from extraterrestrials or some other far-out group."

"Called the Board?"

"That's right. We found notes in his pockets, all about the Board spelled with a capital *B*. How do you know about the Board?"

"He said something about how they needed to be stopped." I took a deep breath. "Now here's what I know. Simmons was a vampire."

"*What?* Please tell me you're joking."

"I'm not. Maybe this is the missing connection, Al, between the vamps and the con. Maybe it's not a con at all. Maybe Hamlyn's being set up."

"By vampires," Al said, the sarcasm heavy in his voice. "Candace, you know and I know that vampires feed off humans, they manipulate humans. They do not use them to get involved in politics. And don't tell me there's a first time for everything."

"We've got to get him out of the casino, Al," I said. "No matter what the real story is, there are just too many people here. There's no way we'll be able to protect just one, let alone them all."

"Agreed," Al said at once. "And already taken care of. Half that conversation in the car was with Randolph. He's agreed to have his big shindig on New Year's Eve out at the lake house instead of at the hotel. He'll have the celebrities there instead of wandering around the Sher. Smaller venue, easier for security to control."

"Not to mention divide and conquer," I said. "Just in case there really is a con."

"Anything new on that?"

"Other than the headache I got trying to under-stand Chet in IT? No."

Al grunted, then gestured toward the door. "Go home and get some rest. We've got a long day to-morrow."

"I'll be here for the day shift."

"And for the night and until the following morn-ing." He sighed. "Provided we still have jobs when the sun comes up."

Eighteen

Tired as I was, sleep turned out to be impossible. A clock was ticking down inside my head, set to explode at midnight tomorrow. I lay in bed, Simmons's anguished face in my mind. Was he just some vampire nut job? Or was there really something out there. Something called the Board? And if there was, how could I find out more about them?

Going back to Ash was not an option. Not only was I afraid I'd want to stay, but when it came to discussing vampire affairs he had completely shut me down. If I was going to discover more about the Board, I was going to have to do it on my own.

After I destroyed my cell phone!

It had been ringing off the proverbial hook. I turned it off after checking voice mail from the first couple of callers, but I knew the calls wouldn't stop. TV and newspaper reporters wanted a quote for their big story about the foiled attack on the senator. I had no idea how they had gotten my cell number, but it didn't matter. I wasn't going to talk to them.

I needed to talk to someone else, someone who would listen and not freak out if I tossed a couple of seriously weird ideas around. *Bibi,* I thought. She was the only one who might understand, the only one left I could trust. I turned my cell back on, called hers before another call could sneak in.

Through the noise that burst out of the phone, I barely heard, "Hello?"

"Bibi?"

"Candace? Speak up! I can't hear you."

"What's going on?"

"Dress rehearsal's over."

She didn't have to say more. I knew the routine. The dancers went to the loudest club in Vegas after a dress rehearsal to take a break before the show opened.

"What's up?" she asked.

"Just checking in to say hi."

"Well, get your butt over here!" Bibi yelled into the phone. "See if you can grab Michael and join us. We're headed for the Irish pub at New York–New York, and we could use another male voice. Besides, I can't believe I haven't met him yet. It'll be fun."

"I have to work tomorrow," I said.

"So do I. It's going to be a new year, Candace. Remember, moving on?"

"Let me see if Michael can get away," I said. "If he can, we'll meet you there."

"See you there," she said, and I closed my cell. It began to ring again. I tossed it on my bed, got up, and went to my closet. *Moving on*, I thought.

The tournament seemed to be on break when I walked by. I saw a man tinkering with a camera laid out on one of the tables. He told me that the tournament had been called for the night because the No-Limits Foundation wanted everyone at the top of their game for the final table tomorrow.

"Michael Pressman?" he asked in answer to my question. "Yeah, he's one of the six finalists."

Thanking him, I walked to where I could get a signal to call Michael's cell. No answer but voice mail. I didn't want to leave a message, so I took the elevator up to the eleventh floor and rang the door-bell for Room 1100.

No answer.

I tried knocking.

Still no response.

Maybe he was somewhere else in the casino, out with his friends. But if so, why wasn't he answering his cell? I checked my watch. It wasn't all that late. Maybe they'd all gone out for a quick bite. Maybe

Michael had tried to reach me, but been unable to get through. I'd had *my* phone off, after all. I drew out the key he had given me. There was nothing that said I couldn't wait in the suite. As I suspected, the key worked in the main door as well as the one for the bedroom. I slid the key in and opened the door.

There were lights on in the foyer, baggage piled against the wall. Michael's friends were probably getting ready to head home as soon as the tournament was over. The living room was dark. A dim light in the dining room glowed from the screen of an open laptop. It beeped and I went over to it. It was Michael's; I recognized the royal flush sticker on the keyboard.

Low Battery Warning flashed across the screen. I started to activate the shut-down sequence, but another warning popped up that files hadn't been saved and would be lost. If I didn't do something, Michael would lose his files when the battery ran down. I clicked on the *Low Battery Warning* screen, then blinked as a brighter image appeared.

It was an outgoing e-mail, but the name on it wasn't his. *Probably just sending a message for one of his friends,* I thought. With only a pinch of guilt, I leaned down and began reading the e-mail. It was a letter of complaint concerning funds that had been delayed being deposited in his account. The address block, like the e-mail address, said it had been written by Michael Irons.

I sat back then, as my security-oriented mind began to take over. The fact that Michael Pressman was sending e-mail for Michael Irons was an awfully funny coincidence. The names were just too close. What else could be in the suite that might tell me Michael's true name? *Prescriptions,* I thought.

I went into the bathroom and opened the medicine cabinet. It was empty, so I opened the bathroom drawers. They were empty, too. The doors beneath the sink revealed a roll of toilet paper and a travel kit, the kind specially designed for carrying toiletries. I pulled it out, unzipped it, and hit the jackpot. Inside was a common allergy prescription. The name on the label was Michael Irons.

Suspicion thoroughly aroused now, I moved quickly to the master bedroom, opened the bifold closet doors. There was a wall safe in the closet wall. All the high-roller suites have them. The safe's door was open and there was a small travel bag inside. I pulled it out, sat down on the floor, and unzipped it. Empty, and so were the pockets. I was about to put it back when I noticed a window where a business card identified the bag's owner. MICHAEL PRESSMAN, SENIOR ACCOUNT MANAGER the card read, over the logo and name of an investment company. This was just like the one Michael had given me.

I slipped my finger into the slot. There was a driver's license behind it. *Very smooth,* I thought. Pretty much the perfect hiding place. The picture on the license matched the Michael Pressman I knew. The name said: Michael Irons.

Well you lying sonofabitch, I thought. It looked like I was a Vegas fling all the way down the line. Michael had seemed so open and natural, it had never once occurred to me he might be using a false identity. I wondered if there was a Mrs. Irons back home in Chicago. On impulse, I slipped the license into my own back pocket, wondering if I could believe one single thing he had told me.

Josh, I suddenly thought. Josh Doyle, the supposed Michael Pressman's very best friend. Such a good friend that he had shelled out a five-figure bankroll so Michael could play in the poker tournament. Josh who had been so eager to ask the cameraman all those questions. I had wanted to talk to him, but Michael distracted me with his offer of a massage. Josh, who was into anything high tech.

Michael and Josh were running the con. Okay, that's part one, now I just had to figure out how the bloodsuckers figure in. First things first.

Al, I thought. But even as I reached for my cell,

the door from the hall to the living room opened, and I heard Michael curse as he found his computer on. Quickly, I turned off the phone. The last thing I needed was for it to go off and give me away. *Okay, Candace, think fast,* I thought. The bedroom door was partially closed, screening me from view.

I got silently to my feet, eased the travel bag back where I had found it. Then, quick as lightning, I stripped and pulled on the hotel robe hanging on the back of the bedroom door. I didn't bother to tie the sash. I tiptoed to the bathroom, put my clothes on the lid of the toilet seat, then returned to the bedroom and pulled open the bedroom door. I struck a provocative pose in the door frame. Somehow, I managed to make my voice light and teasing.

"Honey, I'm home."

Michael spun around, eyes wide. I bent one knee. The robe slipped open to reveal the fact that I was naked underneath.

"I heard you made the final table," I said. "I was hoping we could celebrate." I let my gaze linger on his crotch. "But it's going to be awfully hard to do it if you're way over there."

Hard is right, I thought. He'd just gone from zero to full throttle.

I let the robe gape open a little farther as he came toward me. The second he reached me, I put my hands on him. Pulling his shirt from his pants, keeping my hands moving hard and fast as I went through the motions. That was all they were. Motions. Michael ran his hands along me, then followed them with his mouth. I began to back us toward the bed. He was breathing fast, his body totally aroused.

I climbed onto the bed, letting the robe fall completely open. He followed. But when he reached for me, I held up a hand.

"You're overdressed, Mr. Pressman."

"You could fix that," he said.

I gave a tantalizing laugh. "But I don't want to. I want to watch you do it."

He was more than happy to oblige.

"Now you," he said, his voice husky.

I caught his hand as he tried to run it up my thigh, then pushed it away. "Oh, no. We're playing by my rules today, Michael."

Sliding off the bed, I pulled the sash off and rocked it across my hips, first facing away from him and then facing him. He groaned and reached out. I caught his wrist and pulled it over his head, lashing it to the headboard as he leaned up and pulled my breast into his mouth. Goose bumps crawled across my skin. Only one of us knew the reason why.

"Let me have the other hand," I panted.

With a wicked grin, Michael obliged.

"I sincerely hope this means you're going to have your way with me," he said.

Sincere my ass, I thought. Sexy Michael *Irons* didn't have a sincere bone in his entire body.

I held out my hand for his other arm. He extended it, and I tied it next to the first, making sure I gave an extra tug on the knots. He wasn't going to get himself free without some help. Too bad I wouldn't be around. Then I straddled him, sliding down his body until he moaned.

"A man can always hope."

All of a sudden, I tilted my head as if I had heard something. "Oh, shit," I said. "That's my cell phone. I'm on call. I have to answer it."

"You're hearing things," Michael protested with a groan. "And even if you're not, let it go."

"Michael," I said. "I have to take that. If I don't, I could lose my job. Don't worry. I'll be right back."

I slid off the bed, moved quickly into the bathroom, where I had hidden my clothes. I didn't wait to get dressed, just snatched them up and headed for the front door.

"Candace!" Michael called, and I heard the anger in his voice. "You can't leave me like this!"

"I'll be back as soon as I can," I called. "Meanwhile, just hold that . . . thought."

Then I was out of the suite and running for the

elevator. Security would get an eyeful as I changed, but I was headed to IT anyhow. I slipped into my jeans, checked the back pocket. The driver's license I had palmed was safe and sound. It was time to run a background check on Mr. Michael Irons, and I knew just the man for the job.

Chet was waiting as I entered the IT Department. He grinned and motioned for me to come around the counter.

"Nice to see you again," he said.

I held up a warning hand. "Please, no elevator jokes." On my way down to IT, I had called ahead, to let Chet know what I wanted. Now, I held out the driver's license. "Just tell me what you can about this slimeball."

Chet took the license, considered it for a moment, then moved toward a nearby terminal. "Slimeball info coming right up. Actually, I've already gotten started."

Trying to ignore the seriously annoying computer whine I had heard before, I followed. Chet sat down and began typing in commands. The screen flickered through so many pages so quickly that I couldn't focus on one before he brought up the next.

"Okay," he said, leaning back in the chair after just a few minutes. "First off, your friend Michael

Irons—that's his real name, by the way, does not live in Chicago. Not lately, anyhow. For the past seven years he's lived in the Seattle area at a couple of different addresses. He was employed by Microsoft until about six months ago when he began looking for a new job."

"How do you know?"

"His résumé is posted on several job search sites."

"Can you figure out why he left Microsoft?"

He hit a few more keys, shifted the mouse, and clicked a half dozen times.

"Nothing specific. The circumstances of his departure seem murky. I've got some contacts in Microsoft, but I won't be able to reach them until after the holiday." He glanced at me. "Who is this guy?"

"One of the players at the final table at the charity poker tournament. Under the name Michael Pressman."

Behind his thick glasses, Chet's eyebrows rose. "Interesting," he said.

"What about Josh Doyle? Can you get anything on him?"

"Any other information you can give me as a starting point?"

"He owned an IT company."

"Its name?"

I shook my head. "I don't know, but it was sold

recently. It was in Virginia." I searched my mind. "Petersburg, Virginia, assuming the whole thing wasn't a lie."

"Let's try this," Chet suggested. "I'll go to a site that shows connections *between* different websites. Maybe there's some site that both Irons and Doyle have in common."

Amazed at his artistry with the computer, I put my hands on his chair and leaned over his shoulder. I straightened as the high, pitched sound became stronger.

"They both went to MIT," Chet said. His fingers flew across the keyboard as he jumped from page to page. "Okay, here's the alumni section. It doesn't look as if Michael Irons graduated, but Joshua Doyle was near the top of his class. He majored in electrical engineering and computer science." Chet grinned. "Sounds like someone I'd like to talk shop with."

"I don't think he would be interested in talking to either of us if he knew we were on to them."

"On to them?" He spun in his chair to face me.

"Would these guys have the skills necessary to try and pull off a high-tech con?"

"Yeah, but so do I. Having the skills doesn't make it a given that they're doing something to rip off the casino."

"True, but Josh Doyle was asking all kinds of

questions about the TV cameras, which ones were on when, and how the cameras at the table worked."

"Still not a crime. I know it's suspicious, entering the tournament under an assumed name, but . . ."

"Don't tell me," I said. "This is Vegas."

I began to pace the room. Chet was right. But so was I. There had to be something to make this add up. So much of the Sher's casino was run by computers. Both Michael and Josh—and probably all those friends camping in Michael's room—were skilled with computers. Were they all in on the con?

"Candace," Chet said quietly. "What does Michael bring with him to the poker table?"

I thought for a moment. "He has a special poker chip—not from the Sher—that he calls his good-luck charm. And he has sunglasses to hide any tells."

"Sunglasses? Did you notice anything odd about them?"

"They're heavy," I said. "I'd say heavier than most."

"There's your answer!" Chet threw up his hands as if he expected me to high-five him.

"I hate to sound stupid, but, huh?"

"The table cameras," Chet said at once. "It would be pretty easy to intercept the signals coming from the table cameras—the ones that transmit the cards the other players are holding—then redirect them wherever he wanted them to go. All that would be necessary is a receiver on the same frequency."

"But wouldn't the people supposed to be getting them get suspicious?"

"Anyone with a little bit of knowledge of circuitry could make it appear as if the proper receiver is still the one getting the signal, even when it's also been redirected elsewhere."

"So what does that have to do with the sunglasses?"

"The TV signal could be redirected from the receiver sending it to the sunglasses."

I shook my head. "I still don't follow. If the picture was broadcast on the sunglasses, everyone at the table could see it. They could see it better than Michael."

"Not *on* the sunglasses. *Inside* the sunglasses. Projected by a miniature receiver built into the frames. Then the images would be right in front of Michael along with his own cards. He would know right away if someone was bluffing or had a legitimate hand."

"Is it possible to do something like that?"

Chet glanced at the computer screen. "I would have to say it's possible."

"That has to be the answer. I suspected they had

to be doing something with the cameras, but I never could have figured it out. I owe you a drink. Hell, if you're right, Randolph is going to owe you a bonus!"

"Glad to help," Chet said, as if he saved the casino from a high-tech con every day.

I turned to leave, then paused. "Can I ask you one more thing?"

"Sure."

"How do you put up with that sound?"

"Sound?"

"That high-pitched squeal."

His smile slipped away. He half-turned to the computer as he clicked the mouse and the images on the screen vanished. "You can hear it?"

"Are you serious? It goes through my head like a power drill. If I had to work all day with that sound, I would go mad."

"Guess it's a good thing I'm the one who has to," Chet said, standing up. "If you need anything else—"

"I'll let you know. Thanks, Chet."

"Anytime."

I left the IT section and went to find Al. *Finally,* I had something to tell him.

Al wasn't in his office. A note on the door said he would be in at seven a.m. for the preshift briefing. *Just great,* I thought. He was probably at home, doing what celebrating he could with his wife, Miriam. And Bibi was no doubt wondering where the hell I was. But I couldn't help it. What I knew couldn't wait, but only Al could make the call about how to proceed from here on out. I made a quick call to Bibi, saying I wasn't going to make it to the bar after all. Then I called Al.

Nineteen

I let Candace precede me into her building, watching her closely. Her gaze was turned inward, as it had been since we left the house in the Berkeley Hills, the place where we had witnessed a vampire initiate her human lover into the vampire world. The rite had been exciting and erotic, riveting in its intensity. It was everything I wanted for us.

Tonight is the night, I thought. *There will never be a better time.*

I watched Candace during the ritual. She was mesmerized by the act of utter surrender, profoundly aroused. An arousal that had not abated during our drive home. She was more than ready to move beyond her human possibilities. Something in her had shifted. I could feel it. She was ready to enter my world, to join me for eternity.

I was pretty damned aroused myself.

In silence, I held the door to her apartment building open for her, then followed her inside. Watched as she jabbed the button to summon the elevator, saw the way her fingers trembled, ever so slightly.

She knows, I thought. *She knows this is the night of no turning back. The night we truly consummate our love.*

With its usual annoying *ping,* the elevator arrived and the doors slid open. Candace and I stepped inside. I reached across her, to push the button for her floor, and my hand brushed against her arm. Candace's skin was flushed with heat. Her eyes hazed with desire brought on by no more than her own thoughts. She jerked back, as if startled. And then I watched her change her mind. Watched her desire overcome her spontaneous fear.

Her desire to be mine.

She took a single step forward, and then she was in my arms.

There was nothing tentative about her now. Her mouth was ravenous and eager on mine. I slid my hand down her body, felt the way her legs parted. I rubbed between them, stroking her need, and felt her legs clamp tight around my hand, urging me on.

Candace's body was one sinuous motion of need. Her lust for me, for all that I could bring her, a siren's call. With one impetuous motion, she threw back her head, exposing her throat. Our bodies sliding against each other in the most elemental rhythm of all. I saw the way her pulse danced like lightning across her throat, placed my lips against that throb of life, and bit down. Past flesh, past muscle, seeking the greatest treasure of all: blood.

Candace's body strained up toward mine. I heard her make a single, startled sound. And then we were moving again, our passion so primal no power on earth could stop it now. Her blood was warm and thick inside my mouth, pulsing through my veins as I took it into myself. Made it mine. I stroked against her, urging her body to one last, human climax. I was unbearably aroused now. My lover's body wrapped and shuddering around mine. Her blood in my mouth, in my throat, in my cock.

This is what it means, Candace, I thought. *What it truly means to make you mine. We will be joined forever, now and forever.*

One love. One lust. One blood.

I felt her body begin to tremble, the way her knees went weak. In another moment, her body would cool in the circle of my arms. And then, before she was gone from this world completely, she would feed on me, as a human, for one last time. At that moment, I would finish what we both so longed for. I would end her mortal life and make her a vampire.

Her knees gave way then, and I knew the time had come. Tightening my grip upon her throat, I tried to hold her up. And then, from across an impossible distance, I heard her speak impossible words.

"Ash. Stop. No."

I tightened the grip of my teeth, of my arms, my denial a feral growl in my throat. And suddenly, she was fighting a desperate battle to save her human life. Even as I felt the elevator shudder to a stop, Candace worked her arms up against my chest, put her palms flat against it, and literally tore herself out of my arms.

I heard a sickening, tearing sound. Felt her flesh rend as she pulled her body from my mouth. The impetus propelled her back, out the open elevator doors. She hit the wall of the apartment hallway with a sharp, wet *smack,* then began to slide down. Blood streamed from the open wound at her throat. Her eyes gazed straight into mine. In them, I saw not one trace of passion, not one trace of love. There was only fear and pain and horror.

Do it, Ash, my mind was screaming. *Go after her. Finish what you have started.* Either that, or end her entirely. Those were my only choices.

I couldn't move. I had made a promise. Never to take Candace against her will. In that moment, standing in the elevator watching the woman I loved gaze at me with terror in her eyes, I understood the truth. I would not go back on that promise. Literally could not.

Because I truly loved her.

This is the true power, I realized suddenly. Not what was being offered by the Board. That was a parody, an exercise in self-gratification. Real power was what quivered in the air between Candace and me.

I would not betray. I would protect. Because I truly loved.

I heard a second *ping,* and the elevator doors began to close. The last thing I saw was Candace, sitting in the hallway in her apartment building in a pool of her own blood. And then the doors were closed and both of us were lost.

Twenty

"This had better be good," Al said. After reaching him and convincing him to come back in, I had suggested we meet where the whole mess with Michael began: Ma's Original Diner. This time, I opted for a booth. Less chance of eavesdroppers.

"It's good," I said. Even if it did make me feel lousy. Quickly, I relayed what I had discovered, what Chet had added, and the suspicions that were the result.

"Well, at least there's good news *and* bad news this time," Al commented sourly. "The bad news is you're an idiot—sleeping with the guy. I ought to kick your ass straight into next week and you know it. The good news is, you were sleeping with the guy. If you hadn't been, you might never have known he was lying."

Right on both counts, I thought. "So we pull him, right?"

Al shook his head. "Wrong. Chet has a good point. Lying about your name is not a crime. Hell, in Vegas it's practically a requirement. Unless there's a real Michael Pressman somewhere, it's not even identity theft, though that might be an angle worth exploring. What we need is to catch this guy in the act. That means we've got to let him stay right where he is. At least when he's in the tournament we can keep an eye on him."

"But he's been winning regularly, Al," I said. "And he's the only amateur left. That ought to tell us something."

"Sure," Al said at once. "It tells us he's damn good at poker. No, save your breath," he continued, as I sucked one in to argue. "We're going to do it the way I say or I'm taking this straight to Randolph."

I let the breath out slowly. "That's hitting below the belt."

"You started it." Al snorted. "What the hell were you thinking, Candace?"

"You want me to say it? Fine. I wasn't." I put my head down in my hands. *It was worse than that,* I thought. I hadn't wanted to. The not thinking aspect had been part of Michael Pressman's appeal.

So I had decided the rules didn't have to apply to me. *News flash, Steele,* I thought. *The reason they're rules is that they apply to everyone.*

"What do you want me to do?" I asked.

"The same thing you've been doing," Al replied. "Stay close to Michael Irons."

"He may not be so happy to see me," I said.

Once again, Al snorted. "How you fix things is up to you," he said. "Just stay on him."

"Make up your damned mind, Al," I said.

Al's lips gave a twitch. "That's the Candace Steele I know and love. Now, if it's all the same to you, I'd like to go home to my wife."

New Year's Eve is exciting in Vegas. The casinos are filled to overflowing. Plenty of gamblers, but also just plain people looking for someone to hook up with, so they don't have to be alone at midnight. Booze pours into glasses like cloudbursts in the desert. The staff is looser about letting people get drunk. Everyone has a good time, except those of us whose job it is to make sure they do.

At least I was out of my *I Dream of Jeannie* uniform. For the closing night of the tournament, I got to trade in my pink velvet harem outfit for a tight-fitting black tux. The jacket was plain; the vest, sequined. Hot pants, sheer black hose, and shoes with heels a quarter-mile high completed the ensemble. I was officially assigned to the tournament table, the final round of six, but I still had to elbow my way through the crowds.

"Hey, girlie!" a man old enough to be my grandfather called out. His age was the only reason I didn't ignore him. "How about a drink?" He wagged a bill in my general direction.

I gave him a smile. "I'll have the waitress who's in charge of this area come over as quickly as possible, sir." I would have to give Patti the heads up. I recognized the look in the old coot's eyes. He wanted that bill to buy more than a drink and a smile.

Balancing a tray full of drinks, I continued on toward the tournament table. The whole area had been redone. Yards of billowing fabric gave the area the appearance of a Bedouin tent. Shiny steel posts were set at the corners of a square rigging to hold the brightest lights I had ever seen. The lights were being tested, first aimed at the table and then out toward the crowd gathering on the bleachers to one side of where the commentators would be sitting.

I set my drink tray down near where the players were gathered. Michael came over at once.

"Oh, Michael," I said. "I am so sorry."

"Save it," he said, then gave me his crooked smile. "I thought about being pissed. Okay, I did more than think about it. Then I decided turnabout would be fair play. After the tournament I'll be the one tying the knots."

"I guess I have been pretty naughty," I purred. And if *he* knew the first thing about fair play, I'd eat my sequined vest. Then I added: "I did use the phone call as leverage with my boss for that time off. I told him he owed me as he had interrupted a seriously intimate moment."

"There, you see?" Michael asked. "All's well that ends well."

I'll take you up on that, I thought.

"Excuse me, Mr. Pressman," one of the tournament floor managers said. "They're going to start introducing the players in just a few moments. If I could persuade you to join the others?"

"Sure thing," Michael said. Before I realized what he intended, he leaned down, brushed a quick kiss across my lips. "You're still my favorite good-luck charm," he whispered.

Don't count on it, I thought.

I got out of the way as the director of the cable show called for silence, then I watched as Michael and the other five players were introduced. As I had earlier pointed out to Al, Michael was the only amateur remaining. All the others were pros. There was nothing I could do for the moment. Play commenced. I went back to the bar, requested the drinks the players had ordered. I could see the tournament from where I was standing because of the raised table. I also had a good view of the main doors. If I saw anything funny on the floor, I would call in an APB to Al on the headset hidden in my hair. Everyone on the floor was wired tonight.

It didn't take long for the first guy at the poker table to go all in to the applause and cheers of the audience. Michael called him, there was a shocked silence, then a spontaneous burst of applause. The regular folks were really rooting for their own. The first one out got up from the table, shook hands all around. He definitely handled it like the pro he was. But as he passed me when I walked back toward the table, I could see the fury and frustration in his eyes.

"You!" called the director, waving to me vehemently. "We're taking a break, so bring in the drinks now."

"Yes, sir." I tightened my hold on the tray and took a steadying breath.

In my ear, I heard Al say, "Let's see those nerves of steel, now."

More like nerves of marshmallow, I thought.

Michael and the other players were still seated at the table, chatting as if they were old pals. But I could see the way they were appraising one another. Watching for any sign of weakness. Michael had his glasses tilted up on his head, as did a couple of the others. One of the reasons the glasses were such a great idea is that lots of players wore them.

"Heineken?" I asked the first player, who had long dark hair and a black cowboy hat. I set the glass on the ledge under the table and smiled as he put a hundred-dollar bill on my tray. *You are my new best friend,* I thought. Not just for the hundred, but for supplying the perfect prop for what had to happen next.

The player to the right of Michael had a Bud Light. I set it on the ledge, then straightened up. As I did, I let the hundred flutter to the ground. I made a dive for it, bobbling the tray. In the process, I clipped Michael sharply on the side of his head. His glasses soared off and hit the floor.

"Hey!" he cried. "Watch what you're doing."

"Oh, sir," I gasped out. "I am so sorry."

I stepped back quickly, as if to get out of his way, and heard a satisfying crunch. I had driven one of my impossibly high heels straight through the closest lens. I bent down, as if horrified, slid off my shoe, then yanked the glasses off, cracking the frame right across the bridge in the process.

"What have you done?" Michael's eyes narrowed with fury. He pushed back his chair and started toward me.

"I'm so sorry," I said once more. I was hopping up and down on one foot now, trying to put my shoe back on. The very picture of a hapless, startled cocktail waitress, who knows she's seriously in the shit and will do anything to save her job.

"It was a terrible, terrible accident," I said. "Let me get you another pair. I'll go to the gift shop right now."

The shoe restored to my foot, Michael's glasses firmly in hand, I began to push my way through the crowd. Michael started after me, his hands balled into fists.

"Places!" I heard the director call. The last thing I saw was the cowboy offering Michael his own glasses, while Michael slowly sank down at the table. The commentators were having a field day, really playing up poker players' superstitions. The cameras began to roll.

"Please tell me he's losing," I murmured, as I began to make my way not toward the gift shop, but toward the security office.

"Hold your horses," I heard Al's voice in my ear. "It may take some time."

But it didn't. It didn't take any time at all. By the time I was halfway across the casino, I heard a roar from the tournament crowd. Michael Pressman, the amateur who had beaten all the odds, had just gone down. And I knew why. Chet's theory about how the glasses worked had been right on the money.

"He's out, Nerves," Al said. "Nicely done. Now hurry it up. I've got a couple of the boys ready to head off Mr. Pressman, aka Mr. Irons, at the pass. I want you and the evidence you're carrying to be there when we confront him."

"My pleasure. You got it."

Finally, I thought. *Score one for our side.* Al would ask Michael a few questions, which Michael probably wouldn't answer. We would show him the evidence, and he might talk. Or not. We'd leave the rest to the cops. But we had nailed him, caught him red-handed. Or maybe that should be red-eyed. That was all that mattered. I reached the slots, let the happy shouts of all the big winners buoy me along.

Hey, wait a minute, I thought. There were too many happy shouts.

Slots are a casino's bread and butter. They are notorious money-eaters when it comes to those who play them. So what was all the happiness about? Before I could answer my own question, I heard voices in my earpiece.

"Al, Jones here. There's something going on over here by the Round-Up slots. Everyone seems to be winning."

"Al, Vogel here. Can you send someone from the computer room over here to the video poker? These slots are paying out like ATMs over here."

More voices jumped in, canceling one another, so only bits and pieces came through. Putting my fingers over the earpiece, holding it more tightly in my ear as I tried to sort out the alerts, I looked around. Not *all* the machines were paying out. Some people were sitting there, stunned, as everyone around them won.

I watched a gray-haired woman turn to the young man beside her. She shoved a card into his machine's slot and pressed the button. The wheels whirled and stopped on three 7s. Bells rang, joining the cacophony. Top prize. He pressed the button, and the same thing happened again.

When the gray-haired woman withdrew the card and put it in her own slot machine, she hit the button. The wheels rolled and stopped, and the bells started clanging on top of that machine, too.

The man grinned as he hit the button again on his machine. The wheels whirred . . . and he didn't win.

It was the card!

The Magic Carpet Club card!

I knew instantly what was going on. Michael hadn't been collecting cards to take me to dinner. Another one of his lies! He and his friends had collected a bunch of the cards and had gone from machine to machine, using the cards to reprogram the slot machines' computers. Somehow they were able to change the coding on the magnetic tape on the back of the cards to change the odds of the slot machine. Basically, it was no more complicated than installing a computer virus.

Knowing there wasn't anything I could do standing by the slot machines, I hurried toward the security office. Suddenly excited shouts came from the craps and blackjack tables, too.

I stared. How could everyone be winning there? The Magic Carpet Club cards couldn't change table results.

I went to the closest table, a blackjack table, and watched Nina Padilla, who had been at the Sher since it opened, deal the cards—all faceup—to the six players gathered at the high red-felt tabletop. She scattered the cards around the table with cool efficiency. When she glanced at me, she smiled, then flipped a card in front of her. A ten.

Then she dealt the second cards before setting a

card facedown in front of herself. She gave the players a chance to consider their next move, then asked, "Card?"

Everyone at the table said in turn, "Hit me."

Even the guy with a king and a queen. Was he stupid?

The cards were dealt, and three of the players should have gone bust with a total of more than twenty-one, but all yelled, "Blackjack!"

Nina flipped her hole card up. It was an ace, but she said, "House pays."

"What do you mean? House pays?" I asked. "*You've* got twenty-one. Not the players."

"Candace, what's wrong with your eyes?" Nina pointed to the cards in front of the players who were slapping one another on the back and high-fiving.

I looked at the trio of cards in front of each player. For a second, I was staring at six blackjacks. How could I have been so mistaken? How . . . ? The cards blurred like a lens losing its focus, and I could see what was really there.

What the hell was going on?

The answer came with an icy chill that raced up my spine and clamped itself around my chest. I couldn't breathe.

Vampires! Not just one, but a bunch. *The Bat Pack,* I thought. I turned, straining to look in every direction. The casino was jammed. Hundreds of people were crowding the floor, most of them gathered at the tables and the slots, the others moving forward to join in the play. I couldn't see any Bat Packers, but I knew they were here.

I heard shouts behind me. Winning shouts. I spun to look at a craps table only a few feet away.

A man shouted, "Seven! Again!"

Using my elbows, I shoved my way to the table. The dice showed a one and a five, but the house was paying just like the blackjack table.

Then I saw him. The vampire wolf in Frank Sinatra clothing. Standing by one of the columns with the carved snakes. He was watching the play. He wasn't alone. I knew that even though I couldn't see any other vampires from where I stood. The chill was too strong. There had to be more of them.

This is my worst nightmare come true, I thought. Vampires all over the casino, using their rapport to manipulate the games, the staff, and the players. And stopping them is supposed to be my job. This is exactly what I had been hired to prevent. If things kept up, they were going to take down the Sher, and I was so completely outnumbered that there was no way I could stop it.

"Al?" I called into my headset. It took several shouts before I got his attention.

"Meet me by the machines closest to registration," he barked.

I ran up the steps to where Al was calling orders into his hand mic.

He took the broken sunglasses and shoved them into his coat pocket. "How could this happen? I know the odds can line up against the house, but *this . . .* ?" He shook his head. "It's impossible for so many people to win all at once."

"They aren't. Something's going on." I lowered my voice. *"Vampires."*

"Get them in here!" he answered to a question I hadn't heard. I realized he was listening on several frequencies as he held up a walkie-talkie and barked orders into it. "What in hell are you talking about, Steele?"

I pulled him to the closest table. I picked up the cards of the woman sitting on the end. "Look! She went bust, and yet we're paying out."

He stared at me as if I had gone mad. Nausea rose in my throat as I realized Al couldn't see the truth any more than anyone else in the casino. Everyone but me thought the wins were real. This was vampire rapport on a truly epic scale. But they weren't using rapport to win for themselves. The winners were tourists, locals, high rollers, and dollar bettors. Everyone was winning! Why?

"Al, you've got to clear the floor."

"We can't close the casino when the house is losing."

I grabbed both his arms. "Have I ever steered you wrong? I'm telling you: You have to shut down the casino. Use the poker tournament as an excuse. Say there's too much noise, or something."

"If you're wrong about this . . ." Al began.

"Trust me," I said. "I'm not. Just do it, Al."

He hesitated another second, then went into action. "Get the rest of the backup here. Now!"

I started to follow, then paused. *I'm seeing things,* I thought. In front of me, on the edges of the casino where they wouldn't be noticed, were members of the Bat Pack, including Frank Sinatra who I knew damn well I'd just seen on the other side of the floor.

For crying out loud, they're multiplying! Though the truth was, their garb was the perfect disguise. If anybody even noticed more than one guy in the same getup, they'd figure it was some New Year's Eve gag. The vampires stood, unmoving, as people jostled to get a share of the good fortune; rocks in a flood, not moving, not alive. In their eyes, an expression I had seen just once before. On the face of Simmons, the vampire who had attacked Senator Hamlyn. The one that reminded me of sleepwalking, of being . . . controlled.

Omigod, that's it! I thought, as I felt my body seize with a cold that had nothing to do with the physical presence of vampires.

This was the true core of things. Michael and his friends used their talents to fix the poker game and reprogram the slots. The Bat Pack used theirs to influence the table games. The double whammy—the con within the con. None of it made sense, which is why it was so brilliant. All the action at the Scheherazade was just smoke and mirrors. A colossal show. A Vegas extravaganza that had the Sher's security force running around like headless chickens. Michael and the tournament. Even what was happening now, out on the main floor. The Bat Pack said the action would go down at midnight. They said it was about power. Well, it wasn't midnight yet, and the action here at the casino wasn't about power. It was about money. I knew I was right. All this was just a distraction to deflect security from the real action. The real action wasn't here; it wasn't here at all. It was at Randolph Glass's lake house. And my guess was that the target of this Vegas show was Randolph's powerful guest of honor, Senator Hamlyn.

Go, Candace, I thought. I turned on one high heel and sprinted for the closest door. There was nothing more that I could do at the Sher. I had done my best to alert Al to what was going on. I had to get to Randolph's house fast.

Midnight was less than an hour away. I could only hope I would be in time to stop whatever it was that was about to go down.

Twenty-one

Two years. It has been two years, I thought.

Two years since the night of the Albedo, the night I had tried, and failed, to make Candace irrevocably mine and, in so doing, secure my place on the Board. A failure that had caused me to do the one thing I hated.

Actually, make that two things: run and hide. There were nights when the fact that the Board had driven me to do both still burned like a cinder in my gut.

Let it go, I thought. *You did what needed to be done, on both counts.* And because of it, I had survived. Though I had denied it to Sloane, of course I had had an exit strategy in place. It had existed from the night I was first taken by the Board. My finest antiques put in storage so my business was protected. Bank accounts all over the globe. One call to my secretary put the whole plan in motion. Within the hour, a dozen Ashford Donahues had departed San Francisco, their destinations spanning the globe. The reach of the Board is long, but not even they can be everywhere at once. And so I had gone to ground. Buried my anger, my desire for revenge down deep; nurturing it, like a seed waiting for the light. And my love for Candace had nestled against it, still inextricably bound. Every place I had traveled, every country that had served to hide me, had only strengthened my determination to win her back.

I slid my gold cuff links through the cuffs of my immaculate white shirt, fastened them with quick, economical motions. *Egyptian gold,* I thought. Like every other place that I had traveled, Egypt had yielded up its secrets about the Board to me. I knew the truth now. The members of the Board weren't the only vampires who could invoke the spell for immortality. Any vampire could do that, providing he was strong enough and possessed the Emblems of Thoth.

I could do it, I thought. *I would do it.* The Board possessed one emblem, but that still left two more. With my contacts in the world of antiquities, I was well placed to conduct research. I would find the other two emblems; it was just a matter of time and I would have the ultimate revenge on the Board. I would defeat them and capture the prize they had been striving to possess for hundreds of years. Immortality.

"I still don't understand why you won't let me go tonight, Ash," Dune's petulant voice slid across my thoughts. I stifled a sigh.

This is what comes of being weak, I thought.

I had met Dune the very day I had arrived in Las Vegas. *This vampire walks into a bar . . .* and sees, on the very last barstool, a woman. The woman that he loves. The second he reaches her, puts his hands on her shoulders to turn her around, he realizes his mistake. This woman is not the true, the right one. But by then, it's too late. He is past caring. Even the outer form will be better than nothing at all.

A mistake. I had known it almost at once, from the moment I had felt Dune's blood inside my mouth. I had looked to create solace. Instead, I'd created a liability, a millstone.

"I wish I could," I said, as I turned around, reached for the jacket of my tux. She was wearing the robe I had given her for Christmas, a vivid emerald green. "But, as I explained, your resemblance to Candace Steele is simply too strong. If I take you to Randolph Glass's party tonight, he's bound to notice the resemblance. This will call attention to you, Dune, attention to us, and that isn't what I want."

She moved toward me then, unfastening the sash, letting the robe fall open.

"I know you," she said. "I know what you want. I can still give it to you."

No, you can't. You never could, I thought. I leaned toward her, gave her a kiss on the cheek. "Wait for me," I said. "I won't be too long. Just a little after midnight, and it will all be over."

By the time the last stroke of midnight had faded, the first step in my plan would be complete. And everyone who counts will see it and get my message.

Time to stop running, I thought.

Time to turn the tables.

Time to show my power.

Time to declare war.

Twenty-two

Las Vegas, present
Candace

I shaved a record five minutes off the trip to Randolph's house. It would have been six except when I reached the gates of the gated community, the idiot in the guardhouse slowed me down. It took a little persuasion before he let me through to drive along the winding road that led to the mansion belonging to Randolph and Katherine Glass.

A parking attendant waved me to an area around the side of the house where dozens of cars were parked—Mercedes, Jags, Land Rovers, Porsches, even a Rolls or two. The house itself looked like something from *Architectural Digest*—multilevel and sprawling, with lots of dramatic glass walls. I jumped out of my car and glanced at my watch—eleven-oh-five. I hurried to the front door, hoping I had time to come up with a plan.

Exactly two seconds after I rang the bell, Randolph's butler opened the door. He eyed me up and down, and his mouth formed a thin, disapproving line. "May I help you?" he asked in a precise British accent.

"I need to speak to Ran—to Mr. Glass."

"Mr. Glass is busy."

I showed him my Sher ID badge. "Look, I'm from casino security, and I've got an important message for him."

Somewhat reluctantly, he let me into the foyer. A magnificent Dale Chihuly chandelier with multi-colored glass flowers sent lovely colored reflections onto the cream-colored silk walls and the white marble floors.

"Mr. Glass and his guests are on the pool deck," the butler informed me. "If you'll be so good as to wait here, I'll—"

"Thank you," I said, interrupting him. "I'm sure you're needed here to welcome other guests. I appreciate your taking the time to help me."

He gave me a stiff, reluctant nod. The second he was out of sight, I sprinted through the living room and out the nearest open door.

Cold struck me as if it had congealed into a stone wall. Not the air, which was mild for a December night, but my early-warning system. It was cranked down to arctic. There were definitely vampires around, which made me unhappy, but not crazy. I'd take what I could get.

Waiting for my eyes to adjust, I stepped away from the glass wall. Randolph's "backyard" was predictably immense. Closest to the house was a partially covered "outdoor room" with couches and tables, upholstered chairs and a broad-cushioned platform strewn with silk throws and pillows. On the far side of the yard, I saw a raised deck with an enormous pool, a Jacuzzi, and a long arbor. There must have been close to a hundred people, many of them standing by the edge of the pool where they could look out at the lights of the Strip. I headed in that direction.

I spotted Randolph and his wife chatting with Senator Hamlyn. Katherine wore a simple ivory gown. No beads, no sparkles, just elegant lines accessorized with a simple strand of antique seed pearls. Moving closer for a little eavesdropping, I heard the words "Gaming Commission" and "fast track," but couldn't tell if Randolph or Hamlyn had spoken them. I strained my ears and heard Randolph assure the senator that the fireworks show would go off exactly as planned.

"Just a little glitch in the computer programming," he was saying. "It's being taken care of. I've got someone from the Sher working on it now."

"I'm sure it will be fine," the senator replied. He

sounded distracted, tense. Was he still worried he might be a target? His security was definitely in evidence, but they were pretty much it, I noticed. Just them and me, and I was the only one who knew to look for vampires. I knew they were here. So far, I just hadn't been able to spot them.

And then I saw Ash. His pale hair caught the light from a bright red lantern. He was dressed in black tie like the other guests, but the style looked as if it had been invented just for him. Ash, who told me he didn't give a damn about Randolph and the Scheherazade. Ash, who told me he knew he was in danger, but had taken steps to protect himself. And here he was in the middle of everything.

Frantically, my mind began to race, what I had been trying to accomplish all week: catch up with the action. They were all together now: Randolph, Senator Hamlyn, and Ash. If Ash's presence was due to coincidence, I'd eat my high-heeled shoes. *Stay with Ash. Watch Ash*, I told myself. I slipped behind a thick bush that bordered the arbor. If I could just get close enough. . . .

I stuffed a fist into my mouth to stifle back a cry. The Bat Packers were here, too! Masquerading as waiters, the perfect cover. As I watched, Peter Lawford approached. Ash bent his head, and the other vampire began to whisper in his ear. *How can he let him get so close?* I thought. In the next moment,

Ash nodded, then began to speak in his own turn. I blinked, unable to believe my eyes. The Bat Pack vampire nodded, then moved off. His body language told it all. He looked so deferential. He practically bowed. It was clear that he hadn't come to threaten Ash, but to receive instructions. Or, rather, orders.

Well, fuck me, I thought. That was it. It had to be. Ash wasn't a target. He was calling the shots. The Bat Packers weren't his enemies. They were his soldiers. *That* was the missing connection. The Bat Pack and Ash. They were his own private army. Somehow he had found a way to augment their powers. Their ridiculous affectation was the perfect cover; it made everyone dismiss them as a joke. But there wasn't anything remotely funny about them.

The question was: What did they want?

My mind kept circling back: *Senator Hamlyn.* The senator who had already been attacked by one vampire.

Ash was amassing power in the vampire world. The Bat Pack was proof of that. Did he want to extend that power into the human world as well? Establishing rapport with a United States senator would certainly give Ash power. If that's his goal, he wouldn't try to take out Hamlyn. He'd try to take him, period. It wouldn't require much time to get into his mind, and then to erase any memories he had of what had happened. Ash did that with Bibi. He made her forget nearly twelve hours of her life. He used Bibi to get what he wanted at the time: me. And in his strange logic, he thought I'd be grateful. Now he wants something else; the ability to make humans bend to his will. I looked over at him and in that instant I saw the vampire, not the man. I saw the predator who attacked me in the elevator. I knew my hunch was right.

Poor Simmons wasn't totally crazy. Hamlyn was going to be controlled. By vampires. By Ash.

Not if I can help it, I thought.

A thousand different possibilities began to cascade through my mind, all of which had a chance to work—if I had an entire team on my side. But I was solo. Whatever I did, it had to be subtle and yet distracting enough for me to get the senator safely away from Ash and his cronies.

Distracting . . .

I smiled. Why not a con? Everyone else had been running one this week. Why shouldn't I?

Keeping an eye on the senator, I pulled out my cell, flipped it open, and aimed my finger at the first button on my speed dial.

Before I could push it, pain exploded through my skull. Everything telescoped into blackness. Desperately, I fought to hold on to consciousness. I managed to push myself up on one hand, then hit the ground hard again as that hand was kicked out from under me. Then someone had my ankles, and I was being dragged into the arbor.

I kicked out, hard, and felt the blow connect. I kicked again, heard a yelp of pain, and felt the grip on my ankles let go. But when I tried to get to my feet, I got only as far as my knees. My head swam, and everything spun. Hands on me. Shoved them off. Had to get to my feet. Had to. Then I had done it. Wobbly, but standing, I reached for the silver stakes in my hair, but every movement felt slow, as if I were moving underwater.

In the instant before I could grasp them, I was seized by the front of my jacket and shoved against the rough bark of a tree. And I saw the all-too-familiar face of my attacker.

"Remember me?" Dune snarled, her eyes fierce. "Remember what I promised?" Her lips drew back in a sneer that revealed two razor-sharp fangs.

I jerked my knee up hard, aiming for her groin, but Dune sidestepped the kick easily, and her grip on me tightened.

"He doesn't love you," I said. "He doesn't even want you. You kill me, and you'll lose him forever. You're a mistake. He told me so."

"I don't care. Do you hear me?" Dune answered. "I don't care. All I want is for you to die. You're the mistake, not me. He wouldn't even let me come here because of you. Once you're gone, he'll be free. He'll come back to me then. I know he will. I can give him what he wants. . . . You can't."

She lunged for my neck, but I twisted away, which caused her to shift her balance just for a second. "You mean nothing to Ash," I spit the words in her face trying to rattle her. "You're just his whore." She lunged again, the force of her body was like being hit by a car. She held me in a lethal hug and bared her fangs. I was pinned to the tree. She leaned in closer. I could smell her perfume—the same one I wear. Somehow the idea that she appropriated something as intimate as my scent enraged me. I managed to jerk my leg free and then stamped on her foot, driving my four-inch heel in deep. She pulled back in pain; just long enough for me to free one hand and grab for one of my silver stakes. I slashed the air wildly, hoping the silver would intimidate her and push her back. But the sight of my weapon only made her come closer. She wound her fingers into my hair, pulling my head back so fast and hard that I swear I heard my neck crack. Her fangs pressed my neck and then she went completely still, her eyes open wide. She made a strange, protesting sound. And her body simply disintegrated in front of my eyes, crumbling into a pile of dust.

Behind the spot where she had just stood, I saw

Chet McGuire. His mouth was twisted in a complex expression: fury and disgust and a strange kind of satisfaction. In his hand, he held a silver pen, the one he always kept in his pocket protector.

"Are you okay?" He came carefully toward me. "She didn't..."

"No." I stepped out of the arbor, glanced around. The entire encounter with Dune had taken only a few moments. Except for our whispered, heated exchange, it had taken place in total silence. No one but Chet had even been aware it was going on. Senator Hamlyn was selecting an hors d'oeuvre from a silver tray.

I turned back to Chet. "Thanks," I said. "I just may owe you my life."

"Okay, I just have to ask this," Chet said. "Shouldn't you be just a little more freaked out?"

"When you work security you come up against just about everything," I explained. "Believe it or not, that wasn't my first vampire." There. I had said it, right out loud. "For the record, you don't look all that freaked out yourself."

Chet made a face. "She's not my first vampire, either. I lost my best friend to one about eight months ago."

"Chet. I'm so sorry."

He gave himself a shake, as if to throw off a bad

dream. "Yeah, well, so am I. But I don't figure we have time for a history lesson now."

He reached into his coat pocket and pulled out a small device. The buzz in my ears got louder as he thrust it toward me. Not a buzz, but that high-pitched whine I had heard in the IT center.

"What is that?" I inquired.

"Originally, it was an ultrasonic bat locator," he explained. "I modified it to help me locate and trace vampires, because only vampires react to the sound. Only vampires and you!"

"Chet, I'm not a vampire. I'll explain later. We don't have time. You're here because of the technical problems with the fireworks?"

"Right. Mr. Glass sent for me because there was a glitch in the program, but I got it straightened out."

"So everything's set to go at midnight."

"Yes." Chet's eyes narrowed. "What aren't you telling me? What's going on?"

"I can't explain now," I said hurriedly. "Except to say, watch out for the waiters dressed up like the Rat Pack. They're actually vampires. If I'm right, I think they may make some sort of play for Senator Hamlyn."

I didn't expect Ash would get his own hands dirty, not with his toy soldiers around.

I glanced at my watch. It was eleven-twenty, and

the fireworks would go off at midnight. Maybe, just maybe, there was enough time left for my con.

"I need your help, Chet." I located my cell on the ground, flipped it open, praying it was still intact. It was. "Do you have some paper?" The guy had a pocket protector and a vamp locator, for crying out loud. Dollars to doughnuts he had a pad of paper and a pencil concealed somewhere.

Sure enough. He pulled both from an inner pocket, and I scribbled a few sentences.

"I want you to call the numbers of my most recent twenty voice mails and tell them this," I said, giving the pad back to him. "And call security and see if you can get some more troops over here."

"All right." He looked puzzled. "What are you going to do?"

"I have to find someone," I said.

Chet reached into his pants pocket and pulled out a small silver tube. "Candace, take this," he said, pressing it into my hand.

"What is it?"

"A light I use for working on computers." He twisted one end. "That's how it turns on." The narrow beam was barely visible. "It's not much, but it should help when they turn off all the lights for the fireworks."

"Thanks." I slipped the light into my costume. "Do me another favor?"

"Sure."

"Find me just before the fireworks start."

Music blared as the jazz band began to really let loose. I stood off to the side, clinging to the shadows but staying close to Senator Hamlyn, who was talking with Katherine Glass and another woman who seemed, if possible, even more elegant.

The crowd had grown and now spilled onto the lawn and paths that led from the deck to the house. I checked my watch. It was five minutes before midnight, and aside from the presence of multiple vampires, I hadn't picked up any sign of a direct threat to the senator. That didn't mean it wasn't coming. Only that they hadn't yet put their plan into action.

After leaving Chet with my cell, I had searched the house and grounds for Ash. Nada. He seemed to have vanished from the scene. Which was troubling in its own way. Somehow, I couldn't imagine that he had actually left or that his disappearance was benign. He was lying low, a predator waiting patiently for the kill.

The deck was thronged with couples dancing to the band, and others standing around the food tables and Jacuzzi. The largest and thickest crowd of all was gathering over by the pool, waiting for the fireworks to begin. Randolph Glass appeared at his wife's side. He said something. Both he and Katherine laughed. Then Randolph took Katherine into his arms to dance. Hamlyn was immediately swept into the crowd gathering by the pool.

Shit! The last thing I needed was Hamlyn disappearing from sight. I left the relative safety of the shadows and began to wend my way through the crowd to the pool.

Applause met the end of one song and the beginning of the next. Three minutes till midnight. I glanced toward the living room's glass wall. There was no sign at all that anyone was coming.

Chet appeared at my side. "Ready?"

"As ready as I'll ever be."

"What are we looking for?"

"I don't know. Just keep your eye on Senator Hamlyn.

"Excuse me," I said, edging closer to the senator. There were at least a dozen people between us, and even in heels I couldn't see over most of their heads. Chet, fortunately, was taller.

"Hamlyn's talking with a woman in a black gown," he reported. "And, holy crap, on his left, there's a guy who looks like Peter Lawford moving toward him."

That's the same vamp I saw earlier, with Ash, I thought. The music stopped and the lights dimmed.

I began to push through the crowd, not caring who I bumped or jostled.

"Scheherazade security, let me through," I shouted. But I was too far away, had waited too long. The crowd was thick, everyone packed together to stare toward the Strip. I was barely making any progress. I risked a glance at my watch and another at the windows of the house. No one was riding to the rescue and there was no more time left. My heart sank. Around me, people were shouting drunkenly, "Five . . . four . . . three . . . two . . . one! Happy New Year!"

The music started up again as the first round of fireworks shot up in the air with a fierce explosion. I kept moving, my gaze focused on the senator. "Let me through!" I could hear desperation in my voice. "Please, let me through!"

My eyes blurred as the light was filled with brilliant explosions of light and color and then plunged into darkness. One moment I saw the senator standing by Randolph, but then I caught sight of him being steered by Peter Lawford toward the house.

"Goddammit." I looked around for Chet. He was right behind me. "This is it!" I said. "They're trying to get the senator out. Come with me!" I tugged on his sleeve as I switched on the tiny flashlight.

It was a little easier making our way in this direction. Fireworks were still going off, so most people were glad to let us out so they could move closer to the deck where the view was the best. Although the lights in the outdoor area had been dimmed, I found a door into the living room.

"This way," I said, leading Chet into the house.

The inside of the house was pitch black. I moved slowly, using Chet's light to avoid stumbling into furniture. I thought I heard the senator's voice, but I couldn't be sure. What if they'd already gotten him away? What if . . . ?

I swung the thin beam, hoping to find a lamp or some sort of light I could turn on. And then I felt the bone-chilling cold, a rush of it directly in front of me. Jerry Lewis. Just my luck. I've never even thought the *real* one was funny.

"What did you do with him?" I demanded. "Where's the senator?"

"Expect me to answer you, lady?" the Jerry vampire replied, his grin manic. He clamped a hand around my upper arm and tugged me hard, toward the darkened recesses of the house.

Anger replaced my fear. I don't like being jerked around, especially by a vampire.

The finale of the fireworks show shook the room. The thundering booms and screaming, shrill whistles drowned out all other sound. I struggled to think clearly.

I let the Jerry Lewis vampire pull me across the room. I wanted him to think I couldn't overpower him. He walked steadily and deliberately, dragging me away from the party.

I saw a pale light in a room ahead. My heart sank as I caught a glimpse of the senator being ushered toward the front foyer.

The vampire pulled me down a long darkened hall. He was big and strong. But not strong enough. Time to move, Candace. Time to end his comedy act. Arrogant bastard. He didn't care that I had one hand free.

I took a deep breath. Then I swung the free hand up hard and gave his Adam's apple a hard chop with my closed fist. He made a gulping sound. I didn't give him a chance to recover. I clamped my hand around his necktie and pulled down with all my strength.

He stumbled forward, his knees buckling. Breathing hard, my hand aching, I let go. He hit the wall and spun around. He couldn't keep the surprise from his face. "Damn it, lady," he choked out, struggling to loosen the tie. "I'm not gonna hurt you. I got my orders, you know?"

But I'm gonna hurt you! I told myself. My fingers reached for a silver chopstick. I held my breath and waited for the vampire's next move.

"Hey—!" I didn't expect him to move so fast.

One second he was against the wall, the next he had his hands around my face. "I like the feisty ones," he said, spitting on me with each word. He tangled his fist in my hair and leaned in closer. His lips made a hideous parody of a lover's kiss. I could smell the scent of blood on his breath.

Wait. Wait for the right moment. The kill moment. My heart pounding, I willed myself to wait. The stench of him, his breath nearly suffocated me. He leaned closer. Closer . . .

Now!

As he pressed himself against me, I brought my arm up high behind his back . . . and plunged the silver chopstick deep into his neck.

It made a sick, dry sound like a rake cutting through dead leaves. He made no cry. No sound. No struggle. I could still feel the pressure of him against my body. But he was gone.

I had to be sure. I knelt down to touch the cool marble floor . . . and my fingers sank into a dry pile of dust.

"Chet," I called, hoping that another vampire hadn't attacked him.

He didn't answer and I got to my feet, panic rising. Where was the senator? By this point he might be miles from the house. I could smell the sickening scent of failure closing in on me. I had played my hand and I had lost. Hamlyn was gone. Ash had won.

Somewhere to my right I heard a door swing open. The front door? I tried to orient myself, and there was a flare of light. And then more lights—blinding lights. Great! Lights were what I wanted. Lights that would take away the vampires' advantage and reveal the truth about what was going on. Lights were everywhere as a horde of TV reporters and their camera crews swarmed through the front door and into the living room. "Senator," one of them called out. "Is it true you're announcing your candidacy tonight?"

I followed the line of his gaze and stared in disbelief. The senator was standing in front of the grand piano, with the Peter Lawford vampire next to him. Whatever their ultimate plans, the vampires weren't about to try anything with the major news media around. Their clever disguises would finally work against them. They were simply too noticeable.

"Have you given any thought to a running mate, sir?" another reporter asked.

"Senator Hamlyn," called Lance Weatherly. "What do you want to tell your fellow Americans on the night you make this special announcement?"

Chet appeared at my side, looking worried. "Are

you okay?" he said. "What happened to that Jerry Lewis clone?"

"Chet, I'm so happy you're okay," I said. "Jerry's toast . . ."

"This is amazing," Chet said. He gestured to the crush of reporters and cameras. "You did it."

"Thanks to you," I said. My con, with his help, was going down exactly as I had planned. By calling the last twenty numbers in my voice mail, he had reached all the reporters who tried to get me for a sound bite after the interrupted photo op at the hospital. Chet had given them a tip they couldn't ignore. He said that the senator was announcing here and now that he was running for president.

"I can't believe we really stopped it," I said, realizing that I was trembling with exhaustion. I was relishing the moment. Vampires operate in the dark. Light is always their enemy. . . .

"It's like nothing ever happened. It's all fine," Chet added.

Sure enough, everything was fine. The senator's security men were in their places. Reporters stood in a half-circle around the senator. Hamlyn was in his element, deflecting questions with practiced ease. And I was nearly floating on a private little cloud of elation. I had done it! I had stopped the Bat Pack and Ash.

As I silently said his name, I saw Ash approaching. I tensed and began to move toward him. To my surprise, Ash didn't even look at the senator. Instead, he came straight to me.

"Candace." A half-smile tilted up one corner of his mouth. "How nice to see you. You look lovely."

"You manipulative bastard," I said. "You think I don't know what you are up to . . . I . . ."

Before I could get another word out, his mouth swooped down, covering mine. His arms enclosed me as they had so many times before. My senses filled with the spicy scent of his skin.

"Happy New Year, Candace," I felt him murmur against my mouth.

As if from a million miles away, I heard a voice yell, "Senator Hamlyn. Watch out!"

I yanked myself out of Ash's grip, desperate to push him aside. In front of me, standing directly in front of the senator, I saw my old pal Dean Martin. He was holding the last weapon I would have expected a vampire to use: a gun.

There was a flash of light, an almost deafening explosion. Bright blood bloomed on Senator Hamlyn's immaculate white shirtfront. He dropped like a stone.

The crowd in front of him erupted. Some trying to reach him. Most trying to get away from the possibility of a maniac with a gun. I hurled myself forward, using my elbows viciously to force my way through. Dropping to my knees beside Hamlyn, I stripped off my short tux jacket, tore his shirt open, and pressed my rolled up jacket to the wound, desperate to stop the flow of bright crimson blood.

In the center of his chest, right above the place where his heart worked so frantically to beat, was a tattoo of an image I had seen before: head of an ibis, body of a man. The same symbol as on the back of the picture Ash had given me in San Francisco. And it was red. Blood-red. The color flowing into that of Hamlyn's own blood.

"Miss Steele." All of a sudden, I realized that Hamlyn was speaking. I leaned down close. "It seems you are too late this time."

"Don't say that," I protested. "Help is coming."

Senator Hamlyn closed his eyes. When he opened them again, I knew he was right. Help would never get here in time.

"I think it may be better this way," he said. Then, on one long, slow breath, he gave up the fight for his life.

Twenty-three

"Two vodka martinis and whatever beer you have on tap," I said to Abe, the bartender, as I put my tray on the counter.

"Coming up."

I looked across my section of the casino. It was busy; I had been going nonstop all night, taking drinks to gamblers. In the past week, everything had returned to normal at the Sher. The tourists were coming in to try their luck now that the computer "glitch" had been resolved. A new Magic Carpet Club card was being rolled out in a big promo with giveaways and promises of better comps.

Not that there was any reason to worry about Michael Irons and his partners in crime. They had vanished. In the chaos of New Year's Eve, they had just slipped out. Randolph told Al not to pursue them because he didn't want the news getting out that the Sher's security had been breached.

"Buy a drink for a lady?" asked Bibi as she sat on the stool beside me.

"One sparkling water," I told Abe, knowing Bibi's preference.

Bibi's eyelids were bright turquoise mixed with glitter and her lips a garish red.

"You know, your stage makeup is scary up close," I said with a smile. "Are you trying to keep guys away?"

"Just one." As Abe handed Bibi her water, she added, "He came looking for me this afternoon to tell me he's lonely . . ."

"And what did you say?"

Bibi sighed. "I'm holding my ground. Going back to Randolph won't get me anything but heartache."

I leaned over, gave her a hug. "You know what? I'm really proud of you."

She gave me a lopsided grin. "And what about you? I'm sorry about Michael. We sure know how to pick 'em, huh?"

We sure do, I thought.

Bibi set her glass of sparkling water down on the bar. "Well, I'm off to kick up my heels. Every time I bring my foot down, I'm going to imagine I'm stomping on Randolph." She sashayed off.

If you were smart you'd use Bibi as inspiration, I told myself. She was doing her best to meet her demons head-on. I was still hiding from mine.

In the weeks since Senator Hamlyn's death, I had heard from virtually every media outlet in the country. What could I tell them? That a United States senator had been killed by vampires? That a secret organization called the Board had something to do with it? Not too helpful. After a while the press stopped calling, and I was left with my questions and my anger. I had not heard from Ash. Not once. Clearly, I was a fool to expect him to offer an explanation, but the way he had used me burned in my gut.

I had feared for him, been afraid enough to warn him of the very plot of which he, himself, was the mastermind. And he had let me do it. The fact that he hadn't lied to me outright didn't change what had transpired. He had used my fear, my love, to get what he wanted: me in his bed. Ash had made me feel many things. Never before had he made me feel like a whore.

It's time to stop running, Candace, I thought. I was proud of Bibi. It was time to return to being proud of myself.

*   *   *

Su Li passed me through with just a simple phone call this time. When I stepped off the elevator into the glass-walled living room of Ash's condo, soft music came from speakers set in the high ceiling, and the scent of fresh roses suggested I had entered a strange, night garden. The lights were off, but they came on faintly as I crossed the floor to where a chair faced out to give the occupant a view of the lights on the Strip. Ash was there, holding a champagne flute filled with liquid that captured the reflection of the multicolored neon on the streets below.

"Champagne, Candace?" he inquired, rocking the glass gently.

I resisted the impulse to knock it from his hand. I was here to regain, not to lose, control.

"No, thanks. This isn't a social call, Ash. I've come for what you owe me."

He took a deliberate sip, and I had a sudden moment out of time. *How long had he been sitting there?* I wondered. Watching the lights of the city, waiting for me to come. He had known I would come, of that I was certain.

"And what is that?" he inquired.

"An apology," I said. "Not that I'm likely to get one. So I'll settle for an explanation instead."

"Why the hell should I bother to offer one? You're so certain you have all the answers. Pick whichever one you choose. I'm always the bad guy."

"Of course you're the bad guy," I all but shouted. "You're a fucking vampire!"

With one swift, violent motion, Ash threw the champagne glass straight at the window before us. It hit hard enough to make the pane quiver. Shards of the champagne flute sparkled like diamonds as they fell to the floor. The champagne dripped down the glass pane as clear and cold as winter rain.

"That's right," he said. "That's exactly what I am. I'm a fucking vampire. And you know who I fuck, Candace? I fuck you. And you like it. You come to me, knowing what I am, and then you blame me for it. Well, guess what? It's an old game, and I'm tired of it. You have no idea what drives my actions."

"That's the truest thing you've ever said," I blazed back. "For all I know, it's the only one. *I came to you, Ash.* I thought you were in danger and I came to you, to warn you. I simply could not do anything else. Because I love you. Tell me something: Did it bother you to make love to me that night, knowing I had slept with Michael Pressman? Oh, excuse me, I mean Michael Irons."

He made an inarticulate sound. And I laughed then, the sound wild and bitter. "What's the matter?" I asked. "Did you think I wouldn't take up the bait you offered? Or maybe you thought I wouldn't figure out what you'd done at all. That the whole thing was one big con. It took me a while, I must admit, but I got there in the end. Michael Irons was your little distraction, your little errand boy. You set us up so I wouldn't guess what you were really up to. He seemed so different from you. Funny, how you two turned out to be alike. He's a two-faced lying sonofabitch and so are you."

"No!" he said, striding toward me to seize me by both wrists. Even in the dim light, I could see his face tightening with anger. "What happened between you and Irons is something you did on your own. I used him to set up the con at the casino. He used me to bankroll his entry into the poker tournament. It was business. Nothing more."

I thought this over for a minute, *just business*. The suite at the Sher, even the limo. All my "fun." Ash paid for all of it.

"You used me, Ash, and you didn't even do it yourself. In my book, that makes you a pimp and me a whore."

"No, Candace. It wasn't like that."

"You're wrong," I said. "It was. You had all the knowledge, all the power, Ash. What you did was worse than lie. You withheld the truth, because you knew that telling it would make the difference between satisfying your desires and denying them. You're right. You did fuck me, and it had absolutely nothing to do with love. You've left me with nothing, not even my self-respect."

I pulled against his grip. He released me, but neither of us backed away, backed down. "So, if you'll excuse me, I happen to think an explanation of some kind is in order. Why, Ash? I want you to tell me why."

For a split second, I thought I saw him waver, thought I saw a thousand competing wants and needs in his starshine eyes. Then, his expression shuttered, so thoroughly and completely I could have sworn I actually heard the sound of a door slamming shut.

"I can't do that. I'm sorry."

"Never mind," I said. I stepped away from him then, genuinely uncertain what I would do if I stood that close to him for one second longer. Throw myself into his arms and beg. Slide one of the stakes of silver I always wore in my hair out to plunge it straight through his black and treacherous heart.

"Come to think of it, I'll bet I can come up with an explanation, myself. Could it possibly be safer for me not to know? All you're trying to do is protect me. You have only my best interests at heart.

Would those statements feature prominently on your list of excuses?"

"Yes, damn you," Ash shouted. "And they're not excuses. They're the absolute truth."

I laughed once more. "I used to think you were so remarkable, Ash. So unique. So unlike any other man I had ever known. Just lately, I've found out the truth. You're just like all the rest, vampire or not. You trot out the same lame justifications for your actions and expect the little woman to swallow it whole.

"You killed a man, Ash," I cried. "An important one. Oh, excuse me, you had one of your little Bat Pack soldiers do it for you."

"Hamlyn wasn't what you thought he was," Ash said, his voice tightly controlled. "He was much worse than your run-of-the-mill corrupt politician."

"Are you telling me he was a vampire?"

"No."

"Then what?"

"Let's just say he was being controlled."

"By another vampire?"

"Something like that. I had no choice. Hamlyn had to be eliminated. He was dangerous, Candace, on levels you can't even begin to fathom."

"Of course, not," I said. "I'm not capable of understanding any of it, but you put me right in the middle of it anyway, you condescending bastard.

Ash, you chose the Sher. Why? To protect me or to humiliate me? You know what? I don't care. You can go to hell. I'm leaving. Don't expect me to come back another time."

I started for the door.

"I can make sure you don't do that," he said. His tone stopped me in my tracks. "I can make sure you never leave me, that you never want to go."

"Yes, you can do that," I said. "And do you know what I'll be then? I'll be your human drone. Or your vampire pet, if that's the course of action you choose. Not even *I* expect I would be able to stop you from draining me a second time."

I turned back and walked straight to him, then I lifted my hair from my neck and tilted back my head to expose my throat. I knew what he was seeing: the place where the tattoo did its best to cover up my scars. The ones he had given me in that San Francisco elevator long ago.

"Go ahead," I said. "Get it over with. Make me what Dune was. I put an end to her existence, by the way. Not much choice, as she was doing her best to end mine. Maybe I should have let her kill me and saved us both so much trouble. Personally, I think we both deserve better than this, but it's your choice. You've done such a fine job of proving you're the one in control, why stop now?"

"Damn it!" Ash said. "Damn you. No."

"You are the one who is damned," I replied. I let my hair fall. "And you know what? I've decided I don't want an explanation after all. All I want is to never see you again."

"That isn't going to happen," Ash said quietly. "I am never going to let you go."

I walked to the elevator doors. They slid open without a sound.

"Just answer me one thing," I said, without facing him. "Are you a member of the Board?"

I heard his startled exclamation. Knew that my long shot had hit home. I still might not know what the Board was, but it was clear Ash did. And all of a sudden he was by my side. Swinging me around to face him. The expression in his eyes was wild. Filled with the very last thing I had ever expected to see there: genuine fear.

"Who told you about them?" he said. "How do you know about the Board?"

I yanked myself out of his grip. "You don't give me an explanation, but you expect one?"

He reached for me again, and I danced out of reach. I was in the elevator now. Ash surged forward, blocking the doors with his body. From somewhere deep inside me, I felt a scream begin to rise.

"Answer me, Candace," Ash said. "If you knew Hamlyn was being controlled by the Board, then

you already know too much. Answer me!" he repeated.

I pulled in a shaky breath. "No. Your days of
controlling my mind and actions are over, Ash.
Now get your fucking foot out of the door."

I saw his body ripple, as if it was literally at war
with his mind, his heart. And then, in the blink of
an eye, I knew which one had won. He was beside
me in the elevator, his arms banding around me,
tight, mouth crushing down upon mine.

I swear to God I felt my heart stop. My breath
backed up into my lungs. Ash's mouth was desperate and determined. Coaxing, demanding, wild. I
kept mine still beneath it. To this day, I believe it is
the hardest thing I have ever done. Slowly, slowly,
his touch gentled. His lips on mine became a plea
and a promise. And as they did, I felt my heart
begin to beat once more. I reached up, slid a single
stake of silver from my hair. Brought it down until
the sharp point just touched the exposed flesh of
his jaw. Ash jerked back, a purely involuntary motion, and the point nicked him. I saw a bead of
bright crimson blood well up, then trickle slowly
down his throat.

"You once asked how I would feel if you did not
exist," I said. "Ask me again now."

For what seemed an infinite space of time, he did
not move. I hardly dared to breathe. I gazed up-

ward, he gazed down. Then Ash took one step back, and then a second. By the time he had taken the third, I was in the elevator alone.

"We are not over," he said. "This is not the end of things. We are not done."

I did breathe then, pulling in a single slow and steady breath. "You're wrong. Everything about us is wrong, Ash. Just like everything about us is over and done."

I reached out, jabbed the *down* button on the elevator, and the doors slid closed. The last thing I saw was my vampire lover, his eyes, now and forever like the stars. And down his neck, the thing that lay between us, now and forever. Binding us together, driving us apart.

Blood.

Don't miss this special sneak peek
at the next seductive book in
the Candace Steele Vampire Killer trilogy!!!

Eternal Hunger

It was a stormy night.

I live in Vegas, so I can't exactly also claim that it was dark. I can say this much, however: There's better weather in Hell.

The rain came down in solid sheets, the drops just short of hail but still hard enough to sting. The wind was straight out of a late-night horror film. Some unseen force that should not be sentient but still manages to have a mind of its own anyhow; pushing against me with invisible hands, tearing at my clothing, howling through the city like a long-lost soul. It was the sort of night when anyone with half a brain cranks up the knob on the gas fireplace, slips her favorite DVD into the machine, and curls up on the couch.

So what was I doing? I was pounding the streets of Vegas, soaked to the skin, tracking someone who probably thought the weather was nice.

My name is Candace Steele, and I hunt vampires.

Usually, I do this indoors. I work undercover security at one of the newest casinos in town, the Scheherazade. I look like a thousand other females in Vegas, serving drinks and flashing some skin. In fact, I'm one of a kind. Because while I'm making my rounds, I'm also doing something else: spotting vampires and getting them tossed out on their undead asses if they attempt to cheat the casino.

But tonight I was off, and all I wanted was to go to a movie. I almost got there, too, right up to the ticket window. Then I felt it: a surge of cold straight down my back, one I knew damn well had nothing to do with the storm.

There was a vampire nearby.

Immediately, my adrenaline started to kick in as my vampire-hunting instincts began to take over. I flipped up the collar on my jacket in a feeble attempt to keep the rain from streaming down the back of my neck, slid one of the silver chopsticks I always use to help control my wayward curls out of my hair and into my jacket pocket, and kept on going, hot on the trail of the cold.

Vampire Hunter Rule #1: Never, under any circumstances, go out into the world unarmed. Rule #2: When in doubt, make silver your weapon of choice. Silver is a purifier. A little goes a long way when it comes to vampires.

By the time I reached the far end of the block, I

was completely soaked. The wind was so strong I had to lean into it, as if walking up an incline. But the internal cold I felt still pulled me forward, steady as a lodestone. I crossed the street, stepped up onto the curb, and saw the vampire.

He was young. Not more than early twenties. Wearing a muscle T-shirt and skin-tight jeans that had probably been plastered to his body even before the rain got to them and finished the job. Stepping out from under the cover of a parking garage not twenty paces away, oblivious to the weather, looking entirely too pleased with himself. With his own power. *New kid on the block,* I thought. *On a feeding high.* His eyes slid over me, barely registering my presence. I felt my adrenaline kick up a notch. My biggest weapon in my fight against vampires isn't anything I carry with me, anything external. It's me, myself. The fact that, unaccustomed to humans being able to detect what they are, most vamps literally never see me coming.

As if to prove he was no different than the rest, the vampire in question pivoted on one thick black-booted heel and began to walk away; his arrogance, his enjoyment of his own power, showing in every single stride. It might have been a balmy summer night for all the notice he took of the weather. Water streamed down my face, dripped from the end of my nose.

For ten endless blocks, I trailed the vampire, until I wanted to take him out for no other reason than to take myself out of the wet and the cold. *Come on,* I urged him silently. *Make your move you undead creep. Turn off. Show me where you're going.* The street we were on was still way too public to risk a confrontation, even given the storm.

Do something, Candace, I thought. *Stop following him like some lovesick schoolgirl and make something happen.* If the vampire wasn't going to give me the opportunity I wanted, I was just going to have to make one of my own.

I quickened my pace, sliding a second chopstick of silver from my hair, tucking it into my left-hand jacket pocket. I had one ready and waiting for either hand now.

Come on, I urged him. *Hear me coming.*

Precisely as if obeying my command, he turned around. I let my momentum carry me forward, crashing into him, clutching at him as if he were a lifeline. I pulled him around the corner, onto the side street.

"Oh, thank goodness," I sobbed out. "I'm so glad I found someone."

"Whoa," the vampire said, and then smiled. In the time it had taken our bodies to connect, he had come to the conclusion I posed no threat. How could I? I was only human, after all. Sure, I could have just nailed him right away and been done with it, but that wasn't what I wanted. I wanted to toy with him a little, work him around to just the moment when he could see the end of his existence coming. See it and be powerless to stop it.

"I'm being followed. I think I'm being followed," I gasped out, letting my words tumble over one another even as I leaned into him. I felt his arm snake around my waist to hold me close. If anyone saw us, we'd look like two sweethearts, hurrying to get home out of the rain.

"Please, you've got to help me," I pleaded. "I'm new to Vegas. I'm just a tourist. I got lost—in the storm—I lost my way." I began to pull at him, urging him away from the street corner as if expecting my pursuer to burst into view at any minute. My goal was the center of the block, where the spill from the streetlights left a dark band of shadow.

"Of course I'll help you," the vampire said. "A woman like you shouldn't be on her own. Vegas can be a dangerous town. But you don't have to worry. You can trust me."

In a pig's eye, I thought.

"Oh, thank you," I sobbed out. I stopped moving, dropped my head against his chest as if overwhelmed with relief. "You can't imagine what it feels like to find somebody kind. I've been so frightened. You have no idea."

"First thing we do is get you out of the rain," he said. "And out of those wet clothes."

You are such an asshole, I thought. *Pouring down rain, damsel in distress, and what do you do? You hit on her.*

I giggled then, as if he had actually said something original, and gave a shiver that insinuated me a little closer to his body.

"I just feel so confused," I confessed. "Like I'm having a panic attack or something. I can't even remember the way to my hotel. If I could just be somewhere safe, I'm sure I'd get my bearings back. I'm just so scared, so cold."

"Not to worry," the vampire said easily. "My place isn't far."

It never is, I thought.

"What if he's seen us?" I exclaimed suddenly. I jerked backward, out of the vampire's arms. Instantly, he reached for me, but I scooted out of range. I was in the darkest part of the block now. I wrapped my arms around myself, hugging my elbows, then slid my right hand down and into my jacket pocket. "I could get you in trouble. You might even get hurt. I couldn't bear it if that happened. I would never forgive myself."

"You don't have to worry about that," the vampire said, his voice soothing. He followed me into the shadowy center of the block. He reached for me again, and, this time, I let him bring me close. Palming the silver, I wrapped my arms around his back. He tilted my face up, brushed the water from my cheeks. "Trust me. I can handle anything that comes along."

"Can you really?" I asked, my voice breathless, for all the world as if we were standing together on a night drenched with moonlight instead of wind and rain. I watched the cockiness come into his face.

"You don't have to worry about a thing," he said.

I slid my hand up his back and jammed the silver straight into the side of his neck.

"You know what?" I said. "You're absolutely right."

I had it, then, the moment I'd been waiting for. His eyes went wide with horrified comprehension, his mouth made a round O of astonishment and pain. And then he crumbled into dust.

I heard a sound, then. Behind me. Sibilant, leathery, vaguely familiar, but not readily identifiable. And then there were strong hands against the small of my back, shoving me forward with brutal force, propelling my body straight into the wall of the closest building. Fingers wrapped themselves around my wrist, the hand that still held the silver, slamming it up against the building once, twice, three times. I heard a sharp *crack,* felt a searing pain, cried out even as I heard the silver clatter to the sidewalk. In the next instant, the hands released my wrist to tangle in my sodden hair, propelling my head forward against the building so hard that I saw stars. Blood erupted from my nose.

Cold, I thought. *I'm so very, very cold.*

I knew then what I would see as my attacker spun me back around. He shook me, my head flopping, my neck as limp as a rag doll's.

"Look at me. Look at me, you stupid little bitch," a voice rapped out.

I looked. And found myself staring straight into the second vampire's eyes. Dark as midnight, as the lowest level of Hell. In them, I saw precisely what he wanted me to see: my own death.

Sheer instinct took over then, pushing back even the bone-chilling cold. I was Candace Steele. I'd faced strong vampires before. I was not going down without a fight. I slapped at him, desperately trying to gain even a little room to maneuver, then screamed as pain from my broken wrist sang up my arm. He laughed, backhanded me viciously, releasing his hold on me at the same time. My head snapped sideways and back, connecting with the wall once more. My vision went stark white, then gray around the edges. My ears roared with sudden sound. Slowly, I began to sink down against the wall, my only support. Before I hit the sidewalk, the vampire reached down, seized the lapels of my jacket, and hauled me upright. He yanked the jacket open as if the leather were a dry corn husk, grabbed my hair, pulled my head to one side.

And then his teeth were in my throat.

My whole body spasmed, arcing up on a great wave of pain. My lips opened in a silent cry. My hands scrabbled against his back, trying to gain some sort of purchase, to pull him away from me. He made a sound like an animal, and I swear I felt the grip of his teeth tighten, worrying at my neck like some feral dog. My knees buckled and my legs gave way. Slowly, locked together in our terrible embrace, we sank to the wet sidewalk.

His teeth never relinquished their hold on my neck as he shifted position, turning so that his back was against the wall now. Supporting me as I slid to the ground, cradling me in his lap as a loving parent might a child. Sounds seemed to magnify inside my head. The sound the rain made against the leather of my jacket, different than where it hit the sidewalk. The even, steady rhythm of the vampire's swallows as he drank my blood. My ears rang, then began to pound. Thum *thump*. Thum *thump*. Thum *thump*. *My heart. That is my heart,* I thought. Desperately beating, trying to keep me alive. It wasn't going to work. Nothing was going to work.

I was going to die.

I had a strange, crystalline moment then, a moment out of time. Even as sensation began to leave for good, I felt my whole body, every single part of it, for the very last time. My butt against the vampire's lap, my shoulders and head where they rested against his supporting shoulder and arm. My legs, stretched straight out in front of me, extending past him to rest on the wet sidewalk. The throb of my broken wrist, trapped between us. My head, turned away, facing out toward the street. My free arm extending into space, the hand, palm up. As if they belonged to a stranger, I watched the fingers move, and it seemed to me that they were trying to tell me something. My body was getting it backward, and my hand was trying to give my brain a command. There was something the hand should do. Something important.

Just go for it, I thought. The world was a sea of shades of gray, like an old black-and-white television show. I watched as my pale gray fingers trembled, then jerked toward the darker gray that was the closest jacket pocket. My hand fumbled there for precious, endless seconds, then found its way inside. And, at that moment, my brain caught up. It knew what it was supposed to do now. It was supposed to save me.

In that pocket was my other silver chopstick.

I felt my fingers close around it, and, for one blinding second, there was color in the world once more. A haze of red pain so bright and vicious it made me scream even with the vampire's teeth embedded in my throat. My hand jerked, straight out, the silver chopstick clutched in my fist. My arm shot straight up. Then, as if those two motions had exhausted my last strength, my arm began to fall back down. Against all odds, I felt the tip of the silver chopstick catch, then drag as my arm descended.

The teeth in my throat let go as the vampire opened his mouth to howl, a furious, inhuman sound. He released me, shoving me from him with a violence so sudden I tumbled over backward, the back of my head bouncing against the sidewalk like a rubber ball. Stars wheeled before my eyes. Gorgeous, silver, sparkling. They reminded me of something. A thing that made me want to weep and sing, all at the same time.

And then even they disappeared, and the only thing that existed in the world was the rain, falling down into my open, sightless eyes.